P9-AZV-979

## Praise for
### *Tiger Lillie*

DISCARD

"Reading *Tiger Lillie* is like bungee jumping in a prom dress—breathless, extreme, elegant, a mixture of freefall reflection and being jerked back to heart-stopping reality! I was completely captivated by Lisa Samson's quirky and colorful characters, so tender and down-to-earth, but bold and dangerous when one they love is threatened. You'll never forget *Tiger Lillie*."

—NETA JACKSON, author of *The Yada Yada Prayer Group*

"Lisa Samson has done it again! A superbly told story that immediately captivated me with its loveable and quirky characters. The intricacies of relationship between two completely different sisters provide an intriguing and captivating read—a story that becomes a real page-turner toward the end! Way to go, Lisa!"

—MELODY CARLSON, award-winning author of *Finding Alice, Crystal Lies,* and the Diary of a Teenage Girl series

"Like sprinkles of paprika on a sea of sour cream, *Tiger Lillie*'s colorful characters catch the attention and tantalize the taste buds. I read this novel in one sitting, but I'll not soon forget the cast of flavorful characters—Lillie and Tacy and Cristoff and Gordon. Lisa Samson writes with surprising honesty, genuine love, and indefatigable hope. Make time for this one—you'll love it!"

—ANGELA HUNT, author of *The Awakening*

"Many writers in the genre of Christian fiction shy away from characters who stray too far outside 'safe' conservative lines. Thankfully, Lisa Samson seems to understand that to breathe life into wonderfully flawed characters is to paint a refreshingly honest and compelling picture of the foibles and follies of the human experience. In *Tiger Lillie,* she does just that. Brilliantly."

—CONSTANCE RHODES, founder of FINDINGbalance.com and editor of *The Art of Being: Reflections on the Beauty and the Risk of Embracing Who We Are*

"Wow! What a book! Strong, courageous characters, compelling storyline, hidden truths that jump out and grab you—all in Lisa Samson's marvelous and unique voice. Loved it! Loved it!"

> —GAYLE ROPER, author of *Winter Winds, Autumn Dreams,*
> *Summer Shadows,* and *Spring Rain*

"Nobody writes like Lisa Samson. Not even Lisa Samson! That's because each of her novels is different, exposing yet another aspect of her literary talent. See for yourself in *Tiger Lillie,* a fresh and wonderful addition to her unique body of work."

> —JAMES SCOTT BELL, Christy Award–winning author of *Breach*
> *of Promise* and *A Certain Truth*

"*Tiger Lillie* showcases Lisa Samson's unique ability to write in-your-face fiction. Her vivid characters reach out and grab, providing a contrast between the self-centered mind and the dedicated heart of those who claim His name. This is her best book yet!"

> —LOIS RICHER, author of *Dangerous Sanctuary*

"Lisa Samson creates the most wonderful quirky characters, ones that jump off the page and into your heart. *Tiger Lillie* kept me up reading way too late. Lisa's voice is unlike any other writer out there, and she's addicting. If you haven't discovered this phenomenal writer yet, you're in for a treat with *Tiger Lillie.*"

> —COLLEEN COBLE, author of *Without a Trace* and *Beyond a Doubt*

"Lillie and Tacy, two sisters brimming with *joie de vivre,* delight and then draw us into their life and death struggle with darkness. *Tiger Lillie* provokes thought as it tugs the heart."

> —LYN COTE, author of *Winter's Secret*

"With insight and complexity, Lisa Samson writes a story of God's intricate grace in the heartbreaks of life. *Tiger Lillie* is not to be forgotten."

> —CINDY MARTINUSEN, author of *The Salt Garden*

# lisa samson

best-selling author of *THE CHURCH LADIES*

# Tiger
# Lillie

*a novel*

## WaterBrook
### PRESS

TIGER LILLIE
PUBLISHED BY WATERBROOK PRESS
2375 Telstar Drive, Suite 160
Colorado Springs, Colorado 80920
*A division of Random House, Inc.*

All Scripture quotations are taken from the *Holy Bible, New International Version*®. NIV®. Copyright © 1973, 1978, 1984 by International Bible Society. Used by permission of Zondervan Publishing House. All rights reserved.

The characters and events in this book are fictional, and any resemblance to actual persons or events is coincidental.

ISBN 1-57856-598-7

Library of Congress Cataloging-in-Publication Data

Samson, Lisa, 1964–
    Tiger Lillie / Lisa Samson.— 1st ed.
        p. cm.
    ISBN 1-57856-598-7
    1. Weddings—Planning—Fiction. 2. Married women—Fiction. 3. Abused wives—Fiction. 4. Sisters—Fiction. I. Title.
    PS3569.A46673T54 2004
    813'.54—dc22

                                                    2004009583

Printed in the United States of America
2004—First Edition

10 9 8 7 6 5 4 3 2 1

For my son, my "favorite boy,"
Jacob Patrick.

May you grow up to be a godly, kind,
and gentle man who loves the Lord with all
his heart, mind, soul, and strength.
I love you, buddy.

# Acknowledgments

First, to my Creator, who for some mysterious reason gave me this job to do. I know I could be out in an office, away from my family, and I am ever thankful for the privilege You've afforded me to write. I am ever grateful for Your grace. I deserve none of it.

I began this book several years ago while biting my nails and waiting for the next contract to come through. The person who encouraged me to write this, a very strong-minded, independent woman, is now gone. I'd like to thank my late mother, Joy Ebauer, for keeping this project alive during a very dark time. I do hope you are able to look down, even for a second, and see, Mom.

To Istvàn Palffy I owe a huge debt of gratitude. I found "Stephen" on the Internet. A count in Hungary before communism declared him a Class Enemy, Stephen provided me with a detailed account of his own imprisonment and journey to freedom in 1956. It's a story I'll never forget and one that bears telling in its own right, one my pedestrian skills as a writer would certainly belittle. Thank you, friend.

To my daughter Tyler, who baby-sat Jake and Gwynnie for many hours during the summer I finished this project. You are a precious jewel and a beautiful, strong young lady. I am proud and thankful to be your mama.

To my niece, Melissa Chesser, your help with watching the kids, keeping up my housework, and always doing so with a smile made this easier on us all. Thank you for providing such love to my children. May you always seek God's face.

To my family—Will, Tyler, Jake, and Gwynnie—thanks for seeing this as a regular part of our lives. If any lives are bettered by these words, and I pray some are, the reward is yours. This couldn't be done without you. You give me a deeper heart from which to write.

To Kathy Kreyling, who entered from hard copy to computer my many, many edits, who made this process much less stressful, who caught errors I myself didn't catch, I wish to extend my thanks. The end process was more joyful because of you, Bugg!

And to these people, I owe a great deal: my agent, Claudia Cross, who makes it fun. At Waterbrook: Dudley Delffs, Don Pape, John Hamilton, and all the rest! Erin Healy, my editor whose touch makes all the difference. My Chi Libris friends, especially Jim Bell and Jack Cavanaugh. My family and friends: Lori Chesser, Tim Chesser, Jennifer Hagerty, Heather Born, Chris Burkett, Gloria Danaher, Leigh Heller, Marty Ehrhardt and the Wednesday Afternoon Prayer Ladies, and Pat Reeves for your friendship and prayers. To those who let me write at their establishments: the gang at The Greek Village, especially Jerry and Joan and Becki, and at Main Street Cigar, especially Russ, who welcomed me in his own special way, and Tony, owner and friend who provides community, intriguing conversation, and wonderfully slicing reviews of Stan Remington.

Thank you to my readers! You're the reason why! E-mail me at lesamson@hotmail.com.

# Lillie

I have a skeleton inside of me.

The bizarre, creepy quality of that thought never wanes. As a little girl, I used to catch my mom gossiping about our next door neighbor, a lady named Rexy Van Bibber who wore nothing but medium gray and ordered Chinese carry-out almost every weeknight. After my sixth birthday party, which, as always, consisted of a can of paprika, two large tubs of sour cream, my mother's Hungarian relatives, and Daddy's deaf father, Grandpa Joe (who did, in fact, look alarmingly like Jack Albertson in *Willy Wonka and the Chocolate Factory*), Mom was at it again over poor Rexy. This party, as always, also included gallons of red punch and mouth-blown balloons hanging from the dogwood and maple trees in the yard of the rectory. After the Duncan Hines Red Velvet cake with cream-cheese icing, the mismatched candles, and the strong European coffee, we'd relax out on the buckled brick patio and soak up the purple evening.

I've always loved evening. Even back then, as a chubby, bug-eyed little girl who also loved a good joke, that time of the day sobered me and filled me with peace. I know now it's due to the fact that the clock never stops ticking down and the time for making the day's mistakes draws to a sweet close. Even the circumstances in which to make these blunders fly away, for in the twilight we simply sit and breathe quietly, cross our fingers, and hope the phone won't ring or the Jehovah's Witnesses won't come to the door. Good grief, if their spiel doesn't usher in the loss of all your good intentions, I don't know what does. Must be nice to be one hundred percent right one hundred percent of the time. I'd settle for fifty-one percent myself.

That night, Mom sat and stroked the inside of my forearm. Rexy materialized for a moment at her back door to let out her Persian cat. Mom leaned forward. "Have you noticed the way that Rexy Van Bibber always looks both ways as soon as she steps out her front door? I think she's got a skeleton in her closet." Then she turned to my father, who rocked slowly on an old sliding cedar davenport Mom had painted lime green the year before. The paint didn't weather winter too well. "What do you think, Carl?"

With a twist of his head Carl Bauer listened for the perfect A as he turned the peg on his guitar. Satisfied, he closed his eyes, eyes that had seen my face only until I was six months of age, and even before that, I was just a blur. "Well, Kathy, I don't know, babe. She seems fine to me. A little odd maybe, but certainly not the brooding, mysterious type. You know, just eccentric. Probably nothing more than that."

"Well, *I* think she's got a skeleton in her closet."

Dad shook his head. "Whatever you say, babe. But everyone has some sort of skeleton in their closet, don't you think?"

"Not her kind."

So that's where some people kept their skeletons. The simplicity of the arrangement amazed me. And it made perfect sense to my six-year-old mind. Skeletons, being such ugly things after all, hardly deserved the light of day. The next morning, I proceeded to investigate all of our neatly arranged closets. My mother, Katherina Bajnok Bauer, boxed and labeled everything. She's kept Sharpies in her pocket ever since I can remember. Red for her own items, black for Dad's, blue for mine. And my sister Tacy's birth commissioned that final pen in the Sharpie four-pack, the bright LEGO green, lined up in the confines of her pocket according to age, of course. I never saw her without them back then.

I began the search for my skeleton in the cool recesses of my own closet. Good move, right? I mean, if skeletons lurked in closets, surely they lurked in the closet of their owner. Rexy's obviously spent a little time there. And if Mom was right, it was a doozie. Did she hang it up in one of those vinyl zippered clothing protectors? Or did she arrange it in a box?

The scent of lavender sachet pillows, lemon oil, and cedar weighted the air inside my narrow walk-in closet, and the light bulb discharged a soft, pulsating pink. Clothes, in order of length, subcategory color, subcategory fabric, lined the right-hand side of the skinny cubby: coats, long dresses, dresses, pants, skirts, sweaters, shirts, shorts, and socks. Yes, Mom even hung up the socks, three pair secured by clothespins to one wire hanger. I did have an underwear drawer though. "Some things aren't meant to be hanging in plain view, Lillie," Mom explained the day I asked why boys are allowed to go without shirts but girls aren't. "That's why we have underwear drawers."

Which explains why women don't hang up their bras either, I guess. And these days, mine would take up way too much closet space anyway.

I owned lots of clothing. We all did. Parishioners donated bags and bags, and Mom drew up a chart ensuring we wore at least a few garments from each donor regularly so they'd feel good about their largess. The rest—torn, stained rags, really—she threw out, knowing firsthand how insulting receiving such tatters could be. "It's not good enough for us, but surely, it's good enough for the rector's family," she'd say with a shake of her head.

Floor-to-ceiling shelves checkered the left side of my closet. Shoe-boxes labeled in alphabetical order rested in neat stacks. Having been taught to read in kindergarten, I closely examined the *S* stack, but no mute bone-filled shoebox dwelled there between the *Scenery for Puppet Stage* box and the *Supergirl Dress-Ups* box. No box with *Skeleton* written in incisive, voltage-blue Sharpie letters resided in this proper little nook of our tidy, tiny manse.

Now embarked upon a mission, I hurried down the hallway and into my parents' small, sea blue bedroom.

Maybe parents conferred skeletons upon a child's eighteenth birth-day, which might mean my skeleton waited, gathering a minimal amount of dust, in *their* closet. The same shelving configuration latticed the right-hand side of the long, narrow space. My fingers slid over the smooth sur-faces of the *S* boxes. No boxes marked *Skeletons* there either. What else might they be marked under?

*Family Skeletons?*

*Family. F-f-family. F-f-f-f. F-f-f-f. F.*

So I checked the *F*s for *Family Skeletons* because, knowing my mom, she would have grouped them together to save space.

"What in heaven's name are you looking for, Lillian?"

Oh no.

"Just standing here, Mommy." I shoved my hands in the pockets of my purple overalls and turned to face her, belly thrust forward, feet pigeoned.

Her chapped fingers fluttered back to the nape of her neck where they tightened the knot of her navy blue kerchief. She wiped her hands beside the sharp creases down the legs of her Monday-Wednesday-Friday maternity pants. The aroma of Tide, Mr. Clean, and Clorox puffed out with her movements along with a slight hint of Tabu talcum powder. "You can't fool me, Lillie. You're up to something."

And then, heavily pregnant with my sister, she knelt down on her haunches and settled my squishy, six-year-old body onto her diminishing lap.

I have no beefs with Carl and Kathy Bauer's parenting skills. Other than high expectations, they hardly ever stormed and raged, except for the time I missed Ash Wednesday Mass because I'd lost track of time at the school library. "Lillie, it's a holy day," my father reminded me after mass, during which I'd made a commotion as I ran from the rain into the church, my feet sliding right out from under me there in the center aisle. "I would think you'd learn to take my responsibilities as priest of this parish into consideration." Of course I felt bad. Who wouldn't? When you see a man set his life aside for God, it leaves you almost no leverage for a great retort. Ever.

Ever. Ever.

Besides that, my tailbone hurt for weeks and I ended up with a B on that paper I'd been researching.

As I sat on Mom's lap, I pressed my nose into her full white blouse, the Peter Pan collar ruffling my bowl-shaped bangs. She ran her rough fingertips up and down my slick blond braid. "Come now, Silly Lillie, you know I have mother magic. I can find anything."

Keeping my face buried, I whispered, "I was looking for my skeleton."

"Your what?"

I gazed up into her face. "My skeleton."

"In the closet?" She pressed a hand against her mouth, but amusement bounced around in her sweet nutmeg eyes.

"It's not funny, Mommy. Rexy Van Bibber keeps hers in a closet so I thought maybe that's where you kept mine, too."

Fifteen minutes later, after hefting open the *Britannica,* displaying several diagrams of the human anatomy and explaining the term "a figure of speech," she phoned the church office.

"He's with a parishioner? Oh. But listen to this, Jean." Her laughter, probably mingling with the church secretary's, rustled my eardrum tissue all the way from the old, metal-cabineted kitchen to where I sat on my bed upstairs, examining the knobby bone-bumps on my wrists and ankles.

Well, Halloween never seemed quite as scary after that, I can say. At least not the part skeletons played. And even then I leaned toward jack-o'-lanterns.

I have a skeleton inside of me.

The thought pops up with alarming frequency on first dates, especially those destined for some hall of fame of weirdness, or on nights most likely to make a girl feel she's having an out-of-body experience.

So when Leslie Ferris, the newest male member of the "happening" singles social group I joined a year ago at Chesapeake Bay Baptist, reaches out his hand across the table at Della Notte, I see a skeleton hand. How can I possibly put my skeleton hand inside his skeleton hand? Talk about bizarre and creepy. Holding hands on the first date? Sure. But not with *this* guy. And a second date? Perhaps a few more minutes will open a previously unseen rose, but optimism isn't exactly blooming here in Little Italy's newest, sleekest restaurant, its wide curved window the only smooth thing about the evening thus far.

First of all, Leslie suggested we go Dutch as soon as he flung open the cab door…from the *inside*. Where did this guy's mother go wrong? "I hope you understand, Lillie. But let's face it, a first date isn't the time to make a financial investment."

Great. Here we go again. Curse those stupid bra-burning bimbos who sullied it for those of us nurtured by gentleman fathers, those who realize a female can be honored and served and basically elevated on a pedestal and still be a liberated roaring woman too big to ignore. As Saint Paul, via Dad, said, "There is neither male nor female." But Daddy, now he's special. He actually reads the writing of female Christian mystics (or rather, Mom reads them to him) and passes the books on to me and my sister. I know what a special relationship a woman can have with her Lord. So much more intimate in character than a man can experience. My younger sister, Tacy, loves the mystics, or used to, but since marrying that Rawlins McGovern…well, I won't think about that now.

Second, Leslie asked where I would like to eat, and I answered, "Ban Thai would be nice," and he said, "I didn't have that in mind. Let's eat Italian." Not, "Let's eat Italian, *okay?*" Not, "Thai food is a little spicy for me. Is Italian a viable alternative?" Just, "Let's eat Italian."

I mean, why even ask if my opinion meant so little to begin with, right? And don't I have some say? I mean, I'm paying my own way here!

Obviously he isn't nearly as enlightened as Dad. It's funny that someone who cannot see has a clearer outlook on the stuff of life than anyone else I know. It may not be fair to compare other men to my father, but it is my right.

And now, Leslie's waxing and waning and waxing again about his pet snakes and how expensive mice are getting. But you can get them frozen now, which cuts down on trips to the pet store.

Is he testing me?

Just nervous?

Maybe a little socially backward?

Most important, he is *nothing* like Teddy.

And why does this kind of guy always want to hold hands? Why didn't that cute architect named Cliff make even one physical advance during the entire bevy of Monday evenings I accompanied him to his church-league softball games?

Baptist guys. So free and easy with other people's hearts and emotions. As my Episcopalian father might say, "Nothing a good long dose of liturgy wouldn't fix right up!" And he'd wink. He's been blind for more than thirty years but obviously remembers the power of a good wink. I'm glad. I love Daddy's winks.

But this dating rigmarole hardly proves a worthy antidote to loneliness. Twelve days of my life invested in Cliff, three months of listening for the phone, all for nothing more than twelve ice-cream cones at High's Dairy Store and a couple of drives out to Pretty Boy Dam to stargaze. I thought surely he'd kiss me, but no. Not even a peck on the cheek. At thirty-one, I don't have more than three months to dole out to the noncommittal types. I mean, if a guy reaches forty-two and still lives with his mother, something's just not right. Right?

And looky there. Leslie's wearing huge hiking boots. On a date.

He retrieves his barren hand. "Earth to Lillie. Earth to Lillie."

Earth to Lillie? "Yeah?"

"You were wandering off on me there, sweetheart."

Sweetheart?

I wore a skirt for this? "Tomatoes do that to me, Les. And alfredo sauce always makes me so sleepy I can't concentrate." Which is totally true. See? Should've taken me to the Thai place, boot boy.

Times like these I wish I owned a cell phone so my best friend, Cristoff, could call me an hour or so into each date and fabricate an emergency at work.

"Oh. How about some espresso then?"

Your treat?

"It gives me…gas." Which is totally a lie. I glance leisurely at my watch. We've only been together ninety minutes? Oh Lord, somehow I now see the earthly application of a "day is like a thousand years in Your sight." Or is it the other way around?

"Well, I'll just get some for myself then. Dessert?"

And heels, too. I even wore heels. "No, thanks."

"I'm going to take the cannoli."

The waiter receives the order and Leslie says, "Just bring the check back with dessert. Split it fifty-fifty, would you?"

Fifty-fifty? I didn't even have dessert! Or espresso. In fact, I just ordered ice water and he got Sprite. And my fettuccine alfredo beggars his shrimp scampi by almost half.

With my chin in hand, I let my gaze journey up his blue button-down shirt, over the lump of his Adam's apple, and up to his face. Stopping at his mouth, I peer closely at the scooped bottom lip and I know as sure as I know my own gigantic bra size that scooped bottom lip will never get close to mine. It's not that it grosses me out. But I am afforded no visualization of a future, nothing, only a swirling mist and a total lack of imagination. "Doesn't it weird you out to think you have a skeleton inside of you, Leslie?"

"Say what?"

"There's a skeleton inside of you."

He wipes his lips, eyes darting. "I'm not following you."

"It's not just bones. It's a skeleton. Like, a whole skeleton. Right there. Inside your own body."

"Are you okay, Lillie?"

I dig a twenty and a five out of my purse and lay them by my plate. It's all over! Nothing left to see, folks. Move along! Move along!

"See you at singles group on Wednesday, Leslie."

And I stand to my feet, the sole survivor turning away from the wreckage. But I lied again. I'm not going back to that group. I'm desperate enough without hanging around more desperate people.

I'm not sure what he says to my back. Soon enough, the city streets swallow my deed, and my insignificance strengthens with each step homeward. I'd held out such hope for this one. And for the life of me, I sure can't see why. Daddy's obviously not the only blind one in the family.

I let myself into my old row house after the excruciating, high-heeled, thirty-minute walk home, and I proceed to pump out a few zippy miles on my exercise bike. Hey, I'm plump, not out of shape. Afterward I feel energized enough to reward myself by taking out my contacts and whizzing up a raspberry soymilk shake.

Not that I'd tell anybody else I enjoy the nutty taste of soymilk. It makes me sound so...so natural.

I slide in my socks on the smooth hardwood floors of the hallway back to my bedroom where my planner lies open on the bed. Only nine thirty, and I had blocked out another two hours for this date. Good. Plenty of time remains for a phone call.

Cristoff will love this one! I reach for the phone on my nightstand, dial the number of the apartment on the upstairs floor, and wait for my best friend's answering machine to click to life.

*"My smile is wide.*

*My hat is doffed.*

*You've reached the pad. Of me, Cristoff.*

*So leave your words and make them few*

*'Cause I've got better things to do*

*Like make a return phone call to you!"*

I can't help but roll my eyes every time his greeting chirrups in my ear. Not only does the poetry induce nausea, Cristoff almost never returns his calls.

"Another disaster to record for your book, honey," I report. Yes, report. Cristoff records my dating exploits, in novel form, naturally. Talk about horrible. Passive verbs litter the pages and the words *surreptitiously* and *suddenly* appear over and over again. Daddy would be appalled as would all my undergrad professors, who were heartbroken when I got my MBA instead of an MA in literature. But Cristoff's writing, as well as old movies and Bible study—he loves that Kay Arthur with a passion—keep him home at night, away from the bars and a possible third detox stint. He's also working on a memoir. He hasn't let me read it, and I don't ask for the privilege.

"Hey, honey, it's me. Pick up."

He does. "How bad was it, sweetie?"

Cristoff's voice soothes the open wound of singlehood. Cristoff loves me and I love him. Oh, not in *that* way, of course. He's the brother

I never had. I'm the platonic partner he needs these days. What a family life he endured growing up! Some things you refuse to think about for long or you'll lose your faith, if you know what I mean. We've had this "honey/sweetie" thing going for years, as though we're Lucy and Ethel. Unfortunately, he's Lucy, which makes me—

"I'm lying in bed with a raspberry shake."

"How many prayers of forgiveness so far?"

"Just one."

"So *he* was the jerk this time?"

"Honey!"

"Just calling it like I see it, sweetie. You can be a little…well, disconcerting…to the lesser man, of course."

Sounds good to me. Too good. "Oh please. Let's face it. I'm a geek magnet."

"And you know you write people off too quickly."

"Only when they deserve it."

"And when Miss Thing cops an attitude."

"Okay, Gilbert!" Cristoff hates being called by his first name.

"You need me to come down? It's only nine thirty."

"Nah. Tomorrow's Friday. It's going to be a big day for both of us."

"You know I'll come down if you need me to."

"I know, honey."

"And you even wore a skirt."

"I know. Heels, too."

"Really? Wow. High hopes, huh?"

"Yeah. Bummer, right?"

He yawns. "So what happened?"

"I walked out on him. Just left him sitting all alone in the middle of Della Notte."

"You're usually not rude. He must have deserved it then."

"Not really." I sip my milk shake and pull off my glasses. "He was just a goofball. There's no crime in being a goofball." And I sigh, rubbing the bridge of my nose.

Cristoff pauses, then says, "You posed the skeleton question, didn't you?"

"Yeah."

"I'll be right down."

## 2

## Lillie

Yep, as far as I'm concerned, the Christian singles group scene has gone the way of the girdle. For me anyway. First of all, I do believe loneliness, and not any desire to find God's will, invited me there in the first place. Dreams of a family, a little home with white kitchen cupboards and a blue nursery right next to our soft-yellow bedroom rendered me helpless against my own sorry life. So, being raised as a good Episcopalian, I at least knew where to go for help. The bars held no appeal. God instituted marriage, right? The least He could do was give me a leg up. And the Baptists sure possess a knack when it comes to singles ministries.

But, instead, I've ended up even *less* sure of myself than ever. Well, I'm never going back to Chesapeake Bay Baptist. If all I ask of God is a husband, and He isn't delivering, maybe He has something else in mind. Maybe I'm shooting too low.

Don't laugh. Saint Paul said the same thing!

That poor man. He gets such a bad rap from the bra-burners.

# Tacy

I was swaddled in a blanket.

I sat in a highchair eating from my mother's hand—a spoonful of apricots.

The warm water in the sink accepted my little body and soothed where the diaper had been.

I took a step and busted my eyebrow on the edge of the coffee table.

Mom yelled at me when I colored on the sofa.

I played an angel in the Christmas pageant.

I went to my first day of school and met a little girl named Barb. They served french fries in the cafeteria, and the teacher read us a story from <u>Frog and Toad All Year</u>. I loved the story and the way those two friends stuck together, different but the same.

I lost a tooth.

I won first place in the third-grade art contest!

I won first place in the fourth-grade art contest!

Dad bought me a guitar for Christmas. I hoped my hands were big enough to really learn. He said he started learning when he, too, was ten.

Daddy said I only needed to know three chords, four if I wanted to get a little fancy, to play almost any song I'd want to pick out. D, G, A, E minor. Or was it B minor? I haven't picked up my guitar in years. I picked out that ancient Beatles song "Yesterday" and played it for the relatives at my birthday party. Eleven seemed so old.

J won the sixth-grade art contest!

J got my hair cut short before eighth grade began. But J didn't like it.

## Lillie

The first time I ever saw Teddy, he was sitting in a puddle of oversized clothing, crying by the school door. His mother, Mrs. Gillie, a woman I would come to love almost as much as my own mother, sat down next to him, legs extended, smoking a cigarette and stroking his brown hair. I pranced up the steps, my own mother barely keeping up with me. A kindergartner! I was so ready for school I could barely keep from dancing. I was going to learn to read! Just like Daddy had, years before, before he learned to read with his fingers—a skill, I know now, that isn't reserved just for those with no eyesight.

"He's a little frightened of the day," said Mrs. Gillie, a robust, black-haired woman with thick glasses. "Maybe you could help?"

Shy around unfamiliar adults, I just nodded. She patted the decking next to her, but I sat around on the other side of Teddy. And I don't know why, but I reached out, put my arms around him, and whispered in his ear, "Let's go in together. Let's just do everything together, okay?" That seemed like a good arrangement to me. I didn't know anybody at Churchville Elementary, and to have a ready-made friendship seemed like a great idea.

He looked up at me and grinned a little, and while I couldn't appreciate the deep brown eyes then as I came to later, I knew they held something special that went way down inside. "You mean it?" he asked me.

I still had my arms around him. "Come on, don't be afraid. I'll be with you."

My mother, standing over us, smiled, and I felt so proud. "It's amazing how they mimic what they've heard over and over," she said to Mrs. Gillie.

"That's the truth. And if it's the good things, so much the better. I'm Sally Gillie."

"Kathy Bauer."

They smiled and nodded, for that was in the days when women didn't shake hands, and they acquainted themselves with one another. Meanwhile, I helped Teddy to his feet, showed him my new lunchbox, and held his hand. We walked inside, embarking on a twelve-year sail through oceans, across bays, and down a multitude of rivers, some navigable, others not. I felt as if I'd been given a job to do, like those guys on *Mission Impossible*, and I began to hum the theme song. Teddy joined in, and like the edge of a gentle cool front, something brought change, and it was my hand being tugged.

God, You know I miss him. My heart still reels at the realization that someone so wonderful loved me more than anybody else.

## Tacy

J was so excited the night Lillie took me out for dinner, just the two of us, to Burger King. We ate chicken sandwiches and drank Cokes and we talked. She was so pretty and so strong and was almost finished with her freshman year of college.

My friend Barb turned miserable and depressed during her parents' divorce. J told her J'd give her a makeover one

Saturday night, but she only said, "You just don't understand, Tacy. You think new eyeliner clears up everything." That hurt my feelings, but I was powerless to understand her situation.

Mom told me to sit with Grandma Erzsèbet for a while as she needed to run my Dad to the doctor. It was the first time I was alone in the house without Mom or Dad. Grandma and I played bilingual Scrabble: English and Hungarian. I didn't flaunt my fluent Hungarian in front of Lillie, who never could pick up the language.

Lillie came in one day with her calendar book in hand and told me that the deadline to submit my work for the Towson Art Festival was just around the corner. That summer, she drove me over and helped me unload my canvases, and I really needed her help with that big mother-and-child abstract. We had an ice cream at Friendly's, and she took me over to Walden's and bought me a copy of <u>Lord of the Flies</u>. "It's a little disturbing," she said, "but just goes to show you that kids really do need their parents."

I sang a solo at church on Sunday at the hootenanny mass, as some of the older ones call it. "Take Our Bread" and then right into "On Eagle's Wings." Just me and my guitar. Yep, just the priest's daughter and her guitar.

## Lillie

Far beneath the bridge on which my bare toes rest, the river waters beckon as soundlessly as ever. The soaring steel structure crisscrossed with riveted support beams challenges my eyes as my weak vision skates up the arch.

*You are mine. You are all mine.*

I focus on the blinking orange lights at each corner, their hue reminiscent of the skin of the small jack-o'-lantern I carved yesterday to commemorate the coming of September. The humidity of the estuary coats my throat, wrapping my tongue in the taste of summer's end and the dark settling of the day.

Ah, evening.

I try not to think about the pollution level.

"You ready, sweetie?" Cristoff asks.

"As ready as I'll ever be."

"Get up there then. You'll be fine. You always are."

"You look nice in that tuxedo." Boy, does he! So slender and taut, classic and beautiful. Too bad his looks can't be put to good use on some sweet girl at his church.

"You're not so bad yourself. Now go on, Lillie."

The sparse nine o'clock Key Bridge traffic thickens at the sight of us gathered there. We planned to create this spectacle during the commuter traffic, but one of our clients, a frantic bride waffling between minicheesecakes and pecan tartlets, spoiled that idea. Sometimes I just want to head-butt these silly women, but we can't afford to lose a single account. And so I steady a hand atop the warm cement guardrail and, gripping hard, climb up with firm footing. Not an easy accomplishment in a fancy silk evening gown and a stiff breeze, but again, I'm plump, not uncoordinated.

For several moments, I concentrate on my toenails, lacquered a stainless steel for the occasion to match the bridge, and I breathe deeply. My toes curl around the top of the divider, the small knuckles knobby white angles that mimic the curve of the balustrade. The hardened cement floods my arches, massages my insteps. I love it. I grind them down even more.

A distant siren tightens the muggy air. The rest of those assembled for the occasion observe from ten feet away, nodding me on, necks jerking like park pigeons. I stand tall, the dark pond of land supporting Fort Carroll swallowing my gaze. Overgrown, unused, alone, and obsolete, Fort Carroll invites only the most intrepid adventurer. Maybe someday.

I coil my fingers into my callused palms and stare down. Quite a drop to today's calm Patapsco River. Carefully adjusting my footing, turning my back on the gray liquid mass lined by a golden moon, I look the nearest motorist in the eye, see the shock illuminated by the streetlights, and throw her a reassuring smile, a nod, and a little wave.

"Go, Lillie!" Cristoff yells. "Be a good girl, or we'll all be arrested!"

I knife-throw him a glare. Silly man. Of course we'll all be arrested. We always get arrested.

The lights of the Baltimore Harbor twinkle in the darkness, and the blue dock cranes stand still and silent like monsters in the unfocused pools of brightness illuminating their sturdy structures. The wail of the siren sharpens.

And so I lean back, cross myself, and loosening my toe-grip, I fall in understuffed Raggedy Ann complacency toward the river.

In that moment of helplessness, air caresses me like a tender lover frightened of his own strength. Like Teddy at twelve, reaching out to stroke my arm for the first time. Freedom envelops me as my iron will liquefies, gushing forth from inside a dark place known as "What it takes to be a Strong Hungarian Woman."

Grandma Erzsèbet. My mother, Katherina. My sister, Tacy. Strong Hungarian Women. I fall, liberating myself from their stoic clutch, their grim resolution, their ability to rise above all occasions with smiles on their faces and not a hair out of place.

*I* am the bold one. *I* am the fearless one. *I* am gutsy and strong and daring.

Rrrr.

My ink-blue evening gown flutters in fluid ripples against my skin. The air drafts the flags of fabric upward as, finally, the bungee cord catches and my flight slows. Exiting the fall, I spring upward like a confused Phoenix who'd quite forgotten the rebirth process and went about it all wrong. I tuck my body for the upward wing, then plummet once again. I'd like to tell you it's smooth and graceful, but when I was seven my mother suggested ballet lessons and I laughed.

My compatriots in the Extreme Delights Sporting and Adventure Club cheer, and as I fall once more I hear the pop of a very old cork. Cristoff yells loudest and someone drawls in a fake British accent, "Well, twist it all to Hades and back, we'll just jolly well get arrested too."

Flashing red and blue lights and a couple of state troopers meet me as they pull me over the dividers and onto the dry road. Honey hands me my glasses. The fresh-faced cop can't contain a grudging smile, and his well-done steak of a partner barks, "Who, young lady, do you think you are?"

"I've got a pretty good idea." The Lie-O-Meter buzzes.

"It's just Tiger Lillie, sir," the young trooper says. "Happy birthday, ma'am."

Now that guy knows how to wink. And they've got a nickname for me? Yeah boy!

If they have any brains, they'll mark the day on their calendar and show up before we do next year.

## Tacy

The day I heard from <u>Teen Talk</u> magazine that I was a finalist in their writing contest, Write Stuff '91, I saw all I could someday be coming together. Going to New York. Touring the facilities. A photography session. Oh yeah, the magazine world seemed just so me. Fashion, art, writing, beauty. I talked to Dad about it, about going to school for journalism or something like that, and he liked the idea. He was sitting in his chair, reading a Braille something.

"You would do so well in that profession, Tace."

One day when I told him I just wanted to be a plain old artist or a photographer or something, he said, "You can't make a decent living at that. You need to be able to stand on your own two feet. Just take a look at me and see what happens when you choose a beggarly profession."

I sat down in Mom's chair, next to his, and put my feet up on the coffee table. "Tell me about your first date with Mom again, Daddy." Back when you could see and Mom didn't need to care for you.

I swear his eyes took on a look as though he could see. And maybe he could. Yes, he'd had lots of other girlfriends, "But when I took one look at your mother, I knew those days were behind me for good!"

Mom told me that night as we did dishes, "Boy, was he something," when they started dating. Like the suave, man-about-town type and everything.

As Dad spoke about their dinner out, the way he placed

his hand on hers during the movie at The Grand, I could just picture the two of them together, swaggering arm in arm down Eastern Avenue on their way for drinks and dinner at Haussner's. I believe it was the first time I'd ever really thought of them as carefree, young, and in love.

Lillie arrived home from school after his story. She put down her book bag and kissed our cheeks.

"Good day, babe?" Dad asked.

"Oh yeah. We started <u>Much Ado About Nothing</u>. And I got a copy of <u>The Bell Jar</u> out of the library. Dad, can you believe her use of language?"

My ears started burning. A good burn. I loved it when they talked about books! Lillie wasn't the writer I was, really, but she always loved books. We all loved books.

Lillie had set up one of her craft tables at a small church bazaar, and she asked me to help her man it. I sat there selling all sorts of little trinkets, jewelry, and doll clothes. She paid me ten percent of the profits and put the rest into her school account to pay off her bill.

That night, I sat and read <u>The Bell Jar</u> as she answered phones for doctor's offices who'd signed on with a business she started named Hello There! Answering Service. My sister was a whiz. And I sat beside her most nights, reading and drawing while she answered calls and studied.

She fixed us a cup of tea, and I saw the sadness in her eyes when she sat down across from me at the dining room table. I never knew how she kept so upbeat after Teddy disappeared. Dad felt his way through the room, sat down next to her, and took her hand as though he somehow knew she needed him just then. It was a cosmic experience for me. Dad and Lillie were always so close.

Mom called me into her bedroom, and we read our books, sipped the tea Lillie made, and listened to Beethoven. I felt at peace.

## Lillie

Thirteen years, four months, and two days ago, Teddy disappeared. He said we'd meet at Friendly's for ice cream after graduation, but he never showed up. And Teddy always showed up. Teddy always made good on his promises.

I'll never forget the way Teddy stood up for me the summer we turned eight. As the only girl in the neighborhood, I endured more boy games—cowboys and Indians, marbles, baseball cards, and stickball— than any girl should. And mostly, I liked it. But there we were one day, playing army like we always seemed to do after we tired of riding bikes or roller skating.

Some boys from the next street over didn't deem me combat worthy.

"Hey, they don't allow girls to fight, so neither will we!"

"Yeah!" some of the others answered.

Teddy stood tall. By this time, he looked over all our heads and was easily the nicest-looking boy in school and just the nicest, period, and he was *my* best friend, not theirs, and well, they'd better watch it because that look glittered in his eyes. He always got to be Sarge. "She can't help it if she's a girl."

"That don't mean we have to allow her to play," a boy named Nicolas said, an ugly sneer marring his face. "Girls don't know how to fight, period."

Teddy thought a moment. "Hey, they do too have girls on the battlefield."

"Oh yeah? Where?" Nick asked.

I still stared at the grass, but I looked over to see Teddy thrust out his puny, little-boy chest. "The army nurse! They have army nurses."

"Army nurses!" Scowl, mumble, kick the grass.

"Yep. And Lillie's *our* army nurse."

"No way. She has to be a German nurse."

A German nurse! I wanted to cry. I wanted to run in and tell Mrs. Gillie.

"An American nurse." Teddy took a step forward. "You got anything to say about that?"

I watched him defending me, standing up for me, being my boy hero, my boy wonder, and just then, at that moment, I loved him.

Nick backed down. Nobody stood up to Teddy for long. "Okay, I guess."

The other guys agreed because, well, they knew which boy was the best, and besides, Mrs. Gillie baked the best cookies and scooped an extra half-cup of sugar into her Kool-Aid.

Later that afternoon, Mrs. Gillie invited me over for dinner. She fried up ham steaks, and I sliced the fat from the edge so they wouldn't think me improper.

Mrs. Gillie smiled from her place there at the head of the kitchen table. "Why, hon, look at you, cutting the fat off. Aren't you the proper girl?"

Embarrassed, I said, "Well, actually, I like the fat. I just thought maybe it was the right thing to do."

"Eat however you like here, hon. Think of this as your second home. I mean, you and Teddy here have been best friends since kindergarten. Eat the fat if you like!"

Ham grease had spattered her glasses.

Teddy reached out and touched my hand. "Yeah, that's right, Lillie."

After dinner we viewed a rerun of *Match Game* and laughed like crazy people. I remember thinking if they started making that show again, and I went on and got to the five-thousand-dollar round, I'd pick Richard Dawson as my partner. Yep, I would. Mrs. Gillie swore he was a mind reader.

## Tacy

What a concert that was! The junior-high youth leaders, Jim and Amy, took us down to the Baltimore Blast game, and it was Youth Night. Lots of other church groups went, and they put Saint Stephen's name right up on the scoreboard during one of the breaks. We all cheered. Mr. Jim cheered loudest. He had one of those Baptist voices that rang out in our little Episcopal sanctuary and livened things up.

The local Christian radio station that sponsored the event was giving away free T-shirts so J went down to claim one. J waited in line, chatting with some of the gang when we made it to the table, and the guy giving away the T-shirts, a gorgeous guy, smiled at me. J'm telling you, that smile just went right down into my stomach. He was looking in my eyes and everything.

"Hi, I'm Rawlins," he said.

"Tacy Bauer's my name." And then I giggled, which was so immature, but I couldn't help myself. He was the kind of guy that did that sort of thing to me. Way too old, I knew, but I was just trying to get a free T-shirt. I can't believe it, but I ended up giving him my phone number. I couldn't believe he asked for it. I never did that kind of thing before, as I was only fourteen at the time. Mom always said I looked older than my age. He seemed so nice, like he hung onto every word I said from then on out. Every inane word. I never remembered being so tongue-tied.

He called me the next day and asked me out. His full name was Rawlins McGovern, and I found out he was seven years older than me. Mom and Dad would have had a fit had they known I was talking to a college boy. But I decided they didn't have to know. Besides, he said he went to church and everything, so in the long run they really wouldn't have minded. I didn't want to worry them if I didn't have to. He was interning in the radio station's advertising department, but he planned on assuming a good position at his dad's advertising business someday. That sounded so exciting to me, especially since I wanted to work at a magazine.

Barb and I went to the mall the next day and I bought a pair of lime-green Capri pants like Grace Kelly would have worn. My mother always did like Grace Kelly.

## Lillie

I appreciate the physical body of human beings. Hence my fascination with skeletons and the like, I suppose. But it's a beautiful thing, isn't it? The way the muscles flow like mountain ranges, each bump and sway making utter sense, each mound anchored to a certain point on a bone creating a system of levers and pulleys. What magnificence of planning. And due to this love, this appreciation, I've come to respect Jesus in a way that may be unusual to some. See, He inhabited a body. A body just like mine, minus the female parts and the extra fifty pounds, and He chose to sacrifice it.

If the Incarnation doesn't wow you, nothing will.

Imagine, that cat-o'-nine-tails ripped into those gorgeous mounds of muscle, those perfectly formed, scarlet wads of tissue. Imagine the pain, the very real agony born of very real nerve endings tucked into a neurological network, synapses firing away, firing, firing, blasting sensation of such horrific proportion not many of us can begin to understand.

Imagine the blood spattering like popping oil, wads of flesh flying through the air. I try to picture it, at times, just to appreciate His sacrifice, just to try and not forget and throw around His love and pain like it doesn't really matter in the day-to-day. And I imagine the feeling of a deep scab being ripped away, only that scab covers my entire body and the ripping takes hours.

And even then, am I going far enough? Probably not. Nails into wrists and feet? Dear God. How did You not come down from that cross? How did You stay? What kind of wonderful love is this?

## Tacy

My first date with Rawlins McGovern felt like something from a fairy tale. Unfortunately, I'd never read the actual Brothers Grimm or I might have had a heads-up on the future. I felt guilty because Mom and Dad told me I had to wait until I was sixteen to date, but that was two whole years away. I told Rawlins I was sixteen. He really was the nicest guy. Twenty-one years old. A real man, not like the weird boys in my class who were still laughing during the human anatomy unit in science class. I got ready at Barb's house and he picked me up there. Barb said she'd cover for me if the folks called. I hated to do that to them, but, well, I knew it would all work out fine. Rawlins actually had a car phone. In a blue Miata! His dad partly owned McGovern, Hyde, and Wiley, a really big-time advertising agency downtown. Downtown Baltimore, not Bel Air. In the Signet office tower. And there he was, working at a little radio station to learn the ropes from the bottom up. How cool was that? I couldn't believe he wanted to date me. He told me he'd never seen a more beautiful girl.

He actually had a dress delivered to Barb's house for me. I swear, I looked at least twenty-one in it. It was white with spaghetti straps and a neck scarf. When we drove away from Barb's house, he said, "You have beautiful shoulders, Anastasia." He called me by my full name, wasn't that romantic? "I sent the dress just so I could see them."

Oh man! He was so amazing! Two days before, I worried myself about the school's immature gossip, and suddenly I was dating a mature guy.

But he didn't even reach out to touch my shoulders. I thought he might after going to all that trouble, but he didn't. He just looked at them and flicked his eyes up to look in mine. I can't even explain what it did to me. But that's the way it felt with Rawlins. He was so powerful and wonderful. When he dropped me off, he didn't kiss me or even hold my hand, but he ran a finger down the back of my hand, between the two middle bones, really slowly, and his eyes never left mine and he told me again how beautiful he thought I was. I was so happy.

## Lillie

Cristoff tosses the newspaper onto my desk and I glance up from my planner, watching as he bales his explosive red hair into a ponytail. "If you'd get a cell phone, Lady Nibs, I could have told you about this sooner. We made *The Sunpaper*, Lillie, right on the first page of the Maryland section! Right next to that heroin murder in Patterson Park."

I sip my first taste of consciousness-inducing Coke and push my orange glasses up on my nose. Just couldn't contemplate contacts today. Besides, I love my orange glasses. I love orange. It embodies everything bold and upbeat. I have an orange bedroom, an orange bathroom, and at least ten orange articles of clothing. Today I'm wearing at least four of them, with orange loafers and big orange plastic Wilma Flintstone beads circling my neck.

I'm a nightmare. A size sixteen orange nightmare. I am under no delusion that I'd be allowed as the army nurse in these clothes, German or otherwise!

I tap the paper on my desk. "You sound surprised, honey." We've exploited ourselves this way at least four times a year for the past three years.

Straightening his khaki pants, he perches on the corner of my desk, just an old door on two of my Uncle Jimmy's sawhorses, actually, painted, well, orange. "Oh, honey-girl, I'm just tickled. You know me! And look"—he points to the fourth line down—"there's the plug for our business. Full name *and* the basic location. Free advertising! And we can sure use that. I thought for sure this would catch on more quickly than it has."

"Give it time. We just need that one big account. Or something high-exposure. Like a movie star or something." Like *that* will ever happen in staid and stodgy, provincial Baltimore. Talk about an unorange city. "Until then, we'll just have to tighten our belts and hang on until the line of credit runs out. You got any aspirin? My head is killing me."

"Yeah, I'll get you some in a minute. Just one of those crazy tech companies out in California would give us enough business for a year straight! They do a lot of crazy retreats and meetings and stuff, don't they? How do we get the word out?"

Cristoff is not only my best friend, he's my business partner. We've known each other since seventh grade when, as the new kid, freshly transplanted from Virginia, effeminate and skinny enough to be the offspring of a dogwood tree and a clothesline, nobody else wanted anything to do with him. Well, Teddy and I reached out. Some trio we made once we hit high school. The loud-mouthed, bookish yet athletic girl who paused during every gym class and every lacrosse practice to puff on her inhaler, and Teddy, the love of my life, childhood sweetheart, smarter than both of us put together, taller than both of us put together, and possessing more self-reliance, passion, and daring of spirit than anyone I've ever known. God, You remember how I miss him, don't You? "So what you got going today, honey?"

He looks through my office door to the conference room and the wall-sized whiteboard that organizes Extreme Weddings and The Odd Occasion. "Three days until the Winslow wedding. I'm just figuring up the number of stems I'll need before placing the final order this afternoon. You got everything ready on your end?"

"You know it. The hill behind their house now looks like a pyramid, and you should see the job Pleasance did with the attendants' clothes. They're in the storeroom. A sample napkin came from the rental company. Wanna see?"

"Yepper. I may want to rethink the astilbe in the table arrangements if the dye lot of the fabric is off a bit."

Hard to believe someone who played a sport every season, read all of Francis Schaeffer's writings by the time she graduated from high school, and composed more useless papers on literary themes and comparative analyses of poems and essays in her undergrad program because she couldn't write a lick on her own and didn't dare enter the most orange of all the English programs, creative writing, now spends her days talking about hors d'oeuvres, fabric, flowers, and music. See? Throw that MBA in there and, yep, it isn't any wonder I tang with confusion.

So, here's what I think about God: I think sometimes He gives us innate obstacles directly related to our gifts in order to make us work harder, to rely on Him for improvement, to hone us to a finer, sharper point. Just look at a pencil sharpener if you want to really know what I mean. Those grinding metal rods with lines dug into them. I mean, who hasn't wondered what it would be like, your pinky being small enough, of course, to put your finger in one of those and give it a quick turn?

As expected, Cristoff takes one look at the napkin and runs to his small office at the back of our unit screeching, "No, no, no, no, no, no, no, this astilbe will *never* do now!"

There went my aspirin. At times like this, when his gayness flames more orange than an oil well fire, I feel singed and in some ways a failure.

Man, this outfit is hurting my head! And why did I put my hair into this tight braid? How stupid can I be?

Maybe Pleasance will deliver some painkiller.

It isn't hard to find her. The Amazonian-sized fashion designer paces the floor of the conference/lunch/workroom like some moxie feminine superhero, the cool morning light from the Palladian windows softening her intense brown features. Imagine an elegant, whittled ebony walking stick in goldenrod chiffon, strappy shoes, and an eight-stranded pearl choker and you've got Pleasance Stanley, clothing designer by day, "Stealth Jaguar Woman" by night.

Together, with Cristoff's red hair, we compose a sunset.

The portable phone appears ready to heave its innards out of the antenna, her large hand clutches it so tightly.

"Of course it's fine!" Her airy voice, high, pleasant, and tamed by vocal nodules, contrasts directly with her forceful boxy movements. "No, no. We have people change the fabric all the time, Jaime. Just glad you didn't wait one more week, Jaime."

I roll my eyes at Pleasance as I realize that Jaime Pickerson haunts the other end of that line. Her wedding is scheduled for the beginning of November, only two months away. Romance-book theme. Guess the word *extreme* means different things to different people.

"So you're sure you want to change from Victorian to Regency?" Pleasance Stanley points a finger at me with two quick jabs that say, "You're not off the hook either, girlfriend!"

I pull out one of the mismatched wooden chairs Cristoff had lacquered a bright red and lean my elbows on the old library table he'd marbleized in a shiny, luminous plum. My brain swells as I listen. Cheez Whiz. All that work swirling right down the toilet. And then I remind myself we opened up shop less than a year ago, that red ink threatens to drown us. We must make these changes with smiles on our faces because Jaime Pickerson's father owns eight appliance superstores and two Jaguar dealerships, by gosh by golly.

Pleasance now towers over me on top of the conference table, her high, goldenrod platform sandals shocking the center of the wooden plane via lopsided jumping jacks. I swear the woman could beat Evander Holyfield if he had the guts to fight her. "Well, of course you'll have to speak to Lillian about that. With the mansion already reserved…oh sure, she's right here, honey!"

Talk about light on the feet.

Pleasance literally throws the phone in my direction. Line-drive Frisbee shot toward the gut.

I catch it with one hand.

So there.

"Jaime! Hi! What's this I hear?" Fake voice alert!

And then she rambles on and on. And on.

Jaime Pickerson is the only person I know who can draw in on a cigarette without a break in her speech flow. A bechimnied Tower of Babble, Jaime hosts a conservative political talk show on Radio 680 called "Let's

Kick Butt." I catch it when my schedule allows. Only the most intrepid of callers hang onto the other end of the phone line.

She's my kind of gal.

So I let her simmer on for a bit to buy myself some time, begging Pleasance to go get my Coke off my desk, mouthing, "Aspirin…please," as clearly as I can. She returns a full five minutes later with both, and I swear I uttered less than a dozen words in all that time.

And I thought my headache was bad before this.

I promise myself a trip to the shooting range after work. And I'll look at that target and think, "Jaime Pickerson and every bride in the Baltimore-Washington metropolitan area!" and I'll squeeze off five rounds. And I'll feel better for a full twenty minutes.

Jaime had picked up a Barbara Cartland book about the Regency era, and realized her fiancé Brian looked like a modern Beau Brummel. Cravats explode sexiness if worn by the right man, and doesn't Brian have that timeless appeal, that down-through-the-ages sort of face you see all the time in old portraits but rarely on the street?

Oh, my aching head. I swallow the capsules.

Cristoff, obviously briefed on the news, runs in and plops down at the other end of the table. Drumming his chlorophyll-stained fingertips as he listens, horror widens his winsome hazel eyes. "That girl cannot be serious," he says much too loudly.

I hold a finger up to my lips and emit a glare. I really love to emit a good glare. Emanates self-assurance like a nice long yawn. In two minutes Horace "Peach" Hagerty, catering genius and retired navy man, will glide his pillowy body in, softly demanding to know the menu changes right here and now. I lean back and close the conference room door so he won't hear the ruckus.

Finally, Jaime stops to take a real live breath.

I pounce. "I have to tell you, though, Jaime, that it will be almost impossible to find a different venue for the reception so late in the game, and the balloon rides may be out of the question if you want to keep it authentic."

"You think?" Jaime's raspy baritone voice drops another half an octave.

Pleasance sits down next to me, banging a tome about costuming through the ages onto the table. "Regency, Regency," she mutters.

"Hey, watch it, girlfriend!" Cristoff says. "It took me three days to refinish this table."

"*You* watch it, girlfriend." Pleasance flips pages with her long fingers. "I'm doing a crisis right now."

"Well, aren't we just all?"

Glad he didn't see her doing those jumping jacks!

I hold my hand over the bottom of the phone. "Will you two be quiet?!" I hiss. Yes, hiss. "Good grief!"

I banish their voices from my ears, while, I'm sure, they both roll their eyes. We seem to do a lot of that around here. It's amazing all our eyes aren't hanging out by their optic nerves. Brides.

Brides, brides, brides.

"I'll have to research the balloon rides, Jaime. You did say months ago that authenticity was your priority, didn't you?"

"Well, what about this." Resignation already shades her voice. Good. "If authentic balloon rides are a no-go, we'll stick with Victorian."

"Okay. You want me to go ahead and research it, then?"

Please, say yes. Get Jaime in the library and who knows what theme she'll end up with? Dark Ages? Phoenician? The plays of Arthur Miller? Or more to the point, Vigilante Nuptials.

Jaime sighs. "My schedule is crammed right now. You understand?"

"No problem. I'll do it. I'll get back to you by the end of the day." And I hang up with a quick good-bye before she can change her mind about anything else, or get started on Janet Reno and Waco.

Now Jaime is *too* orange.

Pleasance looks up from her book and runs a hand over the short fuzz of black hair that covers her oblong, aerodynamic skull. "You going to research it? Really? I think balloons have been around for a long time, Lil."

"That's what I'm afraid of. But hopefully the kind they had then just aren't around anymore or are illegal or something. I'll really play up the authenticity thing with that."

"Don't feel too much pressure, sweetie." Cristoff stands to his feet and kisses my cheek. "But we're counting on you. Gotta run." He shuffles his Top-Siders back to his workroom. It still weirds me out the way he's always dressed so preppy and wears it so well.

"Have you eaten breakfast yet, Pleasance?"

She shakes her head.

"Wanna go down to David and Dad's? I'll treat."

"I'll go almost anywhere for free."

I poke my head inside the door of Cristoff's workroom. The filtered morning light of the city gilds the plain white room, a shaft of light high-lighting at a slant the only adornment to the walls—a plain wooden cross. Flowers congest the large cooler we were finally able to lease last month, and the white worktable shines beneath heavy-duty fluorescent lighting. Neat as a pin. For now.

Once he starts building centerpieces, bouquets, and altar pieces, the room will look as though the Wars of the Roses have been fought. And the wars of the lilies, the stephanotis, the ivy, and the coneflowers. Corny but true. I love watching Cristoff's hands when he works. They move with such deft yet gentle purpose, each bloom precious. It's too bad Cristoff and I can't love each other, man and woman. It would make life so much easier for the both of us.

I wipe my brow with the back of my hand. The headache finally begins to subside. "Everything under control now with the table arrangements, honey?"

"Larkspur." He roots around in the refrigerator. "I've decided larkspur will be absolutely perfect."

"Good. David and Dad's?"

"Just bring me back a tomato juice."

He forgets about me that quickly. I turn and leave the room. A tomato juice. Goofy, you know? I mean, who orders tomato juice for their sip-as-you-work beverage?

Pleasance waits by the stairs, a bag the size of an emirate hanging from her collarbone. Naturally it coordinates with her goldenrod platform shoes. Attach wheels and a sail and we could zip right down the center of Charles Street with room for a third person. "I don't feel like waiting for the elevator."

"Me either."

We clop our way down the staircase carpeted in some ancient medallion-littered design and soon cross busy Charles Street. I adore this area of town. My mother used to tell me stories about window-shopping along Charles Street as a teenager fresh from Hungary. The area plummeted to the status of "remember when" for a while, but it's coming back now and this comforts me.

The bells of the basilica ring and a warm breeze glides over Pleasance's head. It makes me think about changing my hair, anything other than the stupid braid I've been wearing since first grade. But all of the Strong Hungarian Women in my family have braided their hair in some form. Our family photo album looks like Medusa and her sisters after a day at the beauty parlor, and I'm not sure whether Hungarians in general or Grandma Erzsèbet in particular favored braids.

Maybe I'll beef up my blond with some more highlights.

Oh, hair, hair, hair. Why do we women waste so much time thinking about our hair? Why don't we revolt, every last one of us, march on Wal-Mart, buy razors, and declare once and for all that bald truly is beautiful?

"You want to go running with me tonight?" I ask Pleasance a while later as we research hot-air balloons up at the Enoch Pratt Free Library a block away from the office.

She shakes her head. "I'm working late on designing a couple of Regency options for Jaime. If you don't mind, LeJeune is coming by after school. He doesn't have football practice today. Stefan is spending the night at my sister's house."

LeJeune is Pleasance's oldest child. Sixteen years old and built like a pro ball player, he speaks so softly I have to bend my neck out of joint to hear him. What an incredible defensive lineman. Ravens material someday, and I'd bet money on that.

"I think Peach is working late tonight too. He'd probably be glad to have Juney hanging around to help him in the kitchen. If he wants to, that is. He's experimenting with beef main courses."

Pleasance pulls down her reading glasses. "Why wouldn't Juney want to?"

"Oh, I don't know. I didn't know if that kind of work is what you had in mind for him."

She screws up her face. "Lillie, you are one weird lady."

"Thanks."

"No, really. You, of all people, with your heritage of paprika and sour cream and, well, other Hungarian ingredients, should know that food preparation is noble"—she sets down her glasses—"*essential.* Like designing masterpieces that sustain and strengthen and give life."

Except she says *life* just like a Baptist preacher. Liiiiiiii-yef.

"You done with your sermon, Bishop Stanley?"

"Oh, you want a sermon?"

"No! No!" Get Pleasance going and she'll pontificate straight into tomorrow.

"I'll tell Peach to expect him," she says.

"Okay. I'm glad Juney's coming over. I like having him around."

"Yeah, well, the boy likes you, that's for sure. Too bad you're so old."

I wave that comment away. A nice, good-looking teenager like Juney Stanley? What could he possibly find winsome in a chubby, garish old gal like me? Then again, African American men are taught from the womb the virtues of a womanly figure. I'd make a great black woman with my bright clothes, curvy bottom, and penchant for jewelry.

Pleasance claims otherwise. She says I overdo everything. And the fact that I love classic rock doesn't help matters either. "Plus, you have no groove. None whatsoever. Not even the littlest bit."

To which I said nothing. Daddy tried to teach me how to dance, and even he, blind as you please, calmer than an early morning lake, rippled with frustration.

Oh well, what can you do, right?

I reach for my planner to see just how much time remains to find out about those blasted balloons! Oh, Lord, please, please, *please* let them be inauthentic, or just make Jaime change her mind back.

To be honest, though, I never really saw Jaime as the Victorian type to begin with.

## Tacy

The day I confessed to Rawlins my true age should have been an indication of things to come. Up until that point, I'd never been sick with fear, but I deserved it. I lied, didn't I?

## Lillie

I lead Daddy down the path in the woods behind the rectory like thousands of times before. He tells me what he's read, I tell him what I've read, and we both get so excited at times you'd think we were running from roller coaster to roller coaster at Cedar Point. My father does love a good ride on an impossibly complicated coaster. The higher the drop the better. I believe I inherited from him my sense of daring, which he never discarded upon growing up. At one time, we actually belonged to a roller-coaster club and have been all over the country. People ask him, "Why do you like coasters so much, with your blindness and all?"

He answers, "Well, do you keep your eyes open or close them?"

Most say, "I close them."

"Well, I don't."

And he gets that mischievous glint in his eyes that has never left him either. He really doesn't seem at all priestly, but no one that I know loves God more than my dad. It's earthy and real and devoted and extremely unmonklike. Teddy, a Presbyterian, told me that the first question in the *Westminster Catechism* goes like this:

Q: What is man's chief end?

A: Man's chief end is to glorify God and enjoy Him forever.

That's Daddy to a *T.* He enjoys God and knowing Him. I mean, a lot of people know *about* God, but Daddy knows Him well. I hope that describes me someday.

So we stroll along in the womb of autumn leaves, and I describe the colors, thanking God that Dad remembers red, that he's seen the might of orange, the strength of yellow, and the promise of green.

"Is the sky that fantastic blue, Lil?"

"Oh yes, that kind you just want to roll around in. There's a very low humidity today."

"Oh yeah. Good breathing. Real good breathing."

"Five p.m. and no puffs on the inhaler."

"Great."

"Big root. Twelve o'clock."

"I thought so." He steps over it easily, as he's done for years now. "Before you tell me about the Hildegarde book, Lillie, let's talk about Tacy. I haven't heard from her in three weeks. You think she's all right?"

We obey an unwritten code. We don't talk much about my sister Tacy's husband Rawlins outright—he's such a thorn—but we always know such questions about Tacy have a deeper meaning.

"I do. And in any case, she's coming to Liberation Day at my house this week."

"Good. Maybe we can steal some time away with her."

To try and deprogram her?

"So tell me about your latest author, Dad."

He chuckles. "I've discovered an author that's not my normal fare, but, well, if you want to know the other side of life…this is it."

"And who is it?"

"Andrew Vachss."

"I've read him. I love that Burke character!"

"Who wouldn't?"

"And his dog. How cool is that?"

"It's the old saying, Lillie: Dogs and children are the key to a good story."

"I like the way he slobbers all over everything."

Dad laughs.

And we begin to discuss the redemptive themes of Vachss's gritty novels, how abused children are saved by an unsavory character and his giant mastiff, how warrior women are always around to lend a hand.

"Do you think there's some sort of Messiah theme, Daddy? Burke as a form of Savior?"

"Well, he's an antihero, Lillie, somewhat of a criminal. So the analogy can't be carried all the way through, I'd say."

Mom always said the most alluring part of Daddy is his mind.

"Can't it? Christ was seen as a criminal by many."

"Hmm. Good point."

Oh man, I love my dad. I love holding his hand. I love knowing that before he found God or Mom he was a ladies' man, that before he went blind he saw more of the world than most people see their entire lives. It's what makes him a good priest now. He's been extended more than one man's share of grace, and so he's got a lot to give away.

I know we're Episcopalian, but I'd have to say that my dad is just plain charismatic. My mom is still nutso about him. The fact that he can't see anything himself sure doesn't make him any less charming in her eyes. But Daddy sees. Oh yes, Daddy sees everything.

As we enter the house after our walk, Mom tucks her arm around his waist and leads him to the dining room for dessert. He slants his arm down across her back to curl around her spare waist. I watch her, small and European next to his baseball American height, his light hair contrasting with her inky tresses. "I made apple crisp, Carl."

Which, since it's his favorite dessert, means: You sexy man, take me tonight.

He leans his head down sideways, touching the top of hers and I see his thumb caress the side of her breast. This is beauty. This is so God-given I want to cry.

"I'm going to the powder room. I'll be right there," I say.

But I watch from the shadows and I see him kiss her mouth and they kiss deeply, like lovers, and at once I am comforted and jealous.

It should be me, I think. Me and Teddy.

## 3

## Lillie

Liberation Day.

It isn't a U.S. national holiday, although the Falkland Islands celebrate Liberation Day on June 14, the holiday birthed in 1982. The Falklands' flag sports a coat of arms depicting a white ram hovering over a sailing ship named *Desire*. Chalk this knowledge up to one too many late nights on the Internet. The crew of the *Desire* discovered the island. *Desire the Right* is the motto. I like that. Especially in this day and age when people feel they automatically have the right to just about anything. I used to think that way, until I lost Teddy. Maybe someone has a right to something, but that doesn't mean it's gonna happen.

But Liberation Day, Bajnok family style, falls on the anniversary of the late Grandma Erzsèbet's birthday. Every fifteenth of September the entire family congregates at my row house to celebrate. We also remember the day in 1956 my mother, neomatriarch of the clan, escaped communism in her native Hungary with nothing but a knapsack, her best friend, and one bicycle.

My younger sister, Tacy, born Anastasia Maria, and her husband, Rawlins McGovern III (God save the king) arrive around ten a.m., bearing a barrel of homemade red-onion sauerkraut. I suspect it isn't really Hungarian because I saw it in an issue of *Gourmet* at Tacy's house at least four years ago. But everyone loves it and now it's part of the tradition.

"Hi, guys!" I let them in through the front door, careful to stand to the side. According to the sizable mound of her stomach and her obstetrician's calculations, Tacy will deliver their first child any day. Maybe the sauerkraut will help get things going.

I kiss the beautiful curve of her cheek, her long, soft blond hair brushing against my forehead. Tacy inherited all the looks and talent, while I received all the athletic ability and business sense. Genetics just aren't fair. We both possess Daddy's love for books and God though. She's an artist. Her framed artwork hangs on all the walls of my house. She hasn't done much since she married Rawlins though. And he ushered her right up the aisle the day after she graduated from high school. My parents wanted them to wait, but Rawlins, being Rawlins, gets whatever the heck he wants, pardon my French. He always claims that what he wants is God's will too, which really bugs me. I mean, does he have a direct line we mere mortals don't? Does God walk with him in the cool of the day? Do the stars align themselves into words that tell him what God is thinking?

Obviously, Rawlins isn't Episcopalian the way he throws around the name of God with nary so much as a thought. It's like God's there to suit him and not the other way around. Tacy isn't Episcopalian anymore either. It's another subject we Bauers don't discuss.

I'm very proud of my baby sister though. At twenty-five she blooms with a womanhood I guess I'll never know myself. A very small part of me relishes in her water-logged ankles.

"You look ready to explode!"

"I know. But Rawlins says the Lord will see fit to let me go on time and not late like Mom did with me."

"Well, you're the sweetest pregnant lady I've ever seen."

"I waited long enough." She tucks wisps of blond hair behind her ear and looks back through the door. "Rawlins, honey, you got that barrel okay?"

"Of course I do, Anastasia. Stop worrying. You know how it affects the child."

Oh please.

Seven years ago, when Tacy married Rawlins, she would have rolled her eyes at that.

Rawlins McGovern is easily one of the best-looking men I've ever seen. He keeps fit after he arrives home from his father's advertising agency by caring for the horses on their small horse farm in Phoenix, Maryland. So he possesses those natural muscles developed by raking hay and baling it and slinging those bales around, by golly. He mostly works without machines because Rawlins is Rawlins.

I watch as he hoists the barrel on one shoulder and scoops the strap of Tacy's "big bag" onto his other shoulder. Until I met Pleasance, I thought Tacy carried the biggest purse in the world.

"You sure you got that okay, Rolly?" I ask.

He hates being called that. I try to say it as much as possible.

He bestows a closed-mouthed smile and nods his thanks as I hold the door. "You want this in the kitchen, Lillian?"

I nod, returning the tight smile, remembering my sister in the tenth grade, before she met Rawlins McGovern. Tacy made honor roll every year, headed up the school newspaper, won writing contests year after year, even that *Teen Talk* magazine one. She entered the Towson Art Festival and won second place against a lot of teachers and college students from Towson State and Maryland Institute. Her skirts flowed and fluttered above either army boots or gladiator sandals. She wanted to be an artist and a writer and a movie star and a chef. Tacy wanted it all.

But I can't blame everything on Rawlins and his hypnotic charm. Tacy chose. And with the McGoverns' wealth, at least her cage glimmers golden.

My heart breaks every time she comes to mind, and sometimes I wonder if my criticism of the entire matter stems from the fact that my plans for a young marriage and a fresh life disappeared with Teddy. Tacy even said as much once.

I trek back to the kitchen, following Mr. Control Freak. I'm telling you, Teddy or no Teddy, this guy stands up as a creep all on his own. "So, have you done the tour of the hospital yet?" I ask Tacy.

"Oh no! Didn't I tell you? We've switched to a midwife now. She goes to our church. Rawlins researched the home-birth route and we're going to go that way."

Rawlins sets the barrel on the glittery pink countertop and washes his hands at the stainless steel sink that's been here since before Grandma Erzsèbet bought the house in '62. "We installed a big whirlpool bath in the master suite. We're planning on a water birth," he says.

What do you say to that?

"Is it safe?"

"Perfectly!" Tacy jumps in. "Right, baby?" She hands Rawlins a paper towel she pulled from her purse.

Rawlins dries his hands, comes up behind my sister and circles his arms around her waist. "Now you know I wouldn't dream of it if it wasn't."

Nauseating.

I retrieve a box of tea for Tacy. "But isn't the whole theory behind that evolutionary in nature? We came out of the water billions of years ago and all that?"

Of course it isn't, but why not have a little fun?

"I've never heard that," he says with a decided shake of his head. "No, Lillian, it's because it makes the transition from watery womb to this world a little less traumatic."

"Must be a big tub then."

Tacy rolls her eyes. Good girl. "It's huge. Almost like a small pool. I don't know how Philly's going to clean it!" Then she blows a weak, guilty laugh that apologizes for being rich and thin—not counting the pregnant belly—and having a full-time housekeeper, while tubby me lives here in dead Grandma Erzsèbet's little row house, working eighty hours a week, trying to get a business going, trying to ease my loneliness and the hanging-on grief and mystery of Teddy with a string of unsatisfactory dates, wishing somehow the blessings I have would be enough.

I'd sure settle for some closure, as they call it these days.

Not that I'd trade places with Tacy for a nanosecond.

I mean, I long to find Teddy himself, or even another Teddy, get married, and have babies so badly sometimes I imagine kicking inside my abdomen. But married and pregnant matter little if Rawlins *"Sleeping with the Enemy"* McGovern is part of the deal.

Honesty, Rawlins scares me. Ever since Tacy became pregnant, he's made her keep a journal of every bite she puts into her mouth, and for several years he's kept track of the mileage on her Range Rover and okayed her visits from the family. "He's just protective, Lillie," Tacy has always insisted.

"So are parole officers," I remember saying. Boy, she sure took offense at that! She clammed up about her marriage after that as well. Not that she offered up juicy morsels to begin with. I guess it really is none of my business, but she's my sister, and aren't we supposed to share those things we wouldn't ever tell another soul?

But she is here with me now and I'm thankful.

Rawlins tells me "a situation" came up in the church and he needs to go help Pastor Cole for a couple of hours, which surprises me. He never lets Tacy out of his sight when we're around, but I guess he figures if he's doing God's work, He'll protect her from the slimy likes of us.

So we putter around the kitchen, Tacy spurning my Lipton and drinking raspberry tea because it's supposed to lessen the severity of the birth pangs. Pangs. She said pangs. We have until four o'clock together when the horde will descend.

"Cool earrings, Lillie."

I touch them to remind myself of what I chose this morning. Oh yes, miniature masks, the New Orleans kind. "Thanks." Pleasance calls them my Pia Zadora jewelry.

Together we prepare *csirke paprikas* for forty. Tacy chops up the onions, carrots, and potatoes because, "Rawlins won't let me touch raw meat since I've been expecting." So I skin and cut up the chickens, all eight of them. Where is good old Peach Hagerty when I need him? He'd do this in a quarter of the time. But I can't afford the "pick of the chix" these days.

As the onions caramelize and the chicken pieces brown, we enjoy the aroma and chat about car seats and the kind Rawlins chose. The smell of paprika causes me to rejoice. Being a Strong Hungarian Woman does have its advantages. And to be honest, since I so identify with my father, it's good to have times like this when my love for Mom refreshes itself. Tacy and Mom have always been close.

While the stew bubbles at a low simmer, I begin the stuffed cabbage rolls, again browning the ground pork and beef because King Rawlins declared it should be thus and so, even from henceforth and forevermore, amen.

Then Tacy and I talk about cribs. Then we talk about strollers. Then we talk about baby pouches and should the baby face out from the mother or cuddle into her warmth?

"What does Rawlins say?" I mix the filling and begin to stuff it into the cabbage leaves as Tacy cuts them from the head after it boils in salted water.

"He's not sure."

"What? Well, hold on a minute while I write this into my planner for posterity! It's something I'll want to remember for years to come—the day Rawlins McGovern wasn't sure of something!"

Tacy drops her chin and peers up at me between her lashes, perfectly mascaraed, of course. "Come on, Lil, he's not that bad. You don't know him the way I do."

"Thank God, Tace!"

"Oh please. How can I complain? He's never even so much as raised his voice to me, Lillie. He's a wonderful provider, and he's so loving and caring."

"He controls every move you make."

She crosses her arms and lays them on her belly, the knife resting on her breast. "You can call it control if you like. I just call it concern."

"What would happen if you told him you'll eat what you please, go where you please, and wear what you please?"

She continues slicing. "It just so happens I think he's right about the food, and I can go wherever I like as long as I tell him. I mean, I don't want him to worry when I'm gone, do I?"

"Whatever, Tace. As long as you're happy."

Her innocent face brightens. "Oh, I am, Lil, really. And with this baby coming—"

"If it doesn't drown on the way out."

She laughs, sets down the knife and pulls me as close as she can, considering her belly. "Everything will be fine." Her fine gold jewelry presses into the flesh of my cheek and I pull back sooner than I want.

Teddy fought for me to be on the boys' soccer team. We were twelve. I'd begun to mature, and he was still taller than the other boys and still more handsome.

"Look, Coach," he said that day at the rec field in Churchville. "She can outplay all of us. The girls' team is hardly challenging. And we can use a wing like her."

I may be chubby, but I can run.

For some reason, everybody found it hard to say no to Teddy, and so I found myself having the best autumn ever, traveling to games, sharing Slurpees with him and Mrs. Gillie afterward. Everyone at school and in the neighborhood teased us and called us girlfriend and boyfriend, but we didn't pay them any mind. Until one day as we walked home from the practice field together, Teddy, carrying both of our shoes, said, "Are we too young to be boyfriend/girlfriend?"

"No."

I'd loved him for years. There could be no other answer.

"We're only twelve, Lillie."

"That's okay."

And that day, Teddy took my hand and I smiled the entire way home.

## Tacy

When I was almost sixteen and anticipating my relationship with Rawlins finally being legal after two years of sneaking around, I could almost taste the relief in my mouth. Sweet sixteen. That was me back then and Rawlins said so too. He would kiss me deeply and mutter, "Ah, you're so sweet." I used to love it when he'd explore my mouth like that, like I was something precious to him. Many times I begged him to do more.

"That's the flesh speaking," he told me. "God made us so this would feel good. But the timing must be proper."

I hoped that meant marriage, but with me being only fifteen, I wasn't about to assume a twenty-two-year-old man was talking about commitment of that magnitude. I'd feel so young at times like that.

But he protected me from a lot of the jerk boys at school who I'd have been interested in, the boys that Barb and

Melanie talked about all the time. I got so sick of hearing their whining and felt so thankful a mature man kept me from worrying about all that. I tried not to say anything to them about Rawlins or to look down on them for liking guys like Jeremy, Brian, and that weird guy Philippe Stanes, who was undeniably a future candidate for the state penitentiary, in the criminally insane ward no less. Besides, Rawlins bought them nice things too, so they liked him well enough.

And then, on my sixteenth birthday, I saw Rawlins's picture in the paper with some socialite on his arm. I freaked out! When he came to pick me up at Barb's house, I had already snipped it out of the paper. I hopped in the car, and after he got in, I held it out. "What's this, Rawlins?"

He took the scrap, and I could tell he was controlling himself because of the way he inhaled a couple of times through his nose. Then he turned to me and cupped my neck with his hand. He went for some warm type of smile, but he missed the mark a little. My memory finds it smarmy. "This is just my lifestyle, dear one. Of course I'm going to occasionally escort women to these type of functions. You don't think I could actually take you, do you?"

How my youth betrayed me. I realized how second-class and insignificant to the world-at-large I really was. I should have broken up with him right then. He didn't even temper his remark with some kind of explanation or reassurance. I should have broken up with him. But I didn't. I loved him. He'd hold me in his arms as I sat on his lap and tell me what a lovely girl I was, how he'd always be there for me. He was so strong and masculine. Not like Daddy.

I loved my dad. But he was so oblivious and content and Mom had to care for him and not the other way around, which, I know, I really know, was probably harder on Daddy than it was on Mom. But still, it wasn't the life I wanted for me. And Rawlins made me feel so protected and safe. He told me that he'd give me the perfect life, that he'd make sure I never had to worry about a thing. Nothing like the life Mom and Dad had. My dad was a great dad, but I didn't want to come home every night to a man so content to have so little. Rawlins wanted it all. And Mom, she got so achy in the shoulders from shelving books all day in that dim library, and her eyesight? Wow, I swore she'd be blind by sixty!

## Lillie

The rest of the Bajnoks begin funneling in from the surrounding areas around four o'clock. We Bajnoks stick close to the motherland. Mom and Dad arrive from Bel Air. Dad, giving me a kiss and hug as warm and big as his soul, settles down at the kitchen table and pulls out a Braille copy of *Imitation of Christ* and a Walkman. He likes to be in the thick of the action, but Sundays never stop rolling around. He greets everyone who makes their presence known and says hi to my cousin Rick before Rick says hi to him. Rick's a natural, nondeodorant type. Fine for him. It's the rest of Baltimore that suffers.

Mom folds me into her strong arms and kisses first the top of my head, then my forehead, then my nose, then my lips, then my chin. And then she says in perfect English, "Everything smells delicious, Lillie."

You'd never know the woman grew up all the way over there.

Her two younger sisters, twins named Babi and Luca, join us in the kitchen for more hugs. I've got the greatest family in the world, and any of my neuroses can only be blamed on myself and maybe what happened to Teddy, because if the expectations have always been high, the resources to meet them were even greater. And then, there's something humiliating about carrying an inhaler with you wherever you go. I can't explain why, but ask any asthmatic, and they'll confess the whole thing embarrasses them. Oh, not in a huge way, but just enough to place a niggling doubt about yourself just behind your forehead. Nobody likes to admit their imperfections, so when yours hangs out there, puffing away, it just eats away the first layer of varnish. And, of course, there's always that big question—"Will I ever get a bad attack and not be in reach of medication?"—and you picture yourself suffocating to death and it's horrible, horrible, horrible.

My aunts kiss me just like Mom did, a tradition Grandma Erzsèbet started in Hungary after my grandfather was murdered by the communists.

Aunts Babi and Luca were only six when they left Hungary, so they've assimilated completely into American culture. Sometimes it feels odd to be so Hungarian and yet so American at the same time. But this is Baltimore, where people hold on to their nationalities like the metal bar on a roller coaster, the only thing that seems to stay put on the wild ride up and down the hills of a changing society. Out-of-towners call us provincial in these parts. They're right.

Cousins and spouses mingle through my two floors at the row house. Babi's youngest hooks up his GameCube to my TV down in the clubroom, and Luca's oldest daughter, twenty-five-year-old Terri, styles hair and manicures nails in my bedroom. Girly squeals of delight whistle from my young female cousins and second cousins, and I decide maybe Terri can do something interesting with my braid.

Dinner, eaten all over the house by men and boys in crew cuts and girls and women in braids, begins in silence. The sister and I done good. Long live paprika. And halfway through, the volume soars as conversations heat up and appetites quiet down—conversations about Mayor O'Malley, the Ravens, or what to do about terrorism. I hear Cristoff sneak up the hall steps to his small upstairs apartment. He won't come in. Our family gatherings pain him, reminding him how insufficient his own family was. His dad, military to the core, didn't realize sons needed affection too, and his mother? Good heavens! The woman could have intimidated Barbra Streisand! They're dead now and I'm not sorry.

Well, I'm not!

Somewhere in the midst of the outside group, a water gun rears its soppy head and my uncles Stu and Jimmy yell in unison, "Knock it off!"

But finally, after the Strong Hungarian Women return the kitchen to the pristine condition in which they had left it the year before, I light some cheap bamboo torches and stick them in sand-filled buckets all around the tiny cement yard. Mom and the aunts pour the wine while I blend milk shakes for me and the kids, and we all congregate around Grandma Erzsèbet's Nightmare, a ten-foot-tall, gangly rhododendron that grows by the back fence. Though she died four years ago of diabetes, it's her legacy to all of us. And I suspect she willed the house to me, her eldest granddaughter, because she may have considered me the least likely to sell the place and leave that bush, her first purchase after disembarking the boat from Ellis Island.

And unfortunately she was right.

It's a strong American bush watered and fertilized by a Strong Hungarian Woman. Grandma Erzsèbet never learned English, but she never regretted the night she followed in my mother's footsteps, tore off those Soviet chains, and fled to freedom.

My uncles yank open lawn chairs from my yard, from car trunks, from any willing neighbor's porch, and we wait in quiet expectation around the Nightmare, torchlight sharpening our Strong Hungarian Features, ready to hear my mother tell the tale of her ride to freedom.

She smiles into my eyes and begins. My gosh, I love that woman. I don't feel the same kindred spirit with her as I do with Daddy, but, truthfully, if I thought for one minute I could be half the woman she is…what? I'd get it through my thick head Teddy is dead? My life would be better? I'd find a husband? I'd be happy?

I don't know.

I pass out sweatshirts and blankets and we all snuggle in for the tale. The night temperature plummets into the forties, nipping at little fingers and causing tennis shoes to slide snugly beneath bottoms.

Mom breathes deeply, her strong posture and stillness demanding silence. The matriarch now, she exudes poise, confidence, and a working, hard-won wisdom. Ten seconds of quiet whisper by.

She begins as though in the middle of the tale, as though she'd already begun in her mind.

"The ÁVH, our secret police, had become extremely powerful. In 1951 things got really bad when they took my father and my brother away. Class Enemies, they were called, because my father was a professor at the forestry university in Sopron. My father died a month into his imprisonment in a work camp south of Budapest. Never a well man, really, the work in the cotton fields did him in. The cold, the rain. It filled up his lungs. It devastated us girls left at home. My mother mourned him until the day she died. She called it homicide."

Mom begins to speak of her older brother, Istvàn. She remembers the lack of news from him, the way all had been silent after his deportation to a work camp. "When he finally wrote to us, he said, 'I see the sun rise each day as we set out toward the fields in the east and set each night in the west as we trudge back to the barracks.'

"You cannot understand it, my dear ones," Mom says from where she stands on my iron back stoop, looking slim and fashionable in gray slacks and a blushing summer twinset only I know she bought at the Goodwill thrift store in Bel Air. "You cannot understand what freedom means until it is gone. Who is an informant? Who is not? Who is friend? Who is foe? It's a mixed up, frightening world of smoke and mystery, and when the mist clears, those around you may still be wearing masks."

The flesh on my arms rises like dotted Swiss when she speaks in this manner. We think we can imagine. We think we all are in some form of slavery, some form of bondage. But we don't know what it's like to look over our shoulder constantly, to carefully consider everything we do and wonder if it is suspect. I steal a look at my sister. Well, maybe some of us do. Rawlins stands behind her by the chain-link fence, a few paces away from us all, leaning stiffly against the railing, arms crossed over his chest.

"It is no way to live. No way for human beings, made in the image of God, to spend their lives. I remember the nights we'd huddle in our attic room, all Grandma Erzsèbet could afford after our house had been seized. She worked at a winery all through the night, and we lay upstairs on a small mattress on the rough wooden planks of the floor. I held my baby sisters in my arms"—the twins nod—"and in the dark I would remember what the priests had said. I was only eight at the time, but I would whisper the portions of the mass that were ingrained upon my memory: 'Behold the Lamb of God which takes away the sins of the world.' And I would pray, 'Have mercy on us. Grant us peace. Lord, hear our prayer.'"

Now, prayer is important to me. I'm single. I'm lonely and I'm often floundering in a world of married people, strollers, Koala changing tables, and gum in the shape of tapeworms. But see, God is with me all the time. He walks beside me, talks with me, and He tells me that Lillian Elaine Bauer belongs to Him. No matter what, which is unbelievable, but upon thought, the only way it can be. For who, by their own performance, can begin to please a Holy God? And so I can easily picture my mother and my baby aunts up there beneath the eaves of the red-tiled roofs of Sopron. I can hear her murmured words of pleading and praise behind the whitewashed walls. And I know that I stand in a line of faith-filled womanhood and I am thankful. Thankful for my faith. Thankful to be a woman.

I mean, who wants to eventually grow ear hair? Not exactly something to look forward to.

"We lived this way for years. Educated by the state. Taught to be good little communists. Doled out hard little hunks of black bread for sustenance. Always feeling cold or hot, never in between. Wearing clothes in conditions we almost never see here in America." She raises her index finger. "But we could not complain about the government or even our living conditions."

"Why, Aunt Kathy?" one of my cousin's children, a boy named Brandon, asks. I think, at five, Brandon is actually listening for the first time. Her words begin to color him in.

"Again, my loves, one never knew who was an ÁVH informant. One never knew who would go running to the secret police, very powerful by this time, in search of gathering some brownie points."

I doubt if they called them brownie points in Hungary. But she's employed that phrase every year, and I always forget to ask her where she learned it.

"Mama took care of Babi and Luca during the day and worked all night. I was with them while we slept. Finally, in 1956, news of a revolution against the Soviets erupted! I was twelve by this time and Babi and Luca were six. The tale of the uprising in Budapest flooded the country like a sweeping wave, as though the stagnant ocean suddenly filled with spring water and washed away the suffocating despair that had encrusted our lives for years."

No wonder Daddy loves this woman. I mean, she's so naturally lyrical.

"Do you remember, Babi?" Luca turns to her twin, who nods in reply, her eyes slick with tears.

Mom nods at them. "We heard our national anthem *'Himnusz'* afresh that October. 'God bless Hungarians with good will and plenty.' It meant more than ever before, even the times I watched those tight-lipped atheist communists endure it during the dark years."

Go, Mom. I like it when she editorializes. And she editorializes because she can now.

"We heard about the way our countrymen had seized the Russian tanks and had fired at the ÁVH. We heard about the horror in the square in Budapest, how the ÁVH had mowed down people like they were nothing more than a flock of lambs."

My mother tells of the first shot fired into the square. How an ÁVH guard had triggered one stray bullet into the crowd. How that stray bullet, that single, deadly shot had pierced the body of an infant in her mother's arms. How the force had thrown the mother backward. How she had walked up to a Russian tank, held aloft her lifeless baby, and screamed. "You've killed my child! Kill me, too!"

"And then bullets rained in a brutal mist upon the masses gathered upon a pavement going crimson. And we fought.

"It was very far away from our little Sopron, but we heard about it in time to feel our hearts swell, to remember, even though I had been but a small child when the Soviets came, what our beloved Hungary had been. We had enough time to relight our lamps of hope, to dream again of a place where we would live in dignity and pride and freedom as true Hungarians."

Luca squelches a sob. Babi lays a hand between her shoulders.

"And"—my mother focuses on each one gathered there amid the bamboo torches, looking each one in the eyes—"we had enough time to feel as though our hearts would break beneath the crushing weight of a disappointment you cannot, here in freedom, imagine, when we heard the news at the beginning of November that the revolutionary forces were squelched. That great Russian tanks came rolling in. That aid was sought from the West. That no help came. That we had been left alone, David against an army of Goliaths."

The Red Army was endless. For every man killed, another one was shoved in line. And another and another. When the Berlin Wall fell, I must say, I was more relieved than anybody I knew outside of my family. Cristoff understood though. And of course, Teddy picked me up, twirled me around and gave a good long hoot. That night, we french kissed for the first time. We were seventeen.

My Uncle Jimmy pours more wine and we await the next part of the tale, the part that still tints my life here in Baltimore, Maryland, USA, the part that ended up inside of my stomach years before as a swollen, abrading question mark.

"I had a friend. Her name was Fruzsina."

Her name is still Fruzsina and she lives up in New Jersey with a guy named Tony. She won't marry him. She's rich and she can't stand his kids, and "There's no way those brats are going to get one penny of mine. Not a single penny." She married well the first time when she came to America.

"One night we knew it was time to leave Hungary. Students from the nearby university, where my father had taught, were mowed down during a peaceful demonstration. We stole a bicycle from the people who lived below us. Fruzsina sat on the seat and I stood in front of her, working the pedals. Austria was only a few kilometers away. It was a cold, wet night. I left a note for Grandma Erzsèbet and I kissed Babi and Luca"—my aunts nod some more—"and I told them to be strong and to stay on their cot. I knew they would. They were such good girls back then."

My uncles both bark out a laugh.

"The moon was hidden by clouds and we set out in the middle of the night. No one followed. No one heard us as we rode along a seldom-used footpath between dormant fields. I prayed inside of my soul, 'Oh, God,' I prayed. 'Let us arrive safely. Please.' An hour later, when the bicycle bounced over the border and into Austria, we were free. Free at last!"

I clap with joy, tears painting my cheeks. Everybody claps. What Mom doesn't say is that her drawers were soaking wet when they got off that bicycle, she was so scared. Some years she tells of the young Austrian couple who gave them shelter. But not this year.

Grandma Erzsèbet, Babi and Luca, and my uncle Istvàn, who had made his way back home during the revolution, escaped two weeks later to join Katherina. The Bajnoks were free.

Every year I gaze upon my mother in wonder and feel my soul gape open, my legs dangling inside the chasm of my own fears, my doubts that if it had been up to me, these precious women would have never crossed the border.

Uncle Istvàn is dead now. I remember his funeral two years ago on the eastern shore of Maryland. He followed in his father's footsteps as a professor of agriculture at the University of Maryland Eastern Shore. I remember thinking of all he had survived only to die of an aneurysm.

He died a free man. That is what he would say if you could ask him about it. Not that we can really comment on our deaths. Can you imagine what one might say?

*Well, now. I suppose, now that I've been through it, and I've seen how unimportant most of my opinions were, or rather, the matters I chose to have an opinion on were so frivolous and ridiculous, for example, why I cared so much that my church had a drum set or that young men not get tattoos, I would have chosen a much different approach. I died in my opinions. And they gave me no comfort at all.*

I can see Rawlins coming to that conclusion.

Well, maybe not.

How about my father? He'd say, "Well, naturally, beyond the obvious rewards of a life of faith, I gambled on the value of a good marriage and it paid off. Yes, I'm dead now, but Kathy was right there, holding my hand as I left, kissing my lips as I drew my final breath. And maybe I didn't save the world, maybe I only really helped a handful of people see things more clearly, but in the end, I died in love."

Me? What will I say? Well, let's face it. It's always easier to project for someone else. All I know is this: I'm not ready to talk about my death, because I don't know what this life is really about yet. Oh yeah, glorify God and enjoy Him forever and all. Sure. But how to do that? That's the biggie, isn't it? And sometimes, I think it's the "enjoy" part that really trips me up. Who am I to enjoy the almighty Creator of heaven and earth? Huh? Tell me that.

4

## Tacy

I hated lying to my mother, but there was nothing else to be done. How could I tell her I'd already been dating Rawlins for two years? As Rawlins said, we'd never get their blessing on our relationship if they found out we'd been forced to keep things a secret for so long. I kept wondering, though, if the blessing would actually mean anything with two years of deception as our foundation. Of course, Rawlins did have a point when he said that, being my intended, he was the head of our "household" and as such, I could follow his lead without worry. God would judge him, not me, and he was willing to bear the responsibility, if indeed, what we'd done was truly deception. "Think of Rahab, the harlot, dear one. Now there's someone who kept a secret."

"She lied, Rawlins."

"Yes, she did. And God used that lie, didn't He? Who are we to question His dealings?"

That sounded a little weird, only I didn't know why exactly or what to say because what happened at Jericho happened, and the Bible never editorialized word one about Rahab's lie to the soldiers of the town. No, Rahab was only praised and given the immense privilege of being an ancestor of Christ. See, things like that in the Bible confused me. I thought of Joseph's brothers selling him as a slave and how the Bible said, "You meant evil against me, but God meant it for good." And it didn't say God allowed it for good, it said meant. As in, "I meant to do that" or "I meant to say that." Purposeful. And that confused me. I struggled so much with the good and evil and God questions. And Rawlins was no help there. He told me to leave the spiritual aspects of life to him. But people have always struggled with that, for thousands of years, and not one person has come up with the defining answer. At least I didn't. Or Rawlins either. As I lay in my bed, knowing I'd introduce Rawlins to Mom and Dad the next day, performing the role of my life, I realized that in the end you accepted God as the truly indefinable being He is, or you muddled along in frustration. I never thought He ever expected us to stop wondering though. I really didn't, despite what Rawlins said. "God doesn't mind our questions," Dad always told us. "And He is more than capable of rendering an obvious scenario, obliterating the need for faith altogether." I looked out my bedroom window at the dome of the night blue sky and saw something beyond fathoming but so worthy of the pursuit.

Being called Rawlins's "intended" also did something for me. I knew then our relationship was destined for permanency. Of course, he reminded me that my lie to him started the whole ball rolling.

A week later, as we sat out on the brick patio behind the manse, Mom and Dad fooled blind, Rawlins said, "You're so beautiful and sweet and trusting, Anastasia. You'd be an easy target for someone who wants nothing more than to take advantage of you."

"Yes, Rawlins, I know."

"Predators take many shapes, dear one." That's what he said.

## Lillie

We try our best at Extremely Odd to blend in with the occasion. I should have asked Pleasance to pencil on my eyeliner, but she was so busy readying the female attendants, dressed like priestesses, that I did it myself. One line meanders upward from my eye, the other wanders downward, lending me an air of confused surprise. And no matter how hard I tried, each attempt worsened the effect. At least the tunic flows loose and comfortable, hiding my padded hips a bit.

I don't really think of myself as an Egyptian princess, but more like Memnet, the nursemaid to Charlton Heston in *The Ten Commandments*. Oh my, when she pulls out that bit of Levi cloth and shows it to Nefertiri, my heart always stops. Poor Memnet. All that dedication only to end up falling from a high porch. There's thanks for you.

Patrice Winslow wanted a dawn wedding. I tried to talk her out of it, the possible, horrible scenarios too numerous to voice, not to mention the one a.m. rising time for us. And considering she is marrying into the family of one of the biggest liquor distributorships on the East Coast, it isn't surprising to see the groom now, dressed like Pharaoh, hurling the contents of his stomach behind the set. I doubt if he and his men even went to bed. And the nightmare begins.

*"So let it be written, so let it be done."*

I'm sure we all pictured Yul Brynner, and only a nauseated guy in a diaper fills the role.

It will all be over by two o'clock, I remind myself as I run over to him with a bottle of Pepto-Bismol. Tear down. Clean up. The whole mystic setup carted away in trucks back down to The Everyman Theater, which went halvesies with us on the pyramid since they'll be doing *Joseph and the Amazing Technicolor Dreamcoat* next season.

Cristoff runs over, dressed in a tunic like mine. No eyeliner for him though. He vowed never to wear makeup again after he decided he loved Jesus more than Bradley and the others, sold his florist shop in Chelsea, and moved back to Baltimore, me, and a church full of happy old ladies in housecoats and knee-high pantyhose down on Erdman Avenue. They're so tickled to have a young man in their midst, one who sings baritone in the choir, provides flowers free of charge each Sunday, and is always the first visitor when one of them has a stint in Bay View Hospital or Franklin Square. Say what you want about gay men, but they sure do have a mind for details others don't.

"The flowers look wonderful, honey!"

Cristoff never hears compliments when he's upset. And judging by the way he points to the two greyhounds we rented for the occasion from some greedy breeder at an astronomical price, he's angrier than poison ivy. The dogs, erect and alert, sit by the stairs leading up to a small platform at the base of the pyramid. Patrice Winslow requested they be dyed black to look like jackals, but after careful research and an "Absolutely not!" from the owner, not to mention a vision of myself scrubbed to a Rexy Van Bibber gray after the dying process, I gladly refused. This breed, Egyptian in origin, has been around for at least twenty-five hundred years, was mentioned in Song of Solomon, and, darn it, if it was good enough for those people, it sure as heck was good enough for Patrice Winslow and her "priestesses."

"Those awful dogs are peeing all over the arrangements by the steps," Cristoff says. "They've even whizzed on the pyramid."

"I told Patrice it was risky, but she insisted." Sometimes you just have to lay the blame where it belongs and work from there. "How are the attendants?"

"Perfect. The larkspur garlands around their necks are the *pièce de résistance*."

"Well, consider the source of inspiration, honey." And I hug Cristoff. He didn't get many hugs as a little guy so I give him all the hugs I can.

He kisses my cheek. "All in all, I think it's going well."

"Two minutes to show time."

You know, every once in a while I schedule time to watch a talk show, and I hear all this "positive thinking" stuff I call "hope speak." Now, I can appreciate the fact that without visualization nothing can be a reality.

But.

Sometimes things you never begin to visualize appear, dreadfully real, horribly unexpected. I see the cat. Darn it, I see a cat.

Just as the morning sun gets a leg up over the horizon and its first beam reflects off some New Age, pyramid-shaped crystal Patrice brought back from a trip to only the Lord knows where; just as the attendants file in two by two with flowing, iridescent robes and extended arms supporting shallow, golden bowls of flower petals; just as the groom, corners of his mouth blushing with carnation pink crescent moons of Pepto-Bismol, takes his place on the platform, his feet spread, going for…yep, Yul Brynner; just as Patrice, in full Nefertiri garb, complete with jangling headdress and shining collar, appears from the patio doors; just as the crystal shines a beam of light so brilliant the guests inhale simultaneously (oh, the precise measurements required to set it up and the price paid for an astronomer to do the calculations!); just as the scene fills so gloriously pregnant with the glorious, inevitable gloriousness of Egypt and its glorious mysteries (yeah, right, I know); two flea-bitten strays in search of that cat tear into the serenity, barking like crazy, and run by the greyhounds, who begin snarling and pulling at the golden chains I'd spray-painted the day before.

Guess the gods weren't looking down in favor on this union. Or who knows? Maybe unexpected cats bring good luck and a happy life after crossing the River Styx. Maybe the appearance of stray dogs at your wedding gives you a free pass on Charon's boat.

This is great. Just great.

"Do something!" Patrice's father bellows from the confines of his tuxedo. (No flowing robes for *him,* thank you, Patrice, and I'll thank you not to tell your father what to wear.)

But I'm already springing forward, a butterball in flowing robes.

Bounding up to the platform, I grab the golden staff of the translucent, New Age "guy" (does one call them priests?) ready to conduct the ceremony, and I chase the strays into the woods behind the estate house, a weald thriving with thorns and sticks. Bugs too.

Oh man, I hate bugs. Teddy always killed the spiders for me.

But, all of this, no match for a Strong Hungarian Woman, right? Well, think again.

I emerge as the couple mumbles their personally written vows, which were cornier than Wordsworth. Ruffled enough to resemble some odd Celtic woodland deity, I shuffle at the rear of the gathering, and no one notices, thank goodness, except Mr. Winslow, who gives me a slow, appreciative nod.

Why didn't I remember to bring Bactine?

## Tacy

I walked with Rawlins into our church. I was always so proud of Saint Stephen's—its robust stone exterior, its curious little bell tower—but Rawlins, who had a thing against Catholicism and actually the whole liturgical tradition, made me unsure. The sun pierced the day too brightly and my smile felt like I'd buttered it on while I fixed my toast that morning.

Afterward he drove me to the restaurant where we all were meeting for dinner. "I'm glad you're a preacher's daughter, Anastasia," he said.

Priest, I thought, he's a priest.

"It's plain to see your father is the driving spiritual force of your home, which, I assure you, will be the way our home will be run. The Bible is clear about wives submitting to their husbands."

I felt a frigid hand clutch my stomach. Mom and Dad were loving partners, and the whole submission thing didn't come up often. But Rawlins just took my left hand and kissed the ring finger and said, "The Bible also tells husbands to love their wives even as Christ loved the church and gave His life for it."

Then he kissed my eyelids and said, "I would die for you, Anastasia. I would lay down my life for you."

I knew I'd never find another guy like him.

He's screaming now, though, and it's chilling my blood.

## Lillie

"Thank God," Mr. Winslow says with a charming smile and a shake of his bald head once the loaded trucks pull away and his stately manner settles back into the relaxed ease it possessed before we arrived to begin setup. "Those dogs gave us at least one moment of normal!"

I laugh. The fathers always crack me up. They rarely understand their daughters, but the fact that they go along with their crazy schemes puts them high up on my scale of good parenting.

He rips out the check from the large binder on his desk and tosses his pen onto the blotter. "Patrice has always been a little, well…extreme."

"You don't have to apologize to me. That's what we're all about."

"Well, I don't know whether I should begrudge your company for giving her the opportunity for an offbeat wedding like this, or if I should praise you for it." He hands me the check.

"What did she say to you before she rode off in that chariot?" It took me five weeks to find that darned chariot.

"She said, 'Daddy, today was a dream come true.'"

I fold the check and stuff it in my Day-Timer, thanking God the office rent will soon be paid and we are solvent for another month. "I guess that says it all."

Mr. Winslow escorts me to my car. "Nice wheels, Miss Bauer. Your business is doing well, then?"

"Oh, me and my Uncle Jimmy fixed this thing up together a few years ago. But as far as the business…we started about a year ago. Thought we'd have more clients by now…but we're surviving. I can't complain too much when I still look forward to work each morning."

"This a '63?"

"Sure is. Good eye, Mr. Winslow."

He whistles low. "I've always loved this one. Can I take her for a quick spin?"

"Only if I can come along with you. Not that I don't trust you, Mr. Winslow. I just hardly ever get to ride shotgun."

I know I'll look back on this moment for years to come, the day the founder of Baltimore Financial took me for a spin in my own car.

A long evening lies ahead of Mr. Winslow, a widower with only Patrice in his quiver. I figure rambling around in that big house all alone is the last thing a nice elderly gentleman like him needs today.

I climb in the old Triumph beside him.

"TR-3." He slides a hand over the steering wheel.

"Sure is. She's a sweet one, too."

"All we need are scarves, Miss Bauer."

"Call me Lillie." I reach into the glove box and pull out my scarf. I hand it to him. "The rules for Boy Scouts and event planners are pretty much the same."

He winds it around his portly neck, the white cashmere bright and soft against his florid, now stubbled face. Then he throws the car into first, and off we breeze down the roads of western Baltimore County. We speed by the white fences and the oak trees about to exchange their green summer shawl for the shiny maroon slicker of autumn. He talks about his company, about his late wife, whom he never really could stomach but after all, she gave him Patrice so he felt completely indebted to her as Patrice was truly the only joy he had these days. "Ah, Sandy. The old gal. Too bad we couldn't really make it work."

I don't know what to say. So I just look forward and keep a smile on my face. I doubt if he talks like this to many people, but it's amazing what folks will say to the wedding planner.

Then he asks, "So what does a young single woman like you do for leisure?" And because he asks in a way I know for certain it isn't some kind of winter/spring come-on, I tell him about the Extreme Delights Sporting and Adventure Club and he laughs, shakes his head, and says, "And my stockbroker says *I've* got guts!"

So we motor on up to Carroll County, eat a piece of homemade apple pie at Baugher's, my treat, and then drive back, the late afternoon sun warming our hair, the pleasant company easing our twin loneliness. Two floating bubbles in the same space of sky.

"Do you have a cell phone?" I ask him.

"One of those dreadful things? No, Lillie. If you can't relax when it's time to relax, you can't do business when it's time to do business."

"I just wonder if I'd do more business with one."

Keeping his eyes on the road, he pats my arm. "Let your work speak for you. It takes time, and you're still in business after a year. Quite an accomplishment if you ask me."

When I drop him off I tell him to keep the scarf. "I want you to remember this for a long time, Mr. Winslow."

"Oh, I will, Lillie. No mistaking that."

The house stands dark except for one lamp burning in one of the front rooms. I wait until he lets himself in, watch as he turns and waves before shutting the door.

And I drive away.

He needed that.


## Tacy

The day the you-know-what hit the fan, as my dad always said, I heard I won second place in the Maryland Arts Committee student contest, and a five-thousand-dollar scholarship. But the victory was short-lived because that night at the supper table the partial truth about Rawlins came out. Before that, they'd had no idea how old he was. I'd let it slip.

Dad wore a sport shirt and jeans and he sat with Mom in the den later. They had no clue I was listening through the heat vent up in my bedroom. "What is it, Kathy? Why in the world would a twenty-three-year-old want to date our precious sixteen-year-old daughter?"

"Well, she is a beautiful girl, Carl, and she's always been a cut above her age group both intellectually and emotionally."

"Can't he get a girl his own age?"

"Now, Carl, that makes Tacy sound like she's second best."

"Not at all. I know men, Kathy. You'd better pray that he hasn't gotten to her already."

"We've raised her better than that."

His voice lowered, but I heard him say, "I got to you, didn't I?"

I don't think I'd ever felt such bitter disappointment in my entire life.

"Just give him a chance. He wants to come over here, to see her properly."

"I don't trust him, Kath."

"Well, frankly, neither do I, but it's better for them to meet here than to go sneaking around."

You guys would know about sneaking around, I thought, suddenly free from guilt. I knew Grandma Erzsèbet raised my mom better than that.

I called Rawlins on the mobile phone he gave me for my birthday and asked him to keep picking me up at Barb's house so we could go make out, but he said it was time to start afresh, to court properly. "Court." That's what he said. He was so funny sometimes, so quaint.

I'd miss his body, the feel of his biceps under my lips. If he'd known how much I adored him, it would have been good-bye Tacy. Flowers arrived for my mother and me the next day. Red roses for me, yellow for her. Daddy cocked an eyebrow.

When Rawlins told me we couldn't kiss anymore, I begged him to change his mind. He gave me all the right reasons and sounded so convincing.

I wanted to cry the next day though. I wanted to wrap my hair around my throat and pull as tightly as I could. I was losing him.

Instead, I slipped a piece of typing paper in Daddy's old Selectric and started writing, writing, writing. It didn't matter what I wrote and none of it would make sense to anybody but me. After that, I worked on a scene for a short-story assignment. Mr. Herring, my Gifted and Talented Creative Writing teacher, said I had potential, but I needed to let go on my first drafts and not get so hung-up on technique.

The next little while it seemed like all I did was write. And sometimes, especially those days when I drove to Loch Raven, sat on its banks with my notebook and the words flowed, I felt ready to explode! Like this joy bubble, pink and iridescent, expanded and thinned and became ever more delicate and ethereal and exquisite. And then sometimes, when my words felt like they were not quite mine, that I'd tapped into something way beyond my measly, insignificant self, the bubble popped and I'd actually want to scream in pleasure. Those days, I likened it to a sexual climax, which I hadn't yet experienced, and now know I never really will. Not in a free-falling, lose-your-breath way.

How fast the thoughts come to me now. It really is just as they say.

5

## Lillie

Entering my old row house, glad Patrice Winslow is now, and hopefully always will be, nothing more than a very odd memory, I decide not to ride the exercise bike. I don't even mix up a fruity shake or call Cristoff. Instead, I boil up a cup of tea and sit beside Grandma Erzsèbet's Nightmare.

Teddy, Teddy, Teddy.

I call the detective on his case, as I do from time to time. He says, "No news, Lillie. He's not coming back, hon. One way or the other. You've just got to move on."

He's right. I know that.

But how can I move on? He was the one. The…One. And no matter how many dates I endure, how many men dance around the corner of my eye, I can't look another fellow straight on. I can't think that just maybe this one will measure up.

I hate it when I fall into the ridiculous pastime of feeling sorry for myself. So I think about Grandma's life before she crossed the border into

Austria. Grandma didn't speak a word of English, but my mother told me all about her job at the winery.

May I never complain again!

We have it so good here.

So on nights after weddings filled with lovey-dovey arms draped around waists and good-byes in cute little suits and foreign cars, or chariots as the case may be, I think about my grandma and all I can say is, "Thank you, God!"

If one was deemed as a Class Enemy after the Soviets took over Hungary, she was pretty much dog doo, and that's not being too harsh or too sickening. The proud wife of an esteemed university professor had been reduced to the graveyard shift. I'd like to report Erzsèbet enjoyed some pleasant job tasting grapes or even turning bottles. Not so. Erzsèbet worked in a cold concrete shed sorting six nights a week, cleaning wine bottles dumped off in large boxes by dour, sour people who drove trucks. Crates and crates slammed in front of her each day, various bottles, stale, sour wine in the bottom of some, the aroma of which would crawl out of the bottles' mouths right up into Erzsèbet's nostrils. Hot in the summertime, freezing in the wintertime, and gloves proved too expensive if the family wanted to eat.

I envision her gray woolen, layered tatters, her braids pinned up under a kerchief. I see cold chapped hands or a sweating brow and never much in between.

And I feel ashamed. And soft. And needy and unthankful. And I remember the sweet little home in which I live, the home that once belonged to Erzsèbet, and think, "How dare I complain?"

But tomorrow will dawn and I'll start moaning about something. I always do.

# Tacy

The day Lillie asked me to help her look good for her old col-legemate's wedding, I felt so important. At the dresser in her room (I can still see that piece of furniture she'd painted orange), I figured out how she could best do her bridesmaid makeup. After that, I simply wound her braid around in a bun at the nape of her neck and it looked perfect with her bone structure. "You can't ask for better than that, Lil. You look so classy."

Her smile at me, reflecting in the mirror before us, did something to me. It made me feel needed and necessary and not just an accessory, a role I'd assumed somewhere back when I was little.

"I hardly recognize myself. You're a miracle worker, Tace. Man, you're talented! You actually gave me cheek-bones!"

Lillie possesses those gentle kind of features ladies wore in old-time portraits, like those pretty, fresh young English noblewomen or something in the days before skeletal super-models. She never could see it though, and maybe I should've tried harder to build her up, but it's too late now, and she's finally got a full life and someone who shines a light on her worth.

People always complimented my looks more than hers, and maybe I was a little more "striking," but feature for fea-ture, Lillie has always been prettier. I blame all that acne she used to have, not to mention having a father who was blind and couldn't compliment her one way or the other. Mom tried, but compliments from your mom, while as important as breath, only serve to let you know someone is on your side. They don't feel like objective truth. A few days later J found some therapeutic makeup for her, and it really went a long way in building up her self-confidence. At least J can go away now knowing J did something for her. When Teddy disappeared, he took all her feminine confidence with him, but it's finally coming back and she deserves that.

J't's amazing how time really does protract at moments like this. The car tips completely over the guardrail. Aren't SUVs silly?

The next day we all went down to the airport to see Lillie off to Woodland Hills, California, wherever that was, near L.A., J think. J started off the day with great excitement. Rawlins drove us all in his big, new Explorer. Lillie shone with anticipation and J yearned to let her borrow my eyes so she could finally see herself with accuracy.

Rawlins took my hand as we walked toward the gate, and Daddy, hanging on to Lillie's arm, was oblivious. Mom just smiled. She liked Rawlins back then. With his money and job and social standing, J think she saw him as my big chance to be a real American. Hungary still haunted her a little too much, and who could blame her? She moved heaven and earth to lose her accent, learning pop songs and memorizing TV commercials, and had totally lost that un-American air we can all spot a mile away. "You be good to him, Tacy," she whispered as we stepped into the boarding area. "Don't let this one slip away from you."

And I wasn't planning on it anyway.

But something disturbed me. He kept laughing at all the fat people. I told him that "God makes people in all shapes and sizes," and he said, "God didn't make them fat, Anastasia. They've eaten their way there all on their own." I told him I thought that he was a little harsh, and he said, "It's a lack of discipline, pure and simple. And Anastasia, don't ever tell me what I am or am not."

I could only hope Lillie didn't hear him. Not that she was exactly fat, but...

## Lillie

I hear a loud crash upstairs. Oh no.

Hollywood always gets it wrong. I've yet to see a realistic-looking seizure on television or in the movies. First of all, the actor shakes way too fast, like some human jackhammer shivering a slow path on the restaurant floor, where epileptic scenes almost invariably occur. Second, they never show the fetal position stage, when this eerie heavy breathing occurs and the mouth foams. If the seizure victim has bitten his tongue or mouth, then blood mixes in, and I have to say it's really quite disconcerting. And third, they usually have the person in the restaurant sit right up afterward and say, "What happened?"

Yeah, right.

So I know *exactly* what has happened and what to expect. I knock over my nightstand fishing for Cristoff's key. There's one on my ring, but I keep one in the drawer for nights like this. Then I grab the portable phone, dialing 911 as I hurry out onto the back porch and up the narrow iron staircase leading to his apartment.

"Honey!" I holler as I let myself in. No answer. Rushing forward, I tell the 911 lady everything. Name, address. My best friend is having an epileptic seizure I say as I swerve into the monastically furnished bedroom, and yes, there he lies yes he's on the floor in a grand mal yes I'm turning him on his side now and the airways are clear so no he hasn't swallowed his tongue or anything yes I think it's been going on for about a minute now you'd think I'd be used to this by now, I say.

"The paramedics are on their way, hon. Stay calm."

I press the off button and throw the phone on his single bed. And I lie down on the floor next to him, curling my body around his like a candy shell. Finally the shaking ceases and he curls up further. My body follows his lines, two Cs close together, and the odd breathing begins. No blood in the foam this time. Good. One time he bit his tongue almost in half.

"I love you, Gilbert." And I lay my arm on his, tucking his hand in mine, feeling his warmth and wishing this kind of thing would never happen to him again.

## Tacy

I had never been that mad at Lillie before. She told me to be careful, that for a reason she couldn't even put her finger on, she didn't trust Rawlins. I told her to shut her mouth. And there we'd been, sitting in her car in front of High's, eating ice-cream cones, everything so nice. She said it was okay I reacted like that, that she figured she would upset me, but sometimes a sister positively has to say something.

When we got home, she walked up to her bedroom, shut the door, and put on her rock-'n'-roll and worshiped at the Teddy shrine.

I called Rawlins and he told me to not worry about it, but I shouldn't ever confide in my sister again because she obviously couldn't be depended upon to see things as they are.

Boy, did I agree.

Boy, was I fooled.

## Lillie

Does anyone get over the love of their life when the next best thing comes along? Does anyone forget the person who stood up for them when no one else would? Does anyone simply refuse to be forever numbered among the lonely and plan accordingly? Move purposefully forward, scientifically, without wavering?

I guess that's what scares me the most about my future. After Teddy, everything else is merely settling for the inevitable. Or at least, that's what it's seemed like so far. How many more dates can I stand? And you know, they only ask at first because of my ample chest. That's humiliating. And the fact that I'm never the prettiest girl in the group, and *never* the slimmest or even just plain slim, they think they're doing me a favor. But the thought of going through the rest of my life alone frightens me. I see a lone casket and one priest. And before that, days consisting of sandwich meals and reruns of *The Golden Girls*. I see lots of volunteering to be done, only to let myself into Grandma Erszèbet's house for…a sandwich and, yep, reruns. Maybe I'll call Tacy's kids, but they'll rarely call me, and after a while, perhaps I'll fear I'm bothering them and their new families. My bones will ache and no eardrum will register my complaints. I'll shine my furniture for no one but me. Keep the guest bedroom at the ready for no visitors.

Nonsense! Daddy would tell me. You'll see the world! Chat with interesting people and learn of their lives, and they'll feel validated because you chose to actually listen, Lillie.

But why? What would that mean in the long run? We are born, we die. In between, the only thing that matters is having loved with a strange and glorious devotion.

This is why Tacy and Rawlins bug me so much. Or really, Tacy. We all could see the handwriting on the wall as clearly as Belshazzar could all those years ago in Babylon. I tried to talk to her about being too young to settle when she was still in high school, but she informed me I was just jealous because I'd never again have a relationship like that.

Rawlins inserted a spite inside her that hadn't been there before. He just as quickly dispatched of it not long after their marriage, and so even the most cursory observation reveals her as the automaton he's engineered. Where went her say-so?

Of course, she was sorry after the argument, because I swear this is true: She shed almost as many tears over Teddy as I did. And the night he disappeared, though she was only twelve, she stayed awake with me there on the patio behind the rectory. And when the sun rose, she hadn't slept a wink either.

I want that Tacy back again.

I've tried to move on. If Teddy's alive, he's felt no compunction to return to me, so it's over. If he's dead, it's over, over. I'm done holding aloft this romantic flame that says, "I will wait for you forever."

First of all, I don't know a real person who's done that sort of thing.

Second of all, I want to love somebody again.

Third of all, and maybe most important, if Teddy came back and found me in love and happy, he'd be glad. He wouldn't want me to pine my life away. No way.

It's amazing the kind of thoughts that whisper about while you're waiting for paramedics to arrive. Here I am, coiled around a man who just had a seizure and my mind is moving along selfishly as usual as though the universe has my name etched upon each star. Poor Cristoff will be so sore in the morning. Stomach muscles he never uses but here will be burning, and then that overwhelming headache and all.

Well, tomorrow's Sunday, and after the disastrous date with Leslie, I'm not all that eager to get to church anyway. I feel awkward enough without that sort of help. I'll probably just walk across the street and hear mass at Sacred Heart. I consider driving out to Daddy's church. At the first mass, they play guitars and the people who have a very deep relationship with Jesus or at least a very expressive form of worship lift their hands high when they sing songs like, "I Love You, Lord" or "There Is a Redeemer." Daddy's fostered that brand of free devotion and fought tooth and nail for a percussion section. He still loves a good beat. My mom bought him earphones a few years ago, declaring her musical tastes had grown up. "Carl, if I ever have to hear another drum solo again, I may just have to leave you!"

Daddy's dead brother played the drums.

A little drum, a little bass, a little playing of the keyboards and so shall your joy come on you like a rush of wind. But, no, the service is just too early and the drive too long after a night in the emergency room. Sorry, Daddy.

Some months ago, I flipped by that charismatic network featuring the makeup lady with the pastel hair, and she said that God inhabits the praise of His people. You can take it from me, despite her error in fashion (and for me to even notice, it must be bad), she's right at least about that.

The first wave of sound from the paramedics' siren jiggles my eardrum. Cristoff lies quiet now, but I could wake him if I chose. He'll have lost track of time, be fuzzed up mentally, and try to do whatever I say.

The paramedics knock on the jamb of the open door. "Hello? Paramedics!"

Thank you, God.

"Back here!"

I jump to my feet, leaving him there on the floor. Man, I hate to do that. Sorry, honey. And I just stand out of their way and answer questions while they do their thing. One of the paramedics is a "little person." It's a shock at first, but he knows his stuff, moves his small hands with skill, and keeps up a genial conversation about his life in Edgewood.

When he finally comes to, Cristoff wants to know what is going on. I run back to his bathroom, examine his pill organizer, and realize that he'd taken his medication that night.

Darn.

Seems as though they haven't regulated the correct dosage of his new meds yet. And he'd been so excited to get off that Stonehenge Dilantin he was taking for years due to that ancient neurologist of his. Of course, I found him a new one. Dr. Tyler rocks.

He's cute, too.

And married.

Figures.

"First clear thoughts I've had in years!" Cristoff had said a few days after starting the Topamax. He'll be furious about this breakthrough seizure once he comes around enough to care.

Off to the hospital.

Grandma's quilt and my pillow lie on the car seat beside me, and I follow the ambulance to Bay View Hospital. The visit won't take too long, unless we're confronted by a burgeoning emergency room. Outside my window the moon shines full in the sky.

Oh well.

Knowing Cristoff will be fine, I pray anyway that God will grant me a lonely waiting room, a silent television, and three armless chairs sitting in a row where I can curl up with my quilt.

## Tacy

I dressed carefully the last day of my junior year because since the seniors already graduated, I was actually a senior. I felt older and excited and ready to take over C. Milton Wright High School. Rawlins, still withholding his kisses, but obviously not his future, called me the night before and said to look outside my window as soon as I woke up. My birthday wasn't until the next week, but he wanted me to have the present for the last day of school.

Mom and Dad and Lillie all heard my scream when I saw the Range Rover, white with tan interior, sitting in the driveway. I was the hit of the class. Rawlins knew I would be. Times like that supplied with me sufficient blinders, I guess.

Oh my. I see nothing but sky. And Hannah Grace? Is she all right? Where's Lillie? Rawlins screams again. Shut up! Just shut up!

I remember the Christmas Eve I read the first chapter of Song of Solomon and how it changed me forever, how I realized the Lord felt such intimate love for me and how I longed to feel that for Him. Maybe I should have thought of Rawlins as I read it, but something didn't ring true when I placed him in the shoes of the lover.

Daddy collapsed the next day on Christmas, two hours after Rawlins, down on one knee, presented me with an engagement ring. All my worrying was for nothing. My father spent a week in the hospital and the tests showed all sorts of things. Chiefly the need for open-heart bypass surgery.

While they were taking care of Daddy, Rawlins accompanied me to the canteen. I put some change into the sandwich machine and began to punch in the numbers for a chicken salad on wheat.

Rawlins pulled my hand away from the key pad, pushed "clear," and punched in a new code. "You've gained some weight over the holidays, Anastasia." He slid open the clear plastic door and removed an apple.

"Rawlins, I haven't had anything since breakfast."

"You want to end up with arteries like your father's?"

The next week was a blur of hospital waiting rooms and

magazines, conversations with strangers, and counting the squares in the carpet patterns. Dad made it through surgery looking pale and bloated, then pink and skinny.

Mom pulled me aside on New Year's Day and asked me how everything was with Rawlins. The message was clear enough.

I spun my engagement ring around my finger and told her not to worry. I would always make sure everything was okay. After he changed my sandwich for an apple, I began to have my doubts. But it didn't matter, did it? And the key in the lock on my cage turned.


The last Sunday of that January, Rawlins asked Daddy's permission for me to begin going to church with him from then on out. Daddy complied, but it hurt him. I know he figured that another sheep would be added to the congregation, not one taken away to another shepherd's flock.

"You'll love Pastor Cole," Rawlins told me as we walked through the bare woods behind the manse, several cardinals coloring the scene. "Now there's a man close to the Lord. A real prophet. I actually saw him work a miracle once."

"You've never talked about him before."

He squeezed my hand. "You weren't ready. But with our marriage in six months, it's time we built our household. That's the way God would have it."

Today I know that he should have said, "the way Alban Cole would have it." But I had no idea what had been happening to my husband-to-be. And I was blinded by his looks, his money, and the things he bought me, like the security I saw in the eyes of my mother.

As it turned out, we didn't really attend The Temperance Church of the Apostles, as the membership was limited and exclusive. But he did a study with the pastor every Sunday afternoon while I sat with two of the women from the church and prayed for the two men inside the pastor's study. I asked Rawlins why we couldn't go to Saint Stephen's in the morning and, boy, did I wish I hadn't. We'd go out for breakfast together instead at what I dubbed Church of the International House of Pancakes.

## Lillie

Cristoff is a very private person, bodily speaking. I've never seen him without a shirt on. Never! In all these years! So when the time came for the exam, I squeezed his hand, kissed his cheek, and asked him if it was just the same to him and all, could I go out and get a breath of fresh air?

I like to give him control. I do. After all he's been through, he deserves a life on his own terms.

One time, shortly after he escaped New York City, he told me, "Lillie, you're the only person who has ever understood me."

Too true.

Cristoff doesn't appear conflicted, but inside, he's the Somme all over again.

Realizing fresh air might be a boon, I amble outside the hospital, cross the wide expanse of dewy lawn, and maneuver onto the ledge of concrete that overlooks the I-895 expressway. Even viewed through chain-link fencing, I adore the traffic of Baltimore City. The concrete road reclines in the desolate gloom of the highway light, but every so often diamond headlights travel their way past, fading momentarily, then flaring to life in the shining ruby of the taillights. Precious people living their lives, probably hurrying home to a family reminiscent of George Bailey and his crew.

Man.

Squeezing the metal links beneath my knuckles, a hollow feeling empties me further. My planner lies forgotten back at the house, nothing scheduled between now and the time they'll finish up with Cristoff.

I look to my left.

About twenty feet away stands a tall man in jeans, a leather jacket, and a very white T-shirt. Easily as tall as Teddy. Hands jammed down in his pockets, standing there hunched-shouldered, he stares at the cars too. Really stares. I watch him. For a while. He stands so motionless it scares me a little bit and I yell out, "You okay?!"

I mean, he appears middle-aged, so I figure he won't think I am on the make or anything, and besides, alleviating unscheduled loneliness is worth the risk of potential humiliation.

As though I pushed a button at an animated wax museum, he comes to life, but without the thunks and whirrs. "Yeah, thanks for asking!"

Wow. How cheerful. He's smiling. I can see the white of his teeth in the darkness.

"How about you, miss?"

"I'm fine." *Miss.* Oh brother. I've obviously got "spinster" written across my forehead.

He turns and ambles in my direction, walking with that peculiar limp that speaks of an artificial leg. Must be a scrappy type. Must have survived something and still found enough left over to be happy about. Must be that I take way too much stock in my abilities to read someone accurately at first impression.

"You visiting someone?" he asks.

"No. Just brought my friend into the emergency room. Epileptic."

He nods. It's hard to see much more than his receding blond hair in the darkness. The hair is shorn close, lending his head the overall appearance of a velour bowling ball.

"What about you?" I ask.

He draws closer. Man, he looks familiar.

"My brother's in there. He's helping me refurbish my old house. Fell off a ladder. Think he might have sprained an ankle."

I cross my fingers and hold them up. "Hopefully no broken bones."

"All you can do is pray when they're in there and you're out here."

He possesses a weathered air, a worldly way of easing himself into conversation, a confidence one doesn't come across even once a year. In fact, I don't think I've ever seen anyone so comfortable in his own skin. And judging by the way that bleached T-shirt achieves some convexity above his belt, I'd say he had learned lessons about what was important well before that leg came off.

So shut up, Lillie. He's said two sentences.

This type of speculation…well…it's why I hate myself when it comes to men. I just don't know how to handle their presence. Maybe I could blame it on my dad. But how can anyone blame anything on a man like my father? But most likely Teddy's to blame. Loving someone for so long during such formative years tends to stunt the development of proper mating instincts.

Or maybe some of us are born awkward and that's that. What can you do, right?

"You going to be here long?" he asks.

"Hard to say. There were about five patients ahead of him, I guess. Your brother going to be all right?"

He waves a hand. "Oh yeah. Stan'll be right as rain soon enough."

Right as rain? That's cute.

He shifts more weight off his prosthesis.

I say, "Speaking of rain, I was just about to get a soda from the machine in the waiting room." I figure I'll extend him an out of the conversation.

"Great. I've worked up a bit of a thirst myself listening to Stan ream himself out for not being careful." His accent possesses an odd cadence. It sounds basically American but different. I can't peg it. "I'll walk you back over."

Well, okay. I mean, why not? This isn't the best neighborhood in the world. It's not the worst either for that matter. Oh, who cares? Why do I need a good reason? He seems safe enough.

Boy, he really looks familiar, even in the dark. But I'd remember that voice if I'd heard it before.


Tacy

On a day in early February Rawlins showed me around the place we would soon make our home as husband and wife. Rawlins gave me the most wonderful bracelet that morning. A solid gold cuff. We were lying in the barn on the property he inherited the previous year from his grandmother. It had been her father's farm and had gone into disrepair, but Rawlins had worked hard, and it was scheduled to be finished just in time for us to move in, and indeed it was. I lay there in his arms beneath several soft, old quilts, fully clothed of course, but I relished in the closeness. I thought he thought of me as a precious flower, that we were gardeners in charge of rare blossoms. I thought he treated me like the most fragile of treasures. He strummed a note deep within the raw part of me and kept me yearning. I remember once hearing a song I thought I'd never heard before, and saying to Mom, "That reaches a place inside of me I didn't know I had."

"It is the Hungarian national anthem."

I convinced myself I felt that way with Rawlins. He, of course, told me all the time we were destined from before the foundation of the world to spend the rest of our lives together. He even hoped we'd die together, which I couldn't help but find romantic then. But now...

I'm ready for this ending now, so very ready.

We lay down together in the barn that April afternoon, and he reached behind him. He pulled a solid gold bracelet out of his pocket. I could smell newly cut hay and fresh coffee in a thermos nearby. A horse whinnied in its stall.

"Rawlins! It's beautiful."

"Put it on, Anastasia. I want to see it on you."

I did. Right around my wrist. He reached out and caressed me from collarbone to wrist, then lightly slid the bracelet up to rest above my elbow. He squeezed it, and although it didn't pain me, or bite into my flesh, it hugged my skin.

"It's beautiful. I love this, Rawlins."

He kissed me then, for the first time in many months, his tongue rounding the corners of my mouth as though we'd never stopped.

I kissed him back passionately, wanting to reassure him that yes, I was his. But truly, I was only a little bit his. I had another love who came to me in the nighttime and told me I was His own. One who had broken the bonds of slavery and called me to be His bride.

I should have left the barn right then and gone on to be the woman my True Love made me to be, but I remembered my mother's grip on my arm that day in the airport, right where the bracelet rested, and it brought me to this day where I may just meet my True Love face to face.

I see earth now, outside my window. The rolling continues and, you know, it really is slow motion, just like they always tell you.

Rawlins's cell phone rings. Probably Pastor Cole. The more that man called, the less I saw of my husband. He'll be livid that Rawlins doesn't pick up. I'd smile if I remembered how.

## Lillie

Twice I flick my fingers with a metallic thump against the top of my Coke can.

"What was that for?" my new ER companion asks.

"You do that so it won't fizz out of the top of the can. It can be quite a drop down to the drawer of these machines." Man I sound like a pedant. Thank You, God, I forgot to pick up my Day-Timer.

He carefully lifts a cup of tea from between the metal wings that anchor the paper cup atop the spill grid. "I don't know why I get tea from these things. It's always grotty."

"You could try the coffee instead."

"I'll keep that in mind, love." He winks. Oh, it's a bit English, the speech. Maybe he had English parents or something.

Now that I can properly see his eyes, I can only compare them to the aquamarine of the waters of Acapulco where I try to cliff-dive at least once a year. Their blue is sheer and endless. I can visualize diving right in, swallowed whole with no bungee cord to pull me out again.

Oh, for pity's sake.

I want to run into the bathroom and hurl at my own foolish romanticism, not to mention the cliché of it.

Teddy's brown eyes had much the same effect though. But Teddy's eyes were earth, begging me to thrust my spade into the soft coolness.

Oh brother, once again! See, this is why I went for the MBA.

Other than the eyes, this man appears quite coarse. Big British features, except for a set of thin lips. Some good looks are so easily defined, the features beautiful in and of themselves. It's obvious. And that's fine. If you like the obvious. Other people, like this man here, well, you can't quite figure out why they're good-looking, but they are. Despite the irregularity of their features, the combination works. You could say the same about Cristoff.

He rubs his sparse blond hair with a confident sweep of his hand, lifts his cup, and says, "Cheers then."

I lift mine and we simultaneously sip. Judging by the look on his face as he sips, I can only imagine it is the exact opposite of my "Ah, Coke" expression. Nothing like the feel of that cold, sweet fizziness sliding down your throat, is there?

He points to my can. "Maybe I should have what you're having."

"Rots your teeth. And with your being English and all, I'd say it's best to take the necessary precautions and leave well enough alone."

He laughs with such verve the other inhabitants of the ER netherworld jerk their heads in our direction. "Good one, sweetheart!" He tips his cup again. "Most people can't detect the accent."

Now *this* guy knows how to say the word *sweetheart!*

"Well, I guess I'm not most people."

"I didn't think you were for a moment." He takes another wincing sip of tea. "So this friend of yours…is he a boyfriend or something?"

"Cristoff?" I laugh. "No. He's my best friend, but there's never been anything…well…you know…"

He nods. "Gotcha, love. Hope it turns out fine for him."

"It will. This isn't the first time we've been here."

He accompanies me into the waiting room. And why are most ER waiting rooms done in shades of teal with rose-colored accents? Even without Pleasance hissing in my ear, I know that's putrid. My outfit— orange T-shirt and baggy khakis—fits that description as well. And wouldn't you know it, the first shoes that caught my eye were my water shoes. I immediately sit down and tuck my feet as far beneath my chair as possible and still maintain a somewhat ladylike pose.

He eases himself into the chair next to mine. "I've spent more than my fair share of time in the hospital."

"Your leg?"

"Yeah."

"How did you lose it?"

He grins. "That obvious, huh?"

"Sorry."

"Nah, don't worry. I lost it in a motorcycle accident years ago."

Ouch. "Oh, wow."

"Worst pain I've ever been in."

"Does it still hurt?" I position my soda beneath the chair next to me.

"Some days. High barometric pressure days."

"And is it true you can still feel your leg there for a while afterward?"

"Oh yeah. And it hurts like...heck."

Oh, good. A gentleman. That's refreshing.

"You still ride a motorcycle?"

"Nah. I'm pretty much a foot-on-the-ground sort of fellow now."

"Can't blame you there."

I study him afresh in the bright lighting. Although weathered and paunchy and worn, a boyish quality skirts the edge. Oh, not pretty-boyish or childish-boyish. Just that freckly, blue-eyed boyish, that unaffected confidence of someone who doesn't know he's supposed to feel a bit awkward in the world, a bit disappointed at how his life has played out thus far. Then again, maybe he wasn't.

His jeans are old yet clean, broken in and faded, and his leather jacket appears as if he'd been wearing it in that motorcycle accident. Doc Marten boots encase his foot and his prosthesis. I wonder how far up the true start of his appendage begins.

So I ask. And I'm not at all scared to ask. Which weirds me out. Shouldn't I be at least a little hesitant?

"Two inches below the knee."

I examine his smooth-shaven face, the color of unfinished cherry wood, wonder what he'd look like with his blond hair grown out, wonder what it would feel like to run my finger down the age line that travels from the side of his nose to the side of his mouth.

I wonder if I will ever see him again and figure probably not. Once when I was about fifteen years old I passed a boy down at Harbor Place. He had long blond hair, huge brown eyes, and the body of a stick bug if that stick bug happened to be wearing Levis. Our eyes met that day and I felt a jolt, and then a sweet taste in my mouth, and I knew then, though I'd seen him for just two seconds, I would never forget that beautiful face for the rest of my life. Teddy and all. Go figure.

"Can I buy you another Coke?" he asks.

"Only if you'll tell me your name."

"Gordon Remington."

"Lillie Bauer."

"A pleasure."

"Yes, it is."

I determine that if he is going to be one of the people I remember for the rest of my life, by golly, I will remember his name. So I repeat it three times in my mind.

We shake hands. A good handshake. Not one of those flaccid fingers-only grasp some men bestow upon women.

"Your brother live in this area?" I ask, unable to think of anything else but desperately wishing to keep the conversation breathing.

"Nah. He's visiting his fiancée. She's from Baltimore."

Oooh, a wedding.

"When's the wedding?"

"Next spring sometime. We haven't really started planning."

"Better get a move on."

"Yeah?"

"If you want a decent place for the reception. Believe me, it's a real pain."

"You plan any weddings before?"

"Oh yeah." I give him my card accompanied by a very brief explanation.

Good. Plenty of fodder for more conversation.

But we move on, talking about motorcycles, sports cars, and the high price of gasoline.

## Tacy

The day Rawlins and I got into an argument over John 3:16 and what was meant by the word "whosoever," something in me died. I realized that for the rest of my life I wouldn't be able to have any decent form of discussion with him about theological issues like I did with Daddy without some huge bugaboo resulting. Daddy loved to talk about the Bible from all sorts of angles. Yes, he was the free-will-of-man sort, but Lillie wasn't, and he respected her opinion. Rawlins and I had been sitting in my car, looking out over Loch Raven, right where the big dam holds back the waters of the Gunpowder.

"Don't tell me what to think, Anastasia!" His face turned

white and his jaw was stiffer than a wooden coat hanger. "You know nothing about these things."

"I've gone to church longer than you have, Rawlins."

He paled further, almost gray with rage. He got out of the car and proceeded to rip the hood ornament off my car, an angel he had installed "for many symbolic reasons" a month before. After throwing it into the water, he reached for his cell phone. I read his lips. "Pastor Cole."

A thirty-minute conversation ensued, him sitting down by the bank, his back turned to me. After some time, waiting for the grilling I would get, I quietly got out of the car and walked toward Sanders's store, where I called Lillie.

Not today, I said to myself. Today I will have some self-respect.

"Don't say a word, Lillie," I told her upon sliding into her little Civic.

"You okay? That's all I want to know."

"Yes."

When we stepped into the house, Mom ran up to me. "Tacy! Rawlins just called with the most wonderful news! He's building a house right on your property, a cottage for your father and me after he retires! He's sending a messenger around with some floor plans!"

I managed to smile. Lord only knows how.


I remember something I wrote that Good Friday, more of an essay maybe or just the ramblings of a girl's heart. I can actually see it there upon the page, my mind's eye in perfect focus.

J am the woman who has anointed Him for burial. J have sprinkled my tears upon His feet, broken an alabaster box of spikenard, and baptized them with a fragrance He bestowed upon me in the first place. J am growing more and more in love with the precious Jesus, the precious face of God on earth.

J followed Him down the dusty road, aching in sympathy, miserable as the crossbeam, settled across His flayed shoulders, dug into flesh unseamed by a cat-o'-nine-tails.

J watched them nail Him to the cross, and J wept once more at His feet and cried, "J'm sorry, dear Jesus. J'm sorry J did this to You."

And J tasted His precious blood as it ran from His wounds, over my bowed head, and down my face. J love You. J love You.

Soon, yes, Jesus? Soon J will see You?

6

Tacy

Rawlins showed me around the attic where an art studio had been built. A surprise wedding present, the event only a week away. Rawlins assured me I wouldn't have to hold down a job. "You can paint and write and do all the things that you love, Anastasia, all day long, while I'm at work," he told me as we sat in the middle of the glossy pine flooring of the studio, a blanket beneath us, picnic basket to the side. I wanted to believe him. Not about the not-working part, but about the creative part. Because it didn't jibe. Whenever I started talking about what I was painting or writing, he just nodded and then changed the subject as soon as I finished.

But when I had met his parents the summer before, he acted so proud. "She's an artist, Mother." And he lied about my age, or rather, he didn't fess up to it. "So you're in art school?" Mrs. McGovern asked.

"Yes," I replied, not telling her it was Mr. Jay's Art Institute down in Lutherville.

"When do you graduate, dear?"

"In June," Rawlins rushed to say, and it was true, I was set to graduate in June. From high school. I didn't dare ask him about that afterward.

The smell of decaying leaves ekes its way into my consciousness, and I tumble along as though I'm on a ride down on the pier at Ocean City. All those times I relished in the love of my Savior come back to me in that earthy smell, and I feel so happy and bright. I feel Him descend like a lover, and I roll around in the softness of His love even at this moment. Yes, Lord, I'm Yours and You are mine, and I love You. I feel Him with me, this God who loves me so, and I thrill despite the circumstances surrounding His visit. I did not ask for this, but He comes nonetheless.

I trust He's with Hannah Grace now too.

## Lillie

"Yes, I gave him the business card, Gilbert!"

For someone holed up in an emergency room only two days before, Cristoff seems awfully perky.

"I wish he hadn't left before I got done with the doctor. 'Touch your nose with your left index finger. Good. Now touch your nose with the right index finger.'" He mimics doctors beautifully. Just the right touch of concern mingled with that feline aloofness ninety-eight percent of them seem to possess.

"Look, the guy's British. I don't think they go in for extreme weddings."

"Well, let's face it, sweetie, we can plan *un*extreme weddings as well. In fact, they would be a piece of cake."

Too true.

"I did what I could. He said his brother would be getting married next spring; I handed him my card. Anything more would have been pushy, Gilbert. We need to have a bit of class here." That'll get him.

Since we almost always work on Saturday, the office is closed on Monday. I'd already kept my Monday morning appointment at the shooting range and had climbed a wall or two down at the athletic club. I always feel like a fat spider doing that, but oh well.

Cristoff and I lounge together on webbed lawn chairs in my back-yard. Right beside Grandma Erzsèbet's Nightmare. She'd be proud of me, the way I handle seizures. I'm a little proud myself.

My tiny back lot, fenced in by chain link, affords me the breath-taking view of the cement alley that flows behind the house and all my neighbors' fenced-in lots, not to mention their sheds, their children's Big Wheels, and their clotheslines.

No Rexy Van Bibbers here on Foster Avenue. I always wondered if Rexy Van Bibber wore gray underthings, too. She's dead now though. And Mom regretted what she said when the lonely woman lived. So bad, in fact, as Daddy had conducted the service at Saint Stephen's, she invited the entire funeral party, which consisted of one aunt and Rexy's son, Earl, to our house after the graveside service. We ate from that deli tray for the next week. Turkey first, then the roast beef, then the ham, then the salami.

Katherina Bajnok Bauer would rather slit her own throat than serve iffy food at her sparkling table.

Cristoff shifts in the chair, turning his face away from the sun. "What did you say the guy's name was?"

"Gordon Remington."

"And you say he looked familiar to you?"

"Yes, honey!"

"And you can't get a handle on it?"

"No. I don't know any British men. Or mildly British in this case. I don't know why he would seem so familiar."

"If you had a cell phone and had the number printed on the business card, it sure would help." His voice contains that tart quality it gets when he's irritated yet holding back.

"Gilbert. Gilbert. Gilbert. Gilbert."

"Stop it, Lillie."

"Gilbert Lee Cristoff."

"You're acting silly."

"Changing your three names to one is silly, honey. *Cristoff.* Like Iman or Sting. But without the fame. That's what's silly."

Cristoff turns up the portable radio. "If you can't beat 'em, drown 'em out."

The station 100.7, Rock Without the Hard Edge, blasts out "Bohemian Rhapsody," with its steady harmonies, the classical influences, the silhouetto of a man, Scaramouch, Scaramouch, can you do the fandango? "I love Queen," I say, because, well, how can you *not?*

"Me too." Still tart. "But then that would be expected, right?"

"Oh, shut up, Gilbert."

The portable phone beside me chirrups. I pick it up and who should it be but Leslie Ferris. Mr. Dutch Treat himself!

"Hi, Lillie."

"Hi, Les."

"How did that New Age wedding go?"

"Pretty good."

"..."

"How was church?" I ask.

"Good. Joe talked about God's best."

"Wish I had heard it."

"..."

"..."

Finally, he clears his throat. "About the other night..."

"..."

He'll have to work for this one. And with my experience, I know whatever comes next could go either way.

"Yeah, well, I've been thinking about it, and I don't think we're meant to go out again, Lillie."

So it's going *that* way. But I'm going to have a little fun, and why not? Wussy guys like him deserve no less, the pansies.

"What do you mean, Les?"

"I really don't think it's God's will."

"Does this have anything to do with the sermon yesterday?"

"Maybe a little."

"You really like that Joe guy, don't you?"

"He's a good man."

"And he's never steered you wrong yet, has he?"

"Not really. I'm sorry, but I thought I should at least call and let you know I wouldn't be calling again."

He could've saved himself the trouble. But he must protect that weird, Christian male ego, the "I've got to be in total control of this situation" tradition handed down by men for ages, men definitely *not* like Daddy. Or I bet even Saint Paul. I've had this conversation before, let me tell you.

"Well, that was nice of you. But it's funny—God didn't say anything to me about you one way or the other."

Cristoff mouths, "You're evil, Lillie!" and I bat the words out of the air.

"Oh," Leslie says. "I'm sorry. I guess I better go then."

"Okay. Thanks for the dinner. Oh, wait! I paid for my own, didn't I? And half of your dessert and coffee."

Now that was uncalled for. Not to mention immature and without class. You know, I have no idea what possesses me at times like this. I don't know why I enjoy making these conversations so difficult for the guy on the other end.

Wait. Yes, I do.

"See you at singles group, Les."

"Uh…yeah, okay."

"Bye."

And I hang up.

Cristoff stares at me. "You know that wasn't right, girlfriend."

I look down at the phone.

"He won't ask another girl out for months." His tone graduates to sweet-tart.

"I know. I'm giving some poor unsuspecting thing some lead time."

Cristoff plops his feet down on either side of his lounge chair. "Want some iced tea? Heavily sweetened."

"Okay."

He returns a few minutes later and hands me a glass with a lemon slice perfectly positioned on the lip. The September sun shines through the amber liquid, illuminating the lemon like a piece of edible stained glass. Cristoff improves everything he touches.

"You know, sweetie, nobody's going to measure up to Teddy," he says, back to his sweet self.

"Someone will."

"No, he won't, Lillie. Not if you continue to worship Teddy's memory."

"How can you say that? I've been back on the dating trail for years now. It's not like I'm not trying."

"You may think you're trying, but you're not. Not really."

"Teddy, was just so…so nice, Gilbert. Wasn't he? And you and me, we had so much going against us. Your, well, *you* know. My weight, my acne. Being a minister's kid."

"Weren't those teenage years awful?"

"Yeah. Let's talk about something else."

He nodded. "But you're not a pizza-face anymore, Lillie."

"Yes, I am, Cristoff. I just found good makeup." Thank you, Tace.

"Well, maybe one day you'll give some guy a chance. I mean a real, sporting chance."

"What about the architect?"

"Did you really want to end up with him?"

"I guess not."

He sips his tea. "I just hope that when the right one comes along, you won't blow it."

I do too. Boy, do I. But I probably will blow it. "I just don't understand men."

"Yes, you do. You just don't give yourself enough credit. Well, actually, Lillie, you give men too much credit. We're very simple creatures."

"And anyway, I'm happy with the way things are, really. Here we are, you and me, honey, sitting by Grandma Erzsèbet's Nightmare, sipping sweet tea and getting a suntan."

"I'm burning."

"Whatever. You know what I mean."

Cristoff sits forward and grabs my hand. "You deserve more than this, Lillie. I'm fine for you now. And you'll always be even more than I need for the path I've chosen. But someday this will all wear a little thin. You'll want to be a mother, sweetie. And you'll be a great one."

He's right. I want to tell him how scared I really am. How much I long to get married. Have a nice husband and a couple of babies. But some things you can't even tell your best friend because they're so enormous, no word in the language is big enough or deep enough, no word groans at the right pitch, the right volume. And the volume changes every other day.

"I love you, honey," is all I can say.

"I love you too, sweetie-girl."

One of my favorite songs bursts its rhetoric from the radio. "God on the Rocks" by Great Guns. Being a preacher's kid, I don't relate to the words at all. But the tune haunts, the guitars amaze, and the drums... well, Daddy likes this song too. No doubt. "I love this song."

"You do?" Cristoff bites into his lemon, wincing. "How can you? This guy was even worse than that Jethro Tull fellow."

"Jethro Tull was the name of the group, honey. There's no *guy* named Jethro Tull!"

"Still, SNAP was no better."

"Well, he converted eventually, although I haven't bought any of his new stuff."

We listen to the existential musings of a British rock star. "So tip your cup, drink your fill, and toast with God on the rocks. It'll soothe what ails, at least for today, drink hearty my friend...tomorrow's always a day away."

"You've got to admit, Cristoff, it's a pretty song."

"I don't have to admit any such thing."

"And my father taught me about existentialism in that song. Which isn't always bad. There *were* Christian existentialists, you know." Why am I discussing this stuff with black-and-white, now-you-see-it-now-you-don't Gilbert Lee Cristoff?

"The guy helped lead almost an entire generation astray."

"Didn't you know? It was the Beatles who did that."

Har.

As I said, Cristoff is down on Erdman Avenue with the ladies, praising the Lord, studying the Bible, and praying, praying, praying. He sees life as bifurcated by a long fence. On one side is right and on the other is wrong, and, girlfriend, that's just the way it is. Snap snap.

I wish sometimes I were more like him.

The announcer booms in his bass voice, "That was the 1975 Grammy winner for best song, written by SNAP, oldest of the Remington brothers, and the leader of the now defunct band Great Guns."

"See? SNAP. One name. It's just goofy, honey."

Cristoff narrows his eyes. "What did you say Gordon's last name was?"

"Remington."

"Didn't you say his brother was named Stan?"

"Uh-huh."

"Isn't that SNAP's real name?"

SNAP. *Great Guns*. Great Guns?

No way.

"You think that's really them?"

"Don't you have the last album the band did?"

I fly off the chair and into my living room. Quickly I flip through my CDs. There it is. *Hell Night Music: Great Guns Greatest*, originally released in 1988, the year I realized I wanted to own my faith, lock, stock, and barrel, and due to Great Guns in a way. Pun intended. But I'm no Christian existentialist, that's for sure.

Ripping open the jewel case, I tear out the booklet, open it up, and there he stands at an easel, Gordon Remington, baby brother of the group, the nonmusical one who designed their famous album covers and went on to become an esteemed artist…in what school of art? I sure don't know. Tacy would. But there he paints, a whole lot leaner, younger, and with longer hair, but unmistakably the guy I'd met in the ER. Blues eyes like that don't change no matter what the mileage.

I holler, running back outside.

"You're not going to believe this, honey." I throw the insert onto his lap.

Cristoff examines it, mouth dropping open wider with each passing second.

"Do you realize what this could mean?" His eyes round. "If we can get this wedding, it'll be *Rolling Stone,* VH1, everybody! It could be the national exposure we need to really get Extremely Odd up and going big time!"

"Big time."

"Did you get his phone number?"

"Of course not. I do have my pride."

"Well, there's only one thing we can do then, girlfriend."

"What's that?"

"Pray, baby doll. We've got to pray."

"So tell me something I don't know."

I think about that pastor, Joe, and I'm sure his sermon was actually good. As Daddy's first choice to practice his sermon on, I know more about homiletics than most women. Joe isn't Dad. And I'm sure Joe's right about God's best and all. It's just a bummer to realize you're *not* God's best for every male that populates the planet. That not only are you *not* the perfect woman, but you are so imperfect as to be inadequate for a lollipop like Leslie Ferris. I tell Cristoff this.

"What makes you think it's really not the other way around?"

"Huh?"

"Maybe Les isn't God's best for *you*, sweetie."

H'm. Maybe. But I'm sure that wasn't what Mr. Earth-to-Lillie was thinking. And that rankles me.

Someday he'll look back and say, "I could have had her for myself, and I blew it."

Yeah, right.

I can't blame Joe and his sermon. Joe's a great preacher, actually. Modern, you know? Wears golf shirts and easygoing loafers to impart the Word of God to his flock each Sunday. I'd peg him around fifty years old, and his wife and kids are involved as much as anybody but not more. The pair protect each other, which I really like. Maybe that's what I want, someone to protect Tiger Lillie.

Gag me.

No, I don't.

Joe preaches all sorts of practical sermons, and usually there's at least one takeaway each time. He cares about his people. Not like Tacy's pastor. Oh man, what a creep! Of course, Rawlins the Jailkeeper thinks the man hung the moon.

Probably literally, even.

## Tacy

I loved life. All the smells and tastes, sensations, and the richness of the color orange. And red, oh yes, I did love red. Behind my closed eyes I often saw a Georgia O'Keefe poppy, as though she got the inspiration for the masterpiece not from the flower, but from the configuration of veins behind her eyelids. I see it now.

I loved life. I really did. I loved the taste of the wind and the salt air when Rawlins sailed me across the Bay to his cabin on the far shore. And I loved his touch upon my back, so fine, and he would sigh as though I were a work of art.

He loved me as much as he could have. Especially once Alban Cole got hold of him. What will happen to that church when we're gone?

7

## Lillie

Too bad I didn't see Stan Remington, a.k.a. SNAP, himself that night. I would have recognized him right away. Something about him always touched me. Honestly, I didn't dwell too heavily on the lyrics other than in discussions with Daddy, but I sensed in them an anger at something much larger than the man who wrote them, a festering discontent that resonated inside me. Maybe not at the same things—like God and established society and big, typical beefs. My gripes had to do with my skin, the sharp eyes of the church people, and having everything I owned labeled with a Sharpie. I'm not that deep a thinker.

Cristoff is right. We can only pray. I find myself talking to God all the time about the Remington wedding, especially while driving. When possible, I allot an hour in the evening just for driving around in my car. So lately my conversations with God seem to be focusing on two things— a phone call from Stan Remington's fiancée and a healthy baby for Tacy.

Unfortunately, I think the scales are tipped, time-wise, more heavily on the Remington matter. Well, after all, Rawlins the Pious is probably praying more than the rest of us put together. I make deals and promises, only to take them back right away because Cristoff always says, "It's better not to vow at all than to make a vow and not fulfill it." He's always telling me I need to read the Bible more, and he's right. Daddy says the same thing but in a softer tone.

A few days ago I found Gordon's phone number in general listing 411, just in case. In the general listing. A surprise. Proof I was right about him not being too full of himself.

It's been over a week since the seizure. The Paxton wedding, another sky-diving extravaganza, went off without any hitch other than the maid of honor chickening out at the last minute, forcing me to do the honors. As I say, whatever it takes. I loved it.

But now it's Tuesday, and so begins another work week. Shivering this morning, I slip on a light jacket on my way out the door. Sometime, behind my back, autumn coaxed the leaves of the dogwood tree in the small earthen square near my front door to a resonating crimson. I'm glad nature doesn't rely on me. I'm glad it's self-starting. My September jack-o'-lantern appears in need of dentures, so I pitch it in the city trash can on the way to the car.

And the air! Oh my. This is my favorite moment of the year. None other compares. I breathe in the coolness, revel in the lack of humidity, see the sunrays jabbing down in shards against the flawless sky. I shiver again and close my eyes, trying to savor the moment, smiling into the change of temperature. Oh, it's one thing for an evening to be cool. It's expected. But for it to linger this long into the waking hours is a treat.

The weekly staff meeting usually consumes our Tuesday mornings.

Peach arrives early and prepares breakfast and we sit around, eat dishes like Eggs Oscar or, this morning, Quail Eggs with Toasted Sesame Salt. From a guy like Peach. I can't begin to count the perks in this business. And yet, as the "business matters" partner, I see dollar signs on everything. Kind of ruins things at times and the others keep telling me this kind of hands-on creativity is expensive but pays off in the end. Only blind faith assures me this is true.

"First round of business," I say after we've eaten, pushed aside our plates and slipped out our various organizational supplies. "Hot-air balloons."

Pleasance ruffles through the pages of a ragged legal pad, muttering, "Pickerson, Pickerson."

Cristoff opens a neatly organized three-ring binder containing color-coded sections, pockets, and hand-drawn pull-out charts. I've tried to teach him Excel. Hopeless.

"Nice ballerina dress, girlfriend," Cristoff says to Pleasance, who's fancied-up in an aqua tulle skirt and a close-fitting ivory tank top. A definite contrast to my jeans and orange T-shirt. I guess she didn't realize it turned cold today.

She tugs Cristoff's ponytail. I had chopped about four inches off it the day before. "Nice hair, girlfriend."

Peach just sits back with an airy burp and pulls a ragged prayer book from his shirt pocket. He's a devout Catholic, attends seven a.m. mass every morning but Tuesdays when he's cooking our breakfast. If Pleasance is right, his ministrations in the kitchen are every bit as holy.

"Okay, guys. I've pretty much found out we can't do authentic balloon rides even for Victorian times."

Peach looks up from his book. "Do I really need to be here for this?"

"Actually, not yet. I can save the catering issues for later. We signed on three weddings this week." They're smaller. But better than nothing.

"Good news." He picks his teeth and stands to his feet. "I'll clear and clean up and then come back. My, that was good."

The rest of us throw out a compliment or two as he clears the dishes. Peach is quiet and very hairy and large, a yeti sort of fellow, but the only time he ever really gets angry at us is when we work late and raid his ingredients. He never writes anything down at our meetings, yet I've never once had to remind him about anything.

"Anyway," I say, once Peach leaves, "they used to burn straw to fuel the balloons back then. Regency, Victorian, whenever."

Cristoff flips to the Pickerson section of his binder. "Are you really sure authenticity is that important to Jaime? Or is it *your* thing, Lillie?"

"Either she'll say she wants the inauthentic balloon rides, or she doesn't, and I'm sorry to say, the answer won't affect her decision to go Regency one way or the other."

Pleasance shakes her head. "She's going to go Regency, I can tell you that. You should have heard her gushing over my new drawings. I have to say, it's a much more elegant time period than all those huge hoopskirts and ribbons and bows. Can you truly picture the host of 'Let's Kick Butt' in a gown that looks like a parade float?"

Ha! "I pictured her more like the Liberty Bell with frosting."

"Has she decided on a color for the attendants?" Cristoff asks.

"Peacock blue!" Pleasance raises a hand almost as if she's praisin' the Lord. "My favorite color."

Cristoff taps his binder with a pen. "Perfect! This will be beautiful. And can you imagine the pictures?"

And here I thought I was doling out bad news. You never know with this bunch.

"You should see the fabric I found, and with those high waistlines and gauzy overskirts. M'm. This will be the most stunning one yet!"

"It's going to be a little awkward in a Victorian setting," I say, experiencing some perverse pleasure at throwing cold water.

But they aren't even listening to me. They bandy about flowers and fabric in great detail. *Ooooo* this and *ohhhhhh* that.

I try again. "And she said she wants me to try to find another place."

More flowers. More fabric. More ideas about party favors.

Right.

Why am I here? Tell me that. Surely we could hire a secretary and I could go back to work for Deutschebank or get a dream job with one of the investment houses down at the Inner Harbor.

They continue to ignore me as well they should, and I doodle an entire page worth of drawings, mostly of flowers and targets and my name over and over. Lillie Bauer, Lillie Bauer.

Finally, I scrape up my planner and head downstairs to Peach's workroom. We only rent the back half of the first floor. It houses the catering department.

Although Cristoff is my best friend, and Pleasance is the only other woman involved in Extremely Odd, Peach and I roost in the same non-eccentric coop. Creative cooking is the part of him that doesn't add up. He's an ex-navy guy without a hint of artistry otherwise.

I pull up a chrome stool to the large, stainless steel worktable. "How's it going, Peach?"

"Finally had enough of those two crazies, huh?" He keeps his back turned as he scrubs our dishes with a sponge on a wand, and his chuckle harmonizes with the water falling out of the spigot.

"I'm way out of their league."

"Yeah, well, someone has to keep their head around here. And you do a good job."

"Thanks." I sit down on one of three stools by the worktable. "How's your Gertie these days?" I love Peach's wife. She's even more of a peach than he is.

Peach places the final fork in the draining board cup. Then he pours himself a mug of coffee, pulls me a Coke from the big restaurant fridge, and hoists himself up on the stool opposite me.

"You can keep a secret, can't you, Lillie?"

"Sure."

"Well, I think The Women's Exchange is going to let some of their waitresses go."

"Really?"

He jerks his head in the general direction of the little place across Mulberry, just a few doors down from our building. It's been there forever. You can buy anything crocheted or decoupaged in the front room and enjoy the best shrimp-salad sandwich you've ever eaten in the dining room in the back. They serve chilled tomato aspic on an iceberg lettuce leaf too, but, well, blech.

When your heels strike the aged floors and you hear the clink of ice as it flows with water into glasses, see the blur of waitresses hurrying in their crisp uniforms, complete with caps, from table to table, you feel a part of something larger, and older and wiser, and with more self-control and honor. You feel like one of the grandmas who raised her brothers and sisters after their mother died during the Depression, or like a librarian from over at Enoch Pratt who faithfully took the streetcar from Catonsville every day for forty years because that was her job and she loved it. You feel like jitterbugging, like wearing an orchid corsage, like sneaking out for a stolen kiss, because when those floors were laid, a kiss was worth stealing. You feel a hollow sadness line the chambers of your heart, a sorrow to be alive in such an age when nothing is special anymore.

"Yeah. Gert's decided she's one of them."

"But she's been there for years!"

"I know. So much for loyalty and all."

"Why are they closing down?"

"They're not. Just a big remodel in the kitchens. May take up to a year."

I gaze around at the spotless kitchen. The business isn't growing as rapidly as I hoped, but still… "Maybe you could use an assistant with you down here on a regular basis? I know Pleasance and Cristoff can always use help with errands and stuff, too."

"What about you though? Could you use some help along those lines? Gert's real smart, Lillie. She may have been a waitress all of her life and all, but she's real smart."

On each forearm, Peach sports tattoos so faded I can't tell what they are. It's hard for him to ask about this job for his wife. And to be honest, he knows as well as anyone that another employee isn't inked into the business plan. But Cristoff taped a three-by-five card, one of many, to his refrigerator that says, "To him that knows to do good and doesn't. Well, that's sin." From the book of James. Not a direct quote from a reputable translation, he assures me, but I doubt James himself would mind. He'd probably be glad his words were being put to good use, lo, these two thousand years later. Now *my* favorite book is Galatians. I have a feeling it would be James's favorite too. I think he'd be a little miffed to know that some people mistook his letter as a license to judge others.

"Oh, she is smart, Peach. You can see that a mile away."

"She's never been fired in her life. I can't imagine how she'll feel to get that pink slip." He shakes his head, old sagging jowls swaying along with the movement. Peach, you big old basset hound, you.

"Well, she won't have to find out. She's hired, Peach. When can she start?"

"As soon as she puts in her notice across the street."

He smiles. When he bares his dentures and lights go on in the gray eyes recessed beneath brows that remind me of my mother's old powder puff, only not pale blue, well, I experience the same warm feeling as I do watching *Match Game,* or walking into The Women's Exchange supplies.

And so I provided God's answer to the Hagertys' prayers. It comforts me that if God uses me as an answer to other people's prayers, He's working on someone else to answer mine.

## Tacy

Rawlins showed me around the new cottage. That's what he called it, "The New Cottage," a three-bedroom home he built for my parents on his property. He paid big money to have it built so quickly.

"I'm going to allow your mother to pick out the details: carpet, cabinets, fixtures, you know, that sort of thing."

"She'd like that." Mother never got to do anything like that. Ever.

"I thought so."

Rawlins could be so thoughtful.

Lillie helped me put on a bridesmaids' luncheon at the church. They all thought I was so lucky, except for Lillie, of course, to be marrying a guy like Rawlins McGovern.

8

## Lillie

When I was little these guys used to travel around and give presentations on creation versus evolution. They'd project films at the fundamentalist churches, hand out booklets, and talk about the fossil record and "the canopy." Everyone would go downstairs afterward to the fellowship hall, eat some cake, drink some punch, and believe the exact same way they did before they even pulled into the parking lot. A friend of mine from school took me to her church for one of those meetings. Most of us knew in our hearts God created the world, we just didn't know the scientific ins and outs. Some of us remembered the scientific evidence they proposed, and some of us, like me, just kept our beliefs simple. God created the world because I know it in my heart. If you don't like it, lump it. I suspect most of them forgot the fodder they received for conversations they would have with all those militant evolutionists out there waiting for discourse.

God created the world because, well, to believe in the other would require a different kind of faith, a faith in man's ideas, which, as we all know, can't be trusted. Can you imagine looking at the veins of a maple leaf, the paws of a baby lion, the eye of a bee, the way a cat lands like a pool of fur; can you imagine biting into a peach, feeling the winter sun on your face, or hearing anything Beethoven ever wrote, or Elton John for that matter, and thinking nothing but time and chance brought all of this about?

Time I can deal with. Who knows how long it took Him? I couldn't care less whether it's a literal six sunrise–sunset days. But chance? No way.

Personally, I like to imagine the Godhead dancing to a rhythm and tempo of its own, something even grander than a waltz, touching, tasting, smelling, seeing, and hearing, creating wonder after wonder after wonder, and when it's finished, looking upon the handiwork and saying, "This is *great!*"

I love God so much. I love the wonder of God and the mystery of His workings. To trade that for some boring, "Eighty bazillion years ago there was a bang out in space, blah, blah, blah-bitty blah," is simply unacceptable to someone like me, someone with a corny "Footprints" poster on the back of her bedroom door.

Unless, of course, that bang was God's voice.

Let's face it. If a person wasn't *there* at the beginning of it all, and none of us were, it's all about faith no matter what you believe. I'd rather believe God's still alive and well and interested in us. Because if there was, perchance, a random Big Bang, couldn't, perchance, a random Big Suck happen just as easily?

Hah!

I'm not very intellectual. And any physicist would scorn me, but I choose to think of them as those lab-coated nerds in *The Far Side*. I rarely discuss these matters considering I'd be deemed a fool. Perhaps I am. Or perhaps I'm wise enough to know what one can and cannot say for certain.

But earlier today when I held my niece Hannah Grace in my arms for the first time, evolution didn't enter my mind. All I could think was, "This is a miracle from heaven."

The birth in the tub occurred without mishap, despite my doubts. Rawlins refuses to go into any great detail because he doesn't believe in talking about Tacy's private parts to anyone other than Tacy. And I don't even know if he talks about them to her. Fine by me either way.

By the time I arrived, Hannah Grace, age three hours, slept in her mother's arms. Tacy never looked more beautiful. Her long blond braid looped over her shoulder, and at the bottom a pale blue satin ribbon glowed. "This is the happiest day of my life, Lillie," she whispered when Rawlins left the room to get me some freshly squeezed orange juice (from organic oranges, naturally).

"Even better than your wedding day?"

"Easily. But don't tell Rawlins I said so! Just look at her." She handed my niece to me. Hannah felt just like Tacy did when our own mother handed my little sister to me for the first time. I was only six then, but some feelings you never forget.

The warm little curve of the child's behind felt just the same as Tacy's did, and I patted it, hearing the rustle of the plastic pants. No disposable diapers for this baby, Rawlins declared when they first found out they were expecting.

I was in love.

And now we sit together on the deck, the sun setting on her first day of life, and I talk to her, staring into those dark button eyes I know right well aren't focusing, but she sees me anyway, right? She knows I love her and will do anything for her. I tell her exactly that. I don't make a vow, due to Cristoff's advice, but I whisper, "You've got me for good, baby girl. You can always rely on Aunt Lillie to take care of you."

## Tacy

When the cottage was almost finished, Mom and I walked through, hand in hand, both wearing cotton skirts and breezy tops. I felt so like her and yet so different, so custodial in a way. She did a beautiful job with the kitchen. Soft-yellow cabinets and even that Corian stuff. I picked out real mahogany cabinetry and green marble countertops for our place. "Only the best for you, Anastasia," Rawlins said. "Only what you want."

Even now, I have to admit it was beautiful. The kitchen designer said I had a real knack for that kind of thing. That made me feel good in a time when I wondered if I'd slipped away completely.

Mom and I stood in the master bedroom, freshly painted a dusty plum.

"I asked Rawlins if I could go work for the ad agency, Mom."

"I already know his answer. Do you think you could paint some murals here for us? It will be a while before we move in—until your father retires, which might be years from now."

"Rawlins said the ad world is too competitive. He doesn't want me to become jaded."

"I was thinking maybe a garden scene in the kitchen."

"Maybe I could sell my paintings."

"Or do trompe l'oeil. Here would be a good place to start."

"I really want to go to college."

Mom looked around. "Of course, the master bath has lots of potential too."

That night the Lord visited me again. It had been so long, but I had cried out to Him several times that day, in my loneliness, my despair, from the recesses of my trap. I felt myself at the bottom of a hole, no rope or ladder to ensure my release.

In the morning I came down to Dad, almost completely recovered from his heart surgery, working on a manuscript. A devotional booklet. Well, they still twinkled, his lively blue eyes as he invited me to sit down and have some toast. I watched the way he patted my mother's hand when she laid a plate in front of him and said, "Thank you, Kathy darlin'." Any pressure she exerted on me regarding my marriage to Rawlins was only out of love for my father.

My wedding day. So lovely a June day, I can breathe that air in even now. Lillie's friend Pleasance decorated the church and made my gown. I remember it now so clearly, more clearly than I ever did before. For it was just a blur, but now, in this moment wrapped in between the planes of time, I see the altar, I hear the voices, smell the roses, breathe the air.

When Rawlins took me completely, I felt so old. I was only eighteen? "Oh, God, deliver me. Come to me, commune with me. Draw me, and I will run after You to the fragrance of Your perfume." I prayed that prayer. Over and over and over.

## Lillie

I can barely concentrate on the wedding at hand. Hannah Grace completely occupies my mind. That little cylindrical body, sparse hair that moves as softly with my breath as sea kelp waves in a gentle current. Much the same as infatuation.

But the event, Space Age Nuptials, rocketed to stellar success. Hah!

When some people want extreme, they do mean extreme. The actual ceremony, a bit off-theme, finds me standing in a piercing parlor. It's weird to think that this couple, both public defense lawyers, are having their wedding rings inserted.

I say when wedding rings need be *inserted* something is just a little too wacky. And that's being nice. The ring ceremony occurs behind a screen.

"With this ring"—click!—"I thee wed," by golly. And the poor judge! Well, he seemed a little off kilter too, though I couldn't help conjuring up visions of him marching in some protest or other during the heyday of his angry youth.

I can't imagine their wedding night will be at all exciting now. Did they stop to consider that?

Sometimes I feel I am making a mockery of God's holy ordinance. But hey, at least they're getting married at all! Those bra-burners who

declare marriage is obsolete and will eventually go the way of the perco-
lator possess no insight into the human psyche, the basic need we all have
to simply belong.

Afterward, we descended into some bomb shelter erected back in
the fifties. For my part, not easy to locate. But after a dozen and a half
phone calls that began with an elderly member of the John Birch Society, I found one farther out Route 40, only ten minutes from the piercing joint.

Poor Gert and Peach didn't even sleep last night, fashioning the odd-
est hors d'oeuvres I've ever seen. Somehow they figured out how to make
everything look metallic. All I know is, they wouldn't touch them themselves. So neither did I. At least our clients, Margaret Phelps and Tib
Wheckle, sure knew what they wanted. That makes our job a lot easier.

"What does a bomb shelter have to do with piercings?" Pleasance
asked after our first consultation with the couple. "And why in the world
does she want them all to wear throwaway clothes?"

I shrugged. "I guess they feel that's the wave of the future."

"Well, at least you won't have to worry about sewing them," Cristoff
had said. "Me, I have to make bouquets out of tinfoil and Tupperware.
How am I going to make flowers out of that stuff?"

Peach stepped in at that point, saying softly, "Get some heavy-duty
foil, or disposable roasting pans. And as far as Tupperware goes, the lids
are more flexible than the containers." He scratched his belly looking
awfully pleased with himself as Cristoff made notes.

The bouquets turned out to be the prettiest things I'd ever seen. They
sparkled and shimmered and each glittery petal moved with the delicacy
of a butterfly. I asked Cristoff to arrange me a bouquet for Grandma
Erzsèbet's Formica kitchen table.

The gowns, tailored from trash bags and cellophane, had us laughing for weeks as Pleasance tried new designs. Even Peach was allowed no escape, the maid of honor being a plus-sized, plus-sized beauty. But we managed perfectly. The couple drove away in a Pacer to their honeymoon in some geodesic dome in the Arizona desert with broad, Space Age smiles on their faces.

"Thank the Lord for that colored GLAD wrap!" Pleasance says after the event as we drive toward the city, tired and pleased with the result, however madcap.

"If we could pull off something like this and make it work, we can pull off some aging British rocker's do!" says Cristoff, who is driving the rented U-Haul van. "Has he called yet, Lillie?"

"Would you be the first to know?"

Cristoff pays the dollar toll for the Fort McHenry Tunnel. "I hope Peach appreciates your offer."

"Hey, nobody twisted your arm, honey. You volunteered to help me unload the stuff."

"Yeah. I'm a dufus."

"Well, I'm not," Pleasance says. "I'm going right home to my babies."

Ten minutes later, after dropping Pleasance off at her apartment, Cristoff pulls into the alley and backs the truck up to the rear entrance of our building.

I open my door. "Let me go check my messages real quick." I run up the steps.

The message light flashes and I punch the button.

That warm voice lightens the twilight gloom of my office.

My scream sends Cristoff directly to me in a few seconds flat. He hears the final, "...to make an appointment soon, sweetheart."

"It's Gordon Remington."

He spins a gangly 360 degrees in the air. "Well, if this doesn't deserve a celebration, I don't know what does. What shall we do?"

"How about unloading that stuff?"

He gives me a stiff squeeze of a hug. "It's going to happen, baby doll. I just feel it in my bones."

"You really think we'll get this contract?"

Cristoff crosses his arms over his chest. "It's what we've been praying for."

"And see, having a cell phone didn't matter one iota."

You know, Teddy would have been thrilled for me. For all of us. I'll go home to an empty old row house and whiz up a shake, feeling a solid hope for the first time since Extremely Odd opened its doors. Mom will think it's a good thing, but more out of relief than anything. Daddy will be delighted though. He'll wink and say, "I told you so." Which is true. "Let's celebrate."

After unloading the truck I decide I'm not going home just yet. I think I'll drive out to Bel Air and tell him myself.

He's listening to the radio when I walk in through the never-locked door. The *Prairie Home Companion* show. And why does Garrison Keillor have to sing? It's really not all that delightful, kind of like that uncle or aunt who always insists on starting everybody off for "Happy Birthday to You."

"Lillie?"

He knoweth us by our footfalls.

"Hi, Daddy." I kiss his chamois cheek.

"Good wedding today?"

"Yes. And I have good news. We have the chance of signing on a huge contract for a celebrity wedding."

"No kidding. Who?"

"SNAP, of Great Guns."

"No kidding! Mr. 'God on the Rocks' himself, huh?"

"Wow, good memory."

He taps the side of his head.

"He's a Christian now."

"Not all that surprising. You could see he was asking all the right questions years ago."

My father astounds me sometimes.

"How did this come about?" he asks.

Of course I tell him everything, even how much I enjoyed Gordon's presence. He congratulates me and says he'll be praying and he knows God will reward my faithfulness. And then, "I'm retiring, Lillie."

"Okay, Daddy, I know it's late. But I was just so excited. I had to come up."

"No. I mean retiring, retiring."

Whoa.

"Now?"

"In a couple months. We're going to move into that place at Tacy's. Your mother is tired. We need to rest. God knows, I really would rather not, but…" He shrugs his shoulders.

He's really saying this: I've given up. We're tired of eking out an existence. We're giving up our independence and placing ourselves beneath the surefire rain of Rawlins's "almsgivings."

"Oh, Daddy."

He closes his beautiful eyes and tears slip from between his graying lashes. Oh, God. Oh, please, God. This is Daddy, my sweet Daddy.

"Come live with me," I hear myself say, and I can't believe I never thought of it before. Things always seemed so set. "I'll take care of you."

"Thank you, Lillie."

I expected more, but apparently this is all he needs. Me too.

It takes some doing to convince Mom. After all, she might have been in the lap of luxury, and Rawlins did already build the house, Corian counters and all. Several years ago, of course. But I say this. "You rode that bike out of Hungary all those years ago to end up in slavery to Rawlins McGovern?"

She nods. "All right."

Pretty easy considering I'm dealing with Superwoman.

So I guess I get to move my bedroom down to the basement now. I call Cristoff right away, as my mom brews us some tea. I tell him the news.

"Wonderful idea, girlfriend."

"You don't mind? I mean, you live there too."

"Of course not. To him who knows to do good and doesn't do it…"

"Well, that's sin." Two voices.

Snap snap.

"Will you help me decorate the clubroom in the basement for my bedroom?" I ask.

"You got it, sweetie."

"I'm thinking Arabian Nights."

"Or Barbara Eden's bottle."

Yep, I think that will do. We're good at this sort of thing now. "Mind if I bring Pleasance in on this?"

"She gets a good discount at the Fabric Warehouse, doesn't she?"

"Big time."

"Well, there's your answer then. You know what a cheapskate I am."

You know, Cristoff should have his own show on TLC. *Flower Power with Cristoff.* It's too easy to imagine how great he'd be. Man, I love my friend.

## Tacy

For Christmas the first year of our marriage I gave Rawlins a gift I thought he'd never forget. Our lovemaking was gentle and he was kind and giving, but I wanted more. What came over me, I can't say. Perhaps my own passionate nature consumed me, but that night, I was willing to try anything. I became a wanton woman, stripping for him as he sat in a chair. Hesitating, I said, "Is this okay?"

Even now the memory embarrasses me.

"Marriage is honorable, the bed undefiled. Continue, Anastasia."

I loved the way his eyes feasted on my body, but in the end he was just the same lover. I wanted him to take me just once with a wild, happy abandon. But nothing seemed to work. I wanted to be ravished, caught up in the mighty whirl-wind of desire. The next night, he asked me to do the same thing, only wearing the ruby necklace he brought home with him that evening after work.

It felt dirty then. Wrong.

When I invited his mother for lunch the next week, I wanted to ask if she had experienced the same coolness with

Rawlins's dad. Mr. McGovern seemed so austere. Of course, I would never ask such things. They were none of my business really, and if my prying got back to Rawlins...

The night Rawlins brought Alban Cole home for dinner, I realized things were about to change, that we were going to be allowed full membership in The Temperance Church of the Apostles. Pastor Cole's eyes burned through me, not in a sexual way, but they told me he knew everything and he didn't trust me one bit. I was dismissed soon after dessert.

The two talked long into the night.

I called Lillie to complain. "My life is so different than I thought it would be. I figured we'd join a country club, go out to dinner a lot, make friends. We're in such a beautiful part of Baltimore County. But I am sequestered. We have a housekeeper and a cook. I have nothing to do but read and paint. I'd just like to use the barn loft for that, but I don't want to hurt Rawlins's feelings. Anyway, my artwork doesn't come out like it should these days. I try and try. I try writing my stories and the words are only chunky blocks sitting on the page like firewood."

But she wasn't home and I only left a breezy message on her machine. That was a mistake. I see that now. I realize that was the time I needed to make a move, because not long afterward, it was just too late.

Maybe it always was.

After that dinner with Pastor Cole, Rawlins gave me a portion of Scripture each day to read, and then we'd discuss it at supper each night. Rather, I was allowed to ask him questions and he'd explain. We started with the book of James. Faith without works is dead. I didn't want to tell him what Daddy once told me, that Martin Luther wished to throw the book out of the canon! I missed my discussions with Daddy.

## 9

## Lillie

Talk about your research!

Stan Remington. Stan Remington. Stan Remington. Stan at the periodicals. Stan on the Internet. Stan on the microfiche. I'm telling you, it's hard to take in such fame, such glowing accolades and, even more indicative of his popularity, the vast amount of criticism.

"Sadly entertaining, the *Sex, Sexty-Sex* tour, nevertheless, left me unfulfilled. SNAP's onstage antics, once powerfully agile and animalistic, were no more than a caricature of his early vitality. I expected provocateur. I was disappointed to instead find a servile, aged jack-in-the-box leaping about as if trying to recapture his lost youth and conform to imagined expectation."

Well!

Ouch!

"Poignant and raw, Remington's lyrics, which seem to emanate from his troubled psyche by way of a thesaurus, offer the masses a fast-moving intellectual current in which to swim, flounder, or be cast ashore like flotsam."

You know you must being doing something right when that many people need to vocalize their misgivings about you and your work.

I like Stan though. At least what I'm reading about him endears him to me. Of course, it might all be hype. A lot of his pictures smile at me. Now, how bad can a rock-'n'-roller be who smiles for the camera?

He's extremely orange. Neon orange.

I saw this poster in the music store window the other day. Lots of, I'm sure, famous guitar players touted this foot pedal, and it was obvious some people were pasted in later because some heads were just way too much bigger than others. But here's the thing. They all wore black, sported leather, tattoos, and silver jewelry, were weighted down by mops of unwashed hair.

When they had their picture taken they had to be thinking, "Dang, if I don't look cool."

And then this poster comes out, and whoa, it's like, "Hey, did you all go to the guitar players' uniform store or something?"

I thought how peculiar some guitar player dressed in Dockers would appear on that paper. And I'd think, "Hey, that's *really* different. That's a true individual."

See, here's the bottom line. So the group you hang out with doesn't look like the moms and the dads. You wear weird clothes and makeup or what have you and think "I'm so different." But I defy anybody to actually ensconce themselves in a Goth group or a skater group or the artsy group, and then one day, just walk in rebelling against *them*. Hah. I'd like to see that just once. *That's* courage. Rebelling against authority is so passé. But rebelling against your peers? Now that takes moxie.

I doubt Stan would have looked much different from the other guitarists though, despite the smile. Still, I like him. "I can't believe I get to meet SNAP."

"The last thing you should tell him is that you've always been a fan of Great Guns," Pleasance says. The three of us sit at a large table in the periodicals room of the library, poring over old magazines.

Cristoff slides a copy of *Wake Up!* magazine off a stack he gathered. "The girlfriend's right. By the way, nice hairpiece, Pleasance. Is blond your natural color?"

"Nice button-down. Been moonlighting at T. Rowe Price lately?" Pleasance shoots back, flipping through some obscure British publication. "The last thing we need to do is look as pathetic as we are."

"Well, call 911. I'm about to have a heart attack!" Cristoff blurts out. "Duran Duran is still around. Did you know that?"

Nope.

Pleasance shakes her head too.

"It says right here in *Wake Up!* they have a Web site devoted to them. Ultrachrome, Latex, and Steel, it's called. I'll be right back." And he hurries off to the Internet servers in the other room.

"Sounds like a gay thing," I say.

"Duran Duran?" Pleasance screws up her feline features. "Never heard of them."

"No, the Web site."

"Who's Duran Duran?"

"Mid-eighties, new wavish, lyrics that made absolutely no sense to some pedestrian like me." I pick up an old issue of *Rolling Stone* magazine. SNAP curls his lip on the front cover. So much for all those smiles.

"Lillie Pad, if it came out after 1965, I don't know it."

"They were big news. But I haven't heard anything from them in years." Yep, there he is, the British-rocker bad boy in 1979, the stadium years. I locate the article, but Gordon isn't in the picture of the band. Not that he should be, but a girl can hope. Another Remington brother clenches an upraised fist above his bass guitar. My eyes scan the list of band-member names. The guy with the bass is named Hale Remington.

That's right, Fitz and Hale Remington were identical twins. Hale on bass, Fitz on drums.

"I'll be right back, Pleasance. I need to find Cristoff."

Hunched over and deep into the Duran Duran Web site, his mouth hangs open like it used to when he first arrived at our school. When we used to call him Gilbert.

I sit down. "Remember one of the twins died? It was Hale. What did he die from?"

Cristoff types "Hale Remington death" into a search engine.

"Drowned on his own vomit."

"Oh, great."

"I'm telling you, sweetie, don't bring up much about the band. These people relish their anonymity."

"How do you know?"

He pulls his eyes from the computer screen. "Wouldn't you enjoy just being treated like a regular person after living all that hoopla?"

"I'm treated like a regular person every day. What's so hot about it?"

Cristoff turns back to the Web site. "Trust me on this, baby doll. Act like you know his work but don't get all gushy. He gets gush every day, but genuine artistic appreciation is always welcomed by creative types."

"Okay." I have to trust him because he is one of those creative types. And me? Well, I'm still living at dead Grandma Erzsèbet's and basically haven't changed a thing, except for electronic equipment and a gas grill. (Love that gas grill, and I got it cheap at Watson's end-of-the-year sale. It even has a little burner attached to it for boiling up a pot of sweet corn.)

So Hale Remington should be listed as a taboo subject. Definitely.

Still, drowning on your own puke. Poor Gordon. That must have been hard on the family. I can't imagine having such information about me and mine available to the general public. It's plain scary. I mean, I'd hate the world to know my sister is married to some psycho control freak.

"Cristoff, see if you can find me some kind of profile or interview just on Stan and then print it out."

"Will do."

"And can you do Gordon while you're at it? I don't think it will hurt to get a little background information on him either."

"You got it. Good idea."

I glance at the time. Planning to make the return phone call to Gordon at three thirty, I check in one more time with Pleasance, who has graduated to an old issue of French *Vogue*. I didn't honestly think I'd have her for long on the whole Remington-information-gathering sortie.

"Wish me luck. I'm going to make the callback."

"Break a leg, Lillie Pad. If you had a cell phone you could make the call from here."

Right.

Hurrying back to the office, passing one of the places Edgar Allen Poe used to live, I skid into my office just in time to lift the handset. The wall clock clicks the half-hour and chimes once.

I hesitate, looking at my skeleton hand as it holds the receiver. Can I do this?

Ride that bike, Lillie. You can do it. Over the border, Hungarian

Woman. And don't forget he's got a skeleton inside of him, too. Just like everybody else.

I dial the number, sweat hydrating my forehead. How should I greet him? *Hi, this is Lillie Bauer, remember me?* No. Of course he remembers me. He made the first call, for pity's sake!

First ring.

What about, *Hi, Lillie Bauer here, returning your call!* Not that either. Of course I'm returning his call! Good grief. He knows he called first. No sense in playing that game of "who called first."

Second ring.

Maybe, *Hi, Gordon. This is Lillie!* and just leave it at that. But what if he knows other Lillies?

Third ring.

"Hello?"

"Um, yeah, is this Gordon?"

"Yeah, it is."

"Um, well, I got your message on my answering machine and I thought I'd call."

How stupid can you get? Not much more than that, judging by the dead silence on the other end of the line.

"Who is this?" he finally asks.

"We met in the ER at Bay View."

"Lillie!"

"Exactly!"

"Well, why didn't you just say so?"

"I was going to. In fact, I'd practiced just saying, 'Hi, Gordon, this is Lillie!' just like that, and then I heard your voice and got all frustrated like some stupid star-struck person or something."

He laughs that great "ha!"

"You figured it out then? The music thing?"

The music thing.

"Yeah. And the art thing, of course, which shouldn't be downplayed. I come from a family of art lovers. I thought you looked familiar, but I couldn't place it."

"You liked Great Guns then?"

"Especially in high school."

He laughs again. "That pretty much sums it up all over the world, much to my brother Stan's chagrin."

This actually seems to be going well now. Yeah boy.

"So am I presuming correctly that you'd like to bring your brother and his fiancée around to talk about the wedding?"

"The lady's a mind reader!"

I almost blurt out, "Well, I didn't think you'd called to ask me out on a date." But years of holding my tongue around men keep me under control.

"Do they want something private or a big *Enquirer*-worthy bash?"

That loud "ha!" pushes my ear away from the phone once more. What a cool thing, to just laugh like that. This fluid issue of mirth unable to be controlled even for a second was in all actuality quite alluring. Imagine that. A sense of humor. How sexy.

"They want big. Really, really big."

Thank you, God! Thank you, God! Thank you, God! I do the electric slide—a reception favorite.

Still. "Really? How come?"

"Stan's never really done anything halfway."

"Well, we can sure handle big at Extremely Odd. Extremely big, in fact."

Oh brother. I'm an idiot.

"Good then. I'll call him and we'll set up a time for an appointment. What days are good for you, Lillie?"

"Any day but Friday through Monday."

"That's four days of the week, sweetheart."

"It's an odd business."

"And I thought rock-'n'-roll was crazy."

I open my planner. "How about tomorrow at three? Can SNAP make it then?"

"I'll call him and find out. But I'd really try to call him Stan if I were you. SNAP is a stage name, nothing more."

"Got it." I try to sound cool, but man, how stupid and awkward and, well, non–show biz can a girl be?

"Don't sweat it, love. Everybody does it. I just care enough to give you a heads-up. I'll get right back to you then."

"Sounds good."

And we ring off.

He's so nice. He's so nice. I keep saying the words to myself over and over. To my horror I look down and see that I've hugged my planner against my breast, hiding a furiously beating heart that threatens to just up and lift me off my feet.

To my horror. To my horror.

What if he's like the other twits out there?

Suddenly guys like Cliff the Architect and Mr. Dutch Treat boo and hiss and laugh like scary clowns. What am I doing? Why do I feel like this?

Those guys hadn't broken my heart. I'd broken my own, set my hopes and dreams upon a train track just before the train arrived. And then I blamed the train!

Teddy poured so much love into me for so many years, and I've wasted it on spoiled buffoons who take Saint Paul so literally that women are really just a second-best offering in the life of a dedicated Christian male.

What is wrong with me? Why this desperation? Why this date book pressed to my thumping heart? Oh, God, why all of this? Why am I acting like a junior-high girl? I mean, Gordon has said nothing to lead me on.

Right?


## Tacy

On our first anniversary J asked Rawlins for a baby. He said not yet.

On our second anniversary J asked Rawlins for a baby. He said, "You're still so young, Anastasia."

When Rawlins was away on a trip, one of those convention things for the advertising industry, he told me to stick close to home. But J really wanted to head on down to the ocean, walk the beach, maybe take some pictures. J had a painting in mind and wanted to start on it when J got back. J was sure he wouldn't mind.

The September day flew in and out on a warm breeze. The sand, heated with sunshine, accepted my feet so lovingly. Such a comfort from God overcame me, and J praised Him there on the beach, a blanket spread beneath me. J took pictures, talked to the man at the caramel-corn stand, sketched, and ate Boardwalk Fries. Even the drive home felt supernatural and so important, giving me that assurance that just living was such a noble thing.

When I got home that night from the beach, I picked up my brush and wow! I stayed up all night painting! It was wonderful! I hadn't felt like that in years. It was like dancing. And you know, I felt God's Spirit with me. I really did. I felt Him breathing behind me almost as though He watched and rejoiced with me. I actually painted two canvases. There was something special there finally, something I'd lost years before, as though someone had found a precious childhood toy of mine on some unfrequented byway and sent it to me special delivery. And I knew all that wandering in the desert wasn't wasted. Oh, the plans I had for the next day when I lay down at six a.m., tired but hardly out of ideas. The plans! The next morning, I called down to Towson Art where a friend of mine worked, and he delivered two stretched canvases at lunchtime so I didn't have to stop. It felt more like play than work, that I'd tapped into something holy. I felt so free and wonderful! It seemed like the start of something big in my life. Something huge and wonderful.

Rawlins wouldn't speak to me. He was so angry when he found out I went down to Ocean City. He told me I disobeyed him. That raised my hackles, and I almost called Mom, but then I realized, why bother? She was always so busy with Dad and was finally enjoying herself a little bit these days, what with Rawlins's mom going up to the rectory for a cup of tea a few mornings a month. Rawlins told me he was going to start checking the mileage on my Rover just before he left town. If it was way too high upon his return, he'd know I went "roaming" as he called it. I told him, "Rawlins, I just needed to walk the beach. I love the beach. I wanted to take pictures to paint. You said I could paint. You should see the beautiful pictures I've done while you were away."

He told me, "Not anymore." He locked my studio door and took away the key. "If such fancies tempt you to evil, it's my spiritual duty to protect you. From yourself."

I cried and he just walked away.

Later that night I heard him talking to Pastor Alban and he said, "I did what you said I should do." And I waited, for maybe tears or some show of emotion, just in case, because he seemed to lock the door on me so easily. They got into a discussion on Amos 3:3, where it says something like, "How can two walk together unless they have agreed to do so?" I really thought the discussion would center on Rawlins and me. Hadn't we agreed? Didn't we say our vows? We agreed we were hardly walking together. I was at least ten feet behind, head bowed, in a burqua, the sand swirling between me and him and I was blinded and in all practicality, alone. But no, they talked about how their church must be separate from the world, and not only the world, but other Christians who didn't see things as they. Sounded to me like a kid who wouldn't share his best toys.

When Rawlins told me several weeks previous that we

would have to be rebaptized to join The Temperance Church of the Apostles, I didn't understand. If my baptism was acceptable to God, wasn't that enough? But he said no, this would be a sign of our coming out of the world and into this church, of being pulled yet further from sin and into a glorious light of a more devoted, sin-shunning following of the Lord. Then, after what I did, he doubted we'd be allowed to join. I suspected though, had I been privy to our bank accounts, a sizable chunk would be missing, and not before we'd become full-fledged members.

On Pastor Cole's dictates, Rawlins stayed away for a week. I still don't know where he stayed.

## 10

## Lillie

The Extreme Delights Adventure Club decided a catapult is a very interesting device and worthy of our consideration. Due to the overall
medieval flair of this escapade, Cristoff wears hosen and a leather jerkin.
Ack. This outfit hits a little too close to home, if you know what I mean.
And yet, here we all congregate out in a field in Harford County on the
ancestral farm of one of our members, so who's going to see anyway?

I wasn't about to buy some medieval garb, so I just wear running
shorts, a tank top, and a bed sheet, toga style, over my shoulder. I mean,
catapults go way back, right?

It takes the engineers of the group, three guys from Northrop Grum-
man, a good while to calculate how far away from the haystack to place
the catapult in between flights. With each member of the club, the dis-
tance will differ, due to weight and all. Let's hope they don't have to move
mine too far back, or I'll be too humiliated to sit in that bucket.

They've been launching sandbags for hours now, which is more of a comfort than mere math could ever be.

So I'm enjoying a cup of tea with the others. We've achieved quite the civilized setup here. Wicker furniture, silver service, linens. Oh yes, we're *extremely civilized* in the Extreme Delights Sporting and Adventure Club.

I decide to go first. After all, what do I really have to lose? If I die, well, there you have it. Everyone will be sad, but hey, life goes on in the Bajnok-Bauer clan. It always has. Besides, I'll enjoy the rest of the day all the more. And as the only woman aboard, I do have something to prove.

Oh man, it was great! That initial thrust felt like nothing I've experienced before. One second you're motionless, the next you're shot forward so that you're actually slowing down before your brain computes the initial movement. I loved it. I loved soaring. And all too soon, just after I reached the highest point of the arc, I gained full control of my body. I suspended myself in the usual swan dive position and located the large pile of hay. At the last moment, I tucked my head and shoulders and rolled safely to a stop.

"Did you like it?" I ask Cristoff on our drive back downtown.

"Hated it."

"Oh."

"I may be getting too old for this stuff, sweetie."

"Never."

I downshift, going into a hairpin turn.

Man, I love my car. It takes the Seven Sisters Curves on Harford Road like finger and thumb down a satin throw.

"I mean it."

Yikes. "What?"

"Don't you ever wish you were doing more with your life?"

"Usually I think I'm *too* busy."

"No. I mean important stuff."

"I'm not following you."

"Oh, never mind."

Truth is, I *am* following him, and I'm sorry for him. I tell him that God doesn't see the difference between missionary or mason, preacher or physician, that a job well done is a job well done, and it all glorifies Him in the end. But he won't listen.

Truth is, Cristoff was made for more than event planning. God's gifted him to do something magnificent. Surely, time will bring it about.

## Tacy

J asked him, "Why won't you come home?" J didn't know what was happening to him.

His voice sounded so far away on the phone, farther away than my canvases in my studio. "After your deception, J just need a little time away and you need to think about what you've done, Anastasia. There's family penance to be done."

Family penance? J had no idea what he meant.

"J promise J'll never do it again, Rawlins. J didn't know J was doing anything wrong. Please, please forgive me."

J know J compromised, but J couldn't bear that lonely house anymore. J just wanted things to be the way they were before, hardly normal, but at least familiar.

"Pastor Cole will release me soon."

"Release you?"

"I can't talk about it."

Rawlins was still gone when I began reading the Song of Solomon again. Daddy gave me a book by a seventeenth-century woman named Madame Guyon, a married lady who was eventually imprisoned for her writings because they were so revolutionary about spiritual things, I guess. The book was called <u>Song of the Bride</u>. The title itself spoke to me because, well, I didn't feel like a bride anymore. Not after more than two years of that life and already feeling cast aside. But that first verse of Song of Solomon, "Let him kiss me with the kisses of his mouth." Oh, dear God. My dear Lord. My Bridegroom.

How I cherished that kiss, that union of Your spirit to mine. Forever. I loved You then, and now in this moment as the darkness begins to settle in, I need Your love more than ever before. I need You desperately in this sea of lonesomeness and chill. And maybe expectation.

## Lillie

Confession time. I watch the Style Channel on cable television. Last summer Pleasance asked me to view a rerun of some show about fashion. It had been a particularly excruciating day for me, fashion-wise. Since June had arrived only a few days before, I figured the day justified something floral. After fingering through the hangers of my extremely disorganized closet, I found the last Easter dress ever given to me by Mom and Dad. Thinking the wide lace collar more than appropriate, thinking the stiff tulip-strewn chintz very summery, thinking the pearl buttons that followed each other like ducklings from the dropped waist up to below the collar a classy decoration that saved it from being completely pilgrimatic, I walked into the office only to have Pleasance Stanley cross her two index fingers in the international vampire-defense signal.

The ensuing conversation was just what one might expect. A lot of *what do you mean*s on my part, and even more *come on, Lillie Pad, you don't honestly think*s on Pleasance's part. Finally, just to shut her up I agreed to watch the network and penciled the Sunday afternoon time slot in my planner.

So what began as a desperate attempt on Pleasance's part for the fashion reform of Lillian Elaine Bauer became a source of amusement for the said same woman. Normally, I go about my day oblivious to other women and their looks. Tacy pretty much beats all, so growing up and comparing myself to her automatically put most women way down on the overall beauty yardstick, which pretty much tells you where *I* am: not in the measuring device aisle, not in the hardware store, not even in the dying strip mall the hardware store anchors.

On the Style Channel, however, it's a different matter altogether. After hours of watching those models, acting so confident with those inflated, pouty lips, by golly, well, I've started my own version of *The Foot Book.*

It's all in my mind, of course. But right now, a Brazilian girl with the biggest feet I've ever seen on a woman tops the list. And there's a perverse part of me that takes pleasure in watching them strut down the catwalk, all thin and alive, lithe and graceful, and so very, very pouty, and I look down and…whoa! Look at those red satin T-strap river barges. It takes the phrase *sailing down the catwalk* to a completely new level.

Meow.

And just where do they find pretty shoes that big? Tell me that.

Tacy went through a phase where she wanted to be a model. I'd come home from my day at college, excited about a new assignment in my literature class or thinking up some crazy scheme to make money while fulfilling my marketing assignment, and there she'd be in front of her bedroom mirror, a high-school freshman made up like some torch singer, hair teased in B-52s style and some fashion magazine splayed on the surface of her dresser. She'd place her index finger on something, then look up at her reflection, then look down again and dip a makeup brush into a paint pot. And so on and so forth.

What was she thinking as she stared at her beauty? Did she view herself as a blank canvas, unable to express anything in and of itself? Did she view herself as a beautiful room, furnished and painted just right, only needing curtains and lamps and throw pillows to complete the already wonderful effect the architect and designer had given?

I don't know.

I cannot comprehend owning such loveliness.

But now as then, I'm proud to walk alongside my sister and know that I helped raise this creature, helpless as she seems now that she's given the keys to her psyche to that Rawlins McGovern, God save the king.

When I visited after Hannah's birth, she looked every bit as lovely as the day she married that man. Because she'd dated him so all-consumingly, Tacy hadn't cultivated many friendships, just with Barb and another couple of girls. I stood next to her glory on the day she uttered all of those vows, each word stabbing me in the stomach, the white of her garment, her hair, her skin, her pearls, beaming so wide a magnetism that anything nearby was sucked into its shimmering orbit. And that included me in my french braid, orchid headpiece, and pale-yellow organza bridesmaid dress. But her beauty is not so glorious now that Rawlins chooses the getups. Oh, don't get me wrong, she's classy all right, but absolutely *no* imagination fuels her ensembles.

Well, after church at Daddy's—only two more Sundays for him and less than a day before the big meeting with Remington and company, I am scared to death—I drive out to Tacy's house to get my Hannah Grace fix for the week. I've talked to Tacy on the phone every day since my last visit and she says she's never been happier. She said that kind of thing a lot though, even before Hannah. Rawlins this, Rawlins that. He's so great, great, great. North, south, east, and west, Rawlins, Rawlins, he's the best.

Right.

I often wonder who Tacy's really trying to convince.

I pull up to the gated entry of their house out in Baltimore County. They live near Loch Raven Reservoir, up Dulaney Valley Road and out Jarrettsville Pike. People like me think it's kind of snooty up that way, people like me who grew up in a manse on the outskirts of Bel Air. But to each his own. I don't want to admit to being a reverse snob or anything. And I've met my share of kindhearted wealthy people since starting the business. Perhaps I'm a little jealous as well.

I ride by the main pasture and the spotless stone stables, past the white barn with stone foundations, past the horse-jump things and all that equestrian stuff. Secretly, I'm glad Tacy is allergic to animals and hay and all, because she'd have probably thrown herself into that part of Rawlins's world, forcing me to learn all about it.

The white fences appear new, though they aren't, and the tidiness of the small farm angers me somehow. Beauty in its place.

Oh, Tace.

Mom and Daddy's place sits empty and will remain that way. Score one for moi, Mr. Rawlins McYou-Didn't-Win-This-Time, and ha, ha, ha! The reach of your net has been severely shortened.

Calm down, Lil.

Their farmhouse comes into view.

I'm not big into architecture, so I'm not sure how to categorize Rawlins and Tacy's house. All I know is it's at least 150 years old, stone, symmetrical and tidy, like something in old Civil War photos. Slate roof gleams, windows reflect the gentle blue of the Maryland sky, hearty pansies and mums vibrate in perfectly mulched, weeded, automatically-watered border gardens, not to mention the clean screens of the back porch that overlook apparently new decking, though Rawlins built the trileveled barbecue lounge palace, complete with understated green retractable awning, five years previous.

And there she sits on that very same deck, swinging on a hammock, baby at her breast.

I park near the steps.

"Come on up, Lillie!"

Wow. She looks tired.

"Hi, sweetie." I lean over to kiss her cheek. "How's the baby?"

"Perfect. She's a hungry thing."

"Did she just wake up from her nap?"

"Oh no! I feed her just before she goes in. That way she can fall asleep at the breast."

Well, okay. I don't know much about this stuff. "Sounds good to me."

"Rawlins created our schedule. And guess what? She's almost gained back her birthweight and she's only two weeks old!" Tacy looks so proud.

I round my hand over the curve of Hannah's skull. "She's so pretty."

"I know."

Just then the porch door opens. "Hello, Lillian."

"Hi, Rolly."

"I'm marinating some chicken breasts. Will you share in our supper?"

"Don't you have church here tonight?" I ask. Their church congregates inside their refurbished barn.

Rawlins leans against the railing. "Not tonight. Pastor Cole's mother passed away and he returned to Oregon to officiate at the funeral."

"Okay, then I'd like to stay for dinner."

Tacy's face lights up. "Oh, good!"

"Can I hold her when she's done?" I feel as though I'm asking my dad for the car keys.

Rawlins stands erect. "I'm sorry, Lillian. But she always goes into her crib right after feeding. We'll be rousing her in two hours for wake time. You may hold her then."

And he reaches down as Tacy breaks the suction for the sleeping infant, then whisks her away, back to the lacy white bassinet in the nursery off their bedroom. Tacy tucks herself back in and I feel so young.

Rawlins sticks close by the rest of the day, so I can't ask Tacy how she feels about Mom and Dad's decision to move back to the city with me. But the chicken is delicious, and he makes me a peach soymilk shake. And every once in a while a look of desolation, or what I perceive to be desolation, passes over Rawlins's face in a quick, fly-buzz of an instant, and I find myself feeling sorry for him.

I hate that.

## Tacy

Rawlins finally came home to me, bearing a gift. I was reading the Bible in the living room when he slipped the present out
of a box, a waterfall of white silk, a nightgown, and he slowly
took off my street clothes, one piece at a time, kissing my body
as each part appeared, telling me how much he loved me and
how he wanted me close to him.

"Never leave me again, Anastasia," he muttered into my
neck. And even during the heat of my body's betrayal, that
feeling his hands conjure, I thought, "I never did. You left
me." But his mouth found mine, and it felt different, almost
needy. Before he took me completely, he slid the gown over
my head, then he picked me up in his arms, those arms I
loved to caress for their beauty alone, and he carried me to
the deck, under the stars. I felt this wild abandon, hating him
and needing him at the same time, as if my anger fueled my
passion. And I clawed him and beat upon his back, and he
roared with pleasure. He never loved me that intensely, or
needed anything I could give him. I had waited so long for
that. Something almost human resided in him, but as soon as
we were finished, he saw me tucked into bed and left the
house.

The next afternoon Pastor Cole called to welcome us
officially into The Church. "Now make sure you are reach-
able at all times, Anastasia. A word from the Lord can
come upon me at any moment, and I like to deliver them
immediately."

"All right. Do you have Rawlins's cell-phone number?"

"Of course."

And that was that.

Perhaps the end is near. J seem to have been rolling for ages, but J am peaceful now in the love of Christ.

"Your love is more delightful than wine."

Oh yes, my God. You fill me, heart, soul, mind, and spirit. You fill me completely with the wine of Your love. J delight in You. J delight to know that You have set me apart as Your bride. That in You J find joy and satisfaction, in You J delight myself, and that You look upon me with favor. Oh, my wonderful, beautiful God, that You can see beyond my sin, my stain, my stench, the utter baseness of my humanity, and still reach down to me in my moment of tragedy, astonishes me. Burn within me, ignite me with Your fire and refine me for Your presence. You are like a refiner's fire; burn me, my Savior, until all sin is gone and only You remain.

## Lillie

On my singular visit to Tacy and Rawlins's church I thought I'd stepped into an episode of that time-travel show. Only watched the show once, and it gave me major creeps for some reason. Cristoff said it almost threw him into a seizure the time he viewed it.

The Temperance Church of the Apostles consists of twelve families. No more. No less. Ever. It's supposedly been in existence for more than one hundred years, but I'm not sure I believe it. More likely, that Alban Cole quack started it himself.

There's a waiting list, believe it or not. Not that any family has left in the past few years. But once or twice a decade, a family moves away from the area. I'm not sure what they do for church once they relocate. Nobody talks about a family once they move on.

Insert freaky theme song of your choice here, folks.

Tacy and Rawlins were the last family to join, and I've always suspected the church allowed their membership because they needed a better meeting place. When Rawlins offered to redo the barn, he and Tacy were given "full membership status." I guess full membership status is all they've got. Nothing halfway about The Temperance Church of the Apostles.

The Sunday I visited—the Sunday they dedicated the new sanctuary—I was told to sit just beyond the doorway. I felt unclean, like a leper or something, only without medical excuses. I was just unclean because I was just me. Or maybe it was that I wasn't them.

But even from my folding chair in the vestibule I could see the chapel. Rawlins spared no expense, that's for sure. Stained-glass windows fixed into the freshly paneled walnut walls glowed. Six on each side, one apostle in each window. Up at the front, a window with imagery of the Trinity broadcasted frosted colors on the thick white carpeting. The members had lined their shoes up neatly in the vestibule. It gave me some small comfort to at least see various styles zigzagging down the line.

Twelve backless benches, six on each side of the center aisle, attested to the alertness each member was expected to achieve during the service.

No real altar. Just a big, simple chair stood on the platform at the front, a chair for Pastor Alban Cole.

Come to save the world.

Each of the twelve families, good-looking specimens of vigor and beauty, all Caucasian, sat on its own bench, each bench carved with the name of an apostle. Tacy and Rawlins sat on the Matthias bench at the back left.

Alban Cole, seated in the chair, talked about consecration of the heart and the body that day as they consecrated the sanctuary, which still smelled of new carpet, fresh wood, and stain. I agreed with everything he said, could find no theological fault; nevertheless, I left feeling unwanted, out of place, and dirty, like a bum watching a white wedding from atop a deserted, windswept hill.

"Who is this guy, Tace?" I asked my sister before I left, before the church fish supper began on the lawn surrounding their house.

She shook her head, eyes still glowing at being included in such a gathering. "Rawlins says he began his ministry here on the East Coast up in Hanover years ago. He appeared one day in the streets and began preaching and healing, Rawlins says. He brought Rawlins to the Lord years ago."

"What does he do during the week?"

She just shrugged and gave me a kiss good-bye. I've never asked her that question again or anything like it. Because Tacy still won't know the answer.

That night I accompanied Cristoff to his church on Erdman Avenue. When an obese lady got up with her accordion and sang, "I believe for every drop of rain that falls a flower grows," I wept so hard Cristoff put his arms around me.

But really, if that song were true, I think there'd be a lot more flowers around.

## Tacy

For my third anniversary I asked for a baby again, and Rawlins said, "Anastasia, I'll tell you when it's time."

He rarely slept with me anymore, just on special days like Christmas Eve, my birthday, and when Pastor Cole was out of town. I didn't know what the connection was there. I still don't. But some nights, he'd come home from Bible studies and would remain so silent I couldn't budge more than a few words from him. I knew not to ask him about it.

For my fourth anniversary I didn't ask for a baby. Neither did I for my fifth or my sixth. My days joined together in an unending string of sameness, one day like the next and the next. I began cross-stitching, which seemed to be accepted by the church ladies, and then moved on to embroidering vestments for Alban Cole. As his priestly garments grew more fine, the congregants' church clothing became more and more plain, almost like a uniform. He told us, as we were all blessed with material wealth, that to lay aside our finery when coming into the sanctuary would warrant more blessing from God.

The next New Year's Day, Rawlins told me it was time to start our family. We received the blessing of the church, the congregants praying over us at a special service in the barn sanctuary, Alban Cole's face set like cement, unreadable as always.

Mom and Dad visited the next April to make sure I was well and to offer their congratulations. I still could hardly believe

I was expecting a baby. I waited so many years. Rawlins, I'd ask, please. Not tonight. Please...don't put a condom on tonight. Didn't he realize the shame I felt? Didn't he realize that I knew he wouldn't give me himself? But that was behind me and new life just around the corner. If Rawlins never approached me sexually again, I think it would have been fine. October, I prayed, find your way to me as quickly as you can.

Spring and summer floated by on the thought that I was bringing a child into the world. Perhaps it wasn't the best of worlds, that fake world "the master" created around me. Three servants, two cars of my own, antiques, gold jewelry, silk, crystal, Rolexes, and designer wallpaper. My Master McGovern.

And yet inside me a child grew. My own baby. More mine than my master's for I nourished this baby, I fed this baby with my body and my blood. I would give all for this baby.

I will give all for this baby now.

I search within me. Deep within me for that place where I met with my God again and again when I sought a greater contemplation, an all-consuming fire. I sought to experience Him who created my soul to commune with Him, to dance with the Divine. To enter into His glorious light. And the more I entered in, the more I found; the more I found, the more I sought. Oh, to know Him, to fellowship in my Lord's sufferings, to joy in His holy presence. Jesus, You are all in all.

Lover of my soul, my Master, I am Your bride. I am Yours. Even now.

Rawlins didn't touch me, except for good-bye kisses and the occasional brush of the arm, during the entire pregnancy. He said the church believed a pregnant woman to be unclean. I searched the Scriptures for such a doctrine but could find nothing. I believed my marriage over, but motherhood would surely be enough. Sad enough to say, that was exactly what happened.

## 11

## Lillie

I love Sunday evenings. Especially because we take Mondays off at Extremely Odd. This is my night with Cristoff. We usually eat pizza, rent a movie, cry at the sad parts, marvel at how easy life inside a picture tube is, and applaud actresses who allow themselves to appear like regular human beings on screen—messed-up hair, weight gain, wrinkles—human and beautiful in the dignity surrounding their commitment to playing a role with integrity, serving the part itself, the work as a whole.

Okay, so Cristoff says that. I just say, "Looky there at that Meryl Streep." Or Jessica Lange or Farrah Fawcett, believe it or not. "What a gal. What a woman of the people!"

I am, however, thoroughly offended that the Bridget Jones actress acts like getting up to a whopping 124 pounds is akin to turning into a bovine. Is she serious?

We go retro tonight and watch *Lawrence of Arabia.* I've got to tell you, there is nothing in the world so beautiful as the eyes of Peter O'Toole. I love that man. I love that man. It can get a little boring at times, but I just watch Mr. O'Toole and imagine what it must have been like in those days, when he was young, to have been his wife, to have been caressed by him and loved by him.

Singlehood is so depressing.

The phone rings and we pause the VCR. Pleasance. "Girl, I'm designing you the perfect outfit for Tuesday's meeting with the Remington boys."

The Remington boys. That's her name for them.

"I was just going to go with the brown pantsuit."

*Snarf.*

"Come on, Pleasance. It's not that bad."

"Compared to what? Sackcloth?"

"Hey! I *could* wear something orange."

"Pick me up at eleven thirty tomorrow morning."

Notice the lack of a question mark.


## Tacy

When I held Hannah Grace in my arms the first time, oh, well, even now I can feel the feelings, see that blotchy little face. Even now my heart bloats with that deep-rooted, primal affection only a devoted parent experiences. That tiny life, that spark of divine creation issued forth from me, so unworthy a vessel. And God was kind.

Oh, Lord, be kind to Hannah now. Surround her with so much love for all of her days.

The day Daddy told me why he went into the priesthood coincided with the day I lied to my parents. I told them they couldn't come inside the house because it had just been fumigated, a stupid fabrication, because Hannah Grace was sleeping up in her crib. But I didn't want to share my little haven with anyone just then, for lately God had begun wooing me to a place I needed so desperately, a place of such devotion and calm I knew it was His gift. I hated being pulled from where I'd been called to go, but there they were on the front porch telling me they wanted to see their granddaughter. I knew Rawlins would be furious that I didn't clear it with him first, so I told them to go around back and I'd meet them on the deck. For some reason Daddy got on a "don't waste your life" topic, one I had a hard time figuring out because I didn't know what it had to do with me, really, especially as I had become a mother.

But nevertheless, he told me why he went into the priesthood. I knew he had a brother who killed himself, years ago. Daddy was only nineteen at the time and on a very rough path. Doing whatever kind of drug they had in the '50s. Opium? I didn't want to ask. Drinking a lot, running around with the guys wreaking havoc on their small town. Like something out of Steinbeck, I guess. They called him "the bad seed" and "James Dean" and I could hardly imagine Daddy like that. Daddy! Just unbelievable, this blind priest was the bad seed.

Everybody thought he was the one who "should have" died like that. Not Robert. Carl was the upstart. Carl was the one who ran fast and loose. Carl was the one destined to be plucked from earth like a weed. Well, it jarred something loose, he told me. And it was then, even though he hadn't been born into a religious family, that he found himself inside the local parish, praying. Even before he knew God intimately, before he knew Jesus had died for him, he knew he was called to serve.

It took some time for his lifestyle to follow suit, and maybe a good dose of Kathy Bajnok. Yep, he ran from God for a while, but when God's got plans, he told me, it's best to get with the program. Sooner than later.

And there he sat on my deck, ready to retire, blind and learned and still sassy and still in love with his Lord. Daddy and I had so much in common by then, spiritually speaking, and I had to push him away.

I wanted to tell him I had no way out, really. That if my marriage and family weren't God's program, what was? I wish he'd have just come right out and said what he wanted to say. Maybe we could have put our heads together. Maybe I wouldn't be rolling down this hill right now.

## Lillie

Monday noontime finds me and Pleasance at the discount fabric outlet over in Eastpoint. Although why she had to drag me along, I still can't say. She springs like a lithe cricket from table to table, picking up and unwinding the bolts, touching and rubbing the fabric against her brown cheek.

I point to a length of navy blue something-or-other, and she just waves me away saying, "You've got to wow them, pow them, and show them Lillie Bauer means business."

"Gee, Pleasance. I thought navy blue *was* business."

"Not our kind of business, Lillie Pad. We need romance, imagination, pizazz."

"Panache?"

"Oooh yeah, I heard that! Besides, you already have a navy-blue fancy dress."

I swear she has the contents of my closet memorized.

"Are you sure you're going to be able to get this outfit done by tomorrow morning?"

I don't know what possessed me to ask that. I don't want to wait around for the diatribe. "Let me know when you've decided. I'll be over at McDonald's getting a Coke."

Pleasance doesn't answer because she's already rushing over to a cart two clerks are just wheeling in from the back. When she literally cries, "Oh baby!" at the sight of a raw silk in a deep mustard color, beautiful, no doubt, I exhale a wary sigh and hurry out the door before she grabs me.

Mustard. Just great.

Sometimes I wonder how I got so lucky. I love so many people. Mom, Dad, Tacy, Hannah Grace, Cristoff, Pleasance, Peach. And Gert's a sweetie, too. I enjoy watching her and Peach interact. They work comfortably side by side, their wide derrières swaying with their steps, and when she starts softly warbling some old tune, he joins right in. They usually stop the words at the same place and just keep humming. Peach seemed so isolated down there before, but now Gert's with him and she's taken on the role as receptionist as well. And she likes it.

Well, there you go. Things really do work together for good, I guess.

So as I sit in the booth at McDonald's and sip on my Coke, I pray for a lot of things. But I pray about the meeting tomorrow, that we won't blow this one chance to get Extremely Odd going big time.

Pleasance joins me half an hour later. "I put the fabric in the car."

"The mustard one?"

"You color blind?"

What did I say?

"Ready to go?" she asks.

"Back to your place?"

"Yep. I'll measure and draw the pattern while the soup cooks."

"Soup? What kind."

"Don't know yet. I'll see what I have in."

Boy, I wish I was more like Pleasance.

Pleasance and I met at The College of Notre Dame in an elective course. Children's Lit. We discovered a shared penchant for Madeleine L'Engle and spent hours at the study lounge discussing the time-travel series. One night she invited me over for stew cooked on a Bunsen burner. Clothing designs papered the walls of her studio apartment, a room containing a scarred set of wooden bunks, a daybed, a dinette set, and some bookshelves. This small apartment in the poor section of Towson was all she could afford at the time, but in her way, Pleasance had combined her skills with the offerings at the Salvation Army Thrift Store. I'd never seen a place like that before, a small Aladdin's cave with one rule—don't you ever be turning on that overhead fluorescent light! Juney, and Pleasance's younger son, Stefan, sat wide-eyed on their bunks, eating their stew as we talked about Meg and the gang from *A Wrinkle in Time,* about which of the cherubim was our favorite.

Something clicked that night, whispering long after the boys slept beneath their quilts, and the dream of the business began when I told her about my first bungee jump with The Extreme Delights Sporting and Adventure Club. She asked what I wore, since it was a formal occasion and all, and when I told her about the prom dress I dug out of my bedroom closet, well, her face took on a horrified expression the likes of which I've never seen in real life. My dark-blue chiffon evening gown, the standard bungee gown for eleven years now, resulted.

Pleasance is my friend and I love her. I wonder if I've ever told her that so plainly?

## Tacy

Rawlins was mad at me again for letting my parents stay without calling him.

"What about 'honor thy father and thy mother'?" I said in a moment of bravado.

"Don't throw Scripture at me, Anastasia. I know more about Scripture than you do."

I wanted to say, "Yeah, Scripture the way Pastor Cole interprets it."

But I didn't. God help me, I just couldn't.

I only said, "I'm sorry."

"You know you're supposed to clear all visitors with me first."

"But they're my parents."

"All visitors, Anastasia."

"But—"

And he grabbed my arm. "Are you questioning me?"

Yes! Yes!

But I just hung my head and told him I was sorry yet again. He let go.

Did Rawlins worship the same God as I? The God of love and freedom, grace, mercy, and forgiveness?

He only knows God's laws and His justice.

"I am responsible for you before God. Do you really want me to have to answer to Him someday for your disobedience? Your...your subterfuge?"

Subterfuge? Right now, as the Rover bangs against a tree, the word tickles me.

I was chained to my own home.

"I am the head of this household, Anastasia!"

"I know."

"Go to bed, Anastasia, I'll be up soon. Wear the white nightgown."

Oh, dear God, no. Not now.

I left the kitchen and halfway up the steps he called to me from where he stood at the bottom. "Anastasia, turn around."

I turned. Of course I did.

"If they come again without notice you are not to answer the door."

"Yes, Rawlins."

"Do you understand me, woman?"

"Yes, perfectly, Rawlins."

Woman. He called me woman.

After he took me—I didn't cry that time—when he slept, for he sleeps so lightly, I tiptoed down to the hammock on the deck, wrapped myself in my quilt against the fall chill, and I found God again. And I asked Him why and He only said, "My grace is sufficient. You are cared for, you are loved. By Me."

I poured out my soul to You then, dear God, as I do now, and I asked You to be close to me. To show me Your goodness, to reveal my freedom in You, to realize that no matter what man can put upon me, I am Your child, Your beloved, and no one, not Rawlins, Alban Cole, or Satan himself can ever take that away.

"You shall be free indeed."

And I am free. I hear a great crack, taste metal, and I am released.

Cradle me. Cradle my child, Hannah Grace.

## Lillie

We drive back to Pleasance's apartment after the trip to the fabric store. She drags out the Bunsen burner for old times' sake and spins a Shirley Bassey album while she heats up some chicken and stars. By the time the boys arrive home from school, she's cut the pieces out with those zigzag scissors and begins setting up the sewing machine.

I clear my laptop off the kitchen table so the boys can do their homework. "Are you sure about that mustard color on me?"

"First of all...mustard? Lillie, this is *caramel*."

I examine it more closely. And shut my mouth if she isn't right. Well, that makes it all seem much more acceptable. I love caramel candy.

"I considered making you that all-occasion little black dress, Lillie. It's time for that. But when I saw this fabric, I just couldn't let it go."

"Sleeveless?" I ask. Dear God, please don't let it be sleeveless. Not with these ugly hams I call arms.

"Of course not! Tight three-quarter sleeves, scooped neck baring your shoulder bones—"

"Are you serious?"

"I certainly am. Your neck and shoulders are gorgeous. Now stop interrupting. Cinched waist and a full skirt with a petticoat underneath it."

"What?!"

Nausea literally begins creeping up my throat. But how can I tell her that? She seems so pleased with the idea.

"Lillie Pad, you're going to look like Audrey Hepburn!"

Like that could ever happen! What a shame I can't figure out this clothes stuff for myself.

"Did you like to play dolls when you were little?" I ask her. "Did you make their clothes?"

"Yep. In between beating up the neighborhood boys."

Juney and Stefan complete their homework at the kitchen table, ruffling textbook pages and shuffling notes, asking questions about algebra and biology. Sometimes Pleasance fields the questions to me when she has too many pins in her mouth; sometimes she answers them herself.

"Should we have bagels or something in the conference room tomorrow morning?" I ask above the hum of the fabulous Viking sewing machine we bought when the business started.

"How about pastries? Don't the English like sweets?"

Well...? "They *do* go better with tea, that's for sure."

Juney pops his head up from his books. "Maybe you should call Peach. Isn't that his territory?"

The boy is so right.

Stefan jumps right up to get the cordless phone.

Pleasance has never told me where Juney and Stefan came from in the first place. She does such a good job at mothering, I wouldn't dream of asking about the father of these boys. But I can't help the fact that I wonder. And the fact that I just assume they're illegitimate is horrible.

"If Miss Lillie would deign to get a cell phone, you wouldn't have to bother, Stefan," Pleasance says.

"I don't mind, Mama."

Good boy.

"Thanks, Stefan." I throw a daggered expression at Pleasance. "It'll be cheaper anyway."

"You got that right." Juney nods and smiles at me. And shoot, if Pleasance isn't right! That special little spark of admiration gleams in his light brown eyes and it shoots off flares into mine before he looks down. Aw, bless that sweet boy's heart. Now if that doesn't make a girl feel good, I don't know what does.

Of course, Peach has everything under control. I should have known.


By five o'clock the dress is basically put together and odds are it will fit perfectly. Pleasance informs me it's time to go on home, and being the obedient person I am, I comply.

"You boys stay here," she says. "I need to walk Lillie to her car."

Oh no. A sermon cometh. I can feel it. I have no earthly idea why though.

Before I can grab the door handle, Pleasance lays a hand on my arm. "You white girls need to lighten up."

"Huh?" That sure is out of the blue.

"Really, Lillie Pad. You are so hard on yourself. So you're a size fourteen. Now where I come from, that's just right."

"You're thin. And I'm a sixteen."

"But I've got me a nice booty. And I'm proud of it, girl. Stop worrying about it. Just stop. You are a beautiful woman just the way God made you. You better stop telling Him He didn't do a good job."

"It's easy for you to say, Bishop Stanley. It really is."

"No. It isn't. We all have our things we have to come to terms with."

I cross my arms. "And yours would be...?"

"Look at the size of my hands and feet. Look at my face, Lillie, really. I'm very masculine-looking."

"No...you're not. You're the most—"

"I'm telling you, really look."

So, okay. I examine. She's right.

She grins. "See? I told you so. But I don't go around blabbering about it. I decided a long time ago to do the best with what God gave me. You'd be wise to do the same. You'd maybe begin to stop cutting yourself off at the knees, baby."

"Oh, please, I don't—"

"Get in the car. Just get your womanly, feminine self into the car right now. And tomorrow, when I dress you in something worthy of your femininity, I don't want to hear word one from you, you hear? Go out and get a pair of winter white pumps this evening. You'll be needing them."

I just nod. But I think the whole conversation is Pleasance's roundabout way of telling me to be quiet when I slip on the dress come morning.

"Pleasance? You've never told me about the kids' father."

"I don't talk about it much. It's painful."

"Will you ever want to?"

"Why do you want to know?"

"Because you're my friend, and I love you."

She nods and inhales deeply, looks down. "He was killed in the Gulf War, Lillie."

"I'm sorry."

"Tell me about it. But he left me these children to carry on. Juney looks just like him."

"He's a good boy."

"James was a good man. Anyway, maybe sometime I'll tell you more about him. But it won't be tonight."

On the way back to Highlandtown, after visiting the massive shoe warehouse out in Hunt Valley, I tune into AM radio, and much to my delight Jaime Pickerson is riding some very high horse about something-or-other. I love that woman's voice. Sounds like someone sprinkled coarse cinnamon sugar on her vocal cords and then rubbed them with a sun-dried washrag.

She's talking about guns again. Every once in a while I run into her at the shooting range. More women than ever are buying guns these days, or so I've read. Well, at least they're starting to get into the hands of sane people now. Still, I wonder how I'll feel if I ever have to use one and I pray I won't. It's good to be overprepared sometimes.

"And by the way, listeners, I have an announcement to make! Brian and I eloped!"

"What?!" I scream, reaching for the cell phone I don't own, the cell phone I thought I didn't need, the cell phone whose absence I have lorded over the rest of this technologically dependent world.

"We leave for our honeymoon early tomorrow morning so Les Kinsolving will be…"

Oh man.

In communist Hungary the workers had a production quota set for each of them. They called it a *norma*.

Poor Erzsèbet.

Every night she slogged into her shed knowing her paltry pay would be docked because she'd never be able to sort and clean that many bottles.

"Everyone equal," Mom would say. "True. Everyone equally miserable and poor."

"Some utopia," Dad would agree.

It worked like this: Some bureaucrat buffoon in the Ministry of Planning decided that in one shift a hard-working citizen could surely clean out some unbelievable number of bottles, some bureaucrat who'd never probably set foot in a winery, much less Erzsèbet's winery in Sopron. And from then on, the wages would be set to that quota and her pay based on the percentage of the quota she fulfilled.

The Party of the People, by golly.

"No matter how hard I try, I'm the last in productivity on the list that always goes up on the wall," Erzsèbet would complain to my mother each morning. And then she'd massage her own hands.

12

## Lillie

"First round of business is the Pickerson wedding," I say the next morning, exactly two hours before Remington and company are due.

"They've eloped!" Cristoff, darn him, blurts out before I can, the party pooper.

Peach scratches his belly as Pleasance slams a fist on the table and shouts, "What? I was up until three this morning cutting out fabric!"

"Do you know why?" Gert asks as she arranges teacups and saucers on the teacart she rolled all the way up Charles Street from their tiny row house down in South Baltimore just for this faux British occasion.

"Does it matter?" Cristoff sips his tomato juice and screws the cap back on.

I agree. "We've already spent a bucketload on this wedding." The facade of our bank's building comes to mind.

"What has she said about the balance on her account?" Peach asks.

"She's on her honeymoon, remember?" Cristoff shakes his head. Cristoff has seen the books, the statements, the red ink in which we're treading. We hide it from the others when we can.

I'm such a nincompoop. What in the world was I thinking when I called Pleasance and blabbered on about a little bit of funding, a little elbow grease, and so shall your success as a wedding planner come on you like a surprise inheritance from a long-lost uncle?

I feel hot. "I've got to get out of here." And they let me go.

The black iron steps out back near the loading dock warm my behind, and I close my eyes in the morning sun. And I think.

So how long is too long? How long do you hang in there with a business waiting for it to get going? If I close up shop now, will it have been too soon? Will tomorrow have landed that big account?

Tomorrow and tomorrow and tomorrow.

The fact is, Stan Remington can save us. Really. But for how long? Who wants extreme weddings anyway? What a stupid, stupid idea.

Gentle fingers pull my braid to rest on my back. "Come back in, sweetie." Gentle fingers pat my shoulder.

Oh, Cristoff.

I stand up and turn around. Why does he have to be so beautiful? Why will his love and care go wasted? And he takes me into his skinny arms and holds me close, tender fingers running over my cheek.

And I figure that maybe now would be a good time to cry. How did I, Lillian Elaine Bauer, Strong Hungarian Woman, find myself here?

"It was a bad idea from the start."

"No, Lillie. We'll make it work, baby doll, we really will."

So I allow a few tears their due.

And Cristoff lets me cry. Because Cristoff knows me. Me.

One time, years ago, Cristoff said to me, "I wish I could love you, Lillie. Or rather, I wish I could be *in* love with you."

There were times I wished the same thing.

Grandma Erzsèbet scrubbed floors down in Canton after she, Mom, Babi, and Luca arrived in Baltimore.

"It hurts the knees," she sometimes told Mom when she'd come home after midnight. She'd kiss her eldest child's face as she lay in the dark of the one bedroom they rented in a small boarding house nearby. "But it's warm, Katherina, and the water is warm and I bought a little hand cream for myself."

She bought a little hand cream.

I step into the conference room.

"You're beautiful, Lillie! Look at her, Gert. Ain't she something?" Peach wipes away a tear glistening in the spray of sunlight trailing through the conference room window. Bless that man's wonderful heart.

"Well, call 911. I'm about to have a heart attack!" Cristoff runs over and touches my hair, the very same hair Pleasance pulled back in a subdued french twist. "We've got this contract in the *bag*, sweetie!"

"Well, don't tell me about it; tell Pleasance. It's her doing."

Like this is really me, you know?

I mean, true beauty doesn't require an overhaul like *this*. Although, let's face it, at least I don't need collagen injections or facial reconstruction to achieve this. What we have here is the phrase *working the best you can with what you have* taken to a level I've never before experienced. The team on those talk shows could have done no better than Pleasance.

A cream sash at the waist adds the perfect touch, matching my new pumps.

And she stands there looking like some mentor character in one of those feel-good-movies-of-the-year when her protégée wins the race, earns the approval of the boss, or simply accepts herself warts and all, and all. "See, Lillie Pad? I am a miracle worker!"

And they all clap and I don't know whether to be insulted or not. So I glance at my watch instead. "Ten minutes!" And I pick up my planner from the conference table. "Water on for tea?"

Peach nods. "As soon as we fall out."

"Music?"

*"Best of Bread!"* Gert says. "Peach told me those guys were big back in the seventies."

Cristoff doubles over and excuses himself.

"I was thinking classical, Gert."

"Oh." She looks down.

"Don't you have a cassette tape down there from Victoria's Secret a few Christmases ago?" Peach asks, slipping an arm around her sizable waist.

*Here he comes to save the day!*

"I'll go get it!" She scoots joyfully out on her tan walking sneakers.

"Swatches?"

"Got a bunch." Pleasance.

"And, Peach, refreshments?"

"British tea things ready to go."

I know better than to ask for a rundown.

Cristoff slides back into the room, composed but still the color of a lover's rose.

"Floral? Set design, Cristoff?"

"All our past weddings and"—he holds up a portfolio—"I was sketching ideas all night."

Examining the list in my planner, I say, "Okay, here are the possible themes we worked up. Let me know if I've missed any."

And so I read down the list, alphabetized, naturally. You know, I work with a crazy group of individuals, which this list proves.

"*Ararat: Climb Every Mountain.* This is a joke, right? Mount Ararat?"

"Theme, baby. *Theme.*" Pleasance wags a finger. "Not actuality. And didn't you say Stan got religion? A little Old Testament never hurt anybody. Except maybe the Canaanites."

Quickly before Cristoff engages Pleasance in a theological discussion on the nature of God, I read the rest, ending with, "*Roll Over Beethoven.* Doesn't that seem too, well, *sensual?* You know? I mean he is a rock star. They can make anything seem dirty."

Pleasance looks at the ceiling. "Lillie Pad!"

"Well?"

Peach shakes his head. "It entered my mind, too."

"Cristoff?"

"Me too."

"How about *Get Bach to Where You Once Belonged* instead?" I ask.

"Whoa, Lillie!" Cristoff claps. "Honey, we must be rubbing off on you! That was creative."

"Okay, five minutes to show time. Let's go."

And Peach hurries away to put on the kettle. And Cristoff runs to fetch the nosegay he assembled for the bride. And Pleasance just sits in her seat looking like the Queen of Sheba.

I run to the powder room to check myself out in the mirror. I examine the face staring back at me. Well, just go figure.

I'm not quite sure what I expected, but it sure isn't *this* guy! Stan Remington, larger than life, messy-haired, leather-laden, fist-waving, lip-curling, pale-skinned performer extraordinaire, takes up less vertical space than I do! And Ursula Aitcheson, his myopic, concert violist fiancée hardly fits the description of "the woman who tamed a rock star." I've never seen such sensible shoes in my life and that sweater must have been knitted before the Civil War. She lays her viola case on the table.

"I never leave it in the car. Temperature changes and all. I have rehearsal after this."

"No problem." I imagine her car and the description of her needs regarding said car being, "It gets me where I want to go." I think of my car. "It makes me who I'd like to be."

I hate myself.

I wish everything didn't seem so horribly important. I wish I could just be.

Gordon touches my elbow. "Lillie, I'd like you to meet my brother Stan and his bride-to-be, Ursula."

"A pleasure." I try as natural a smile as possible and I have to admit, I feel like an idiot in my Audrey Hepburn getup. My normal fare would have been much more appropriate for this unassuming-looking bride. I know without a doubt my smile is a failure so I turn quickly and gesture toward the conference table. "Shall we have a seat?"

Stan removes his beret, revealing hair cut just like his brother's. The color, however, reminds me of birch bark, mostly white, with some dark brown hairs congregating in occasional groups. I guess everybody ages, but one simply expects rock-'n'-rollers' demeanors to coincide with their musical expression.

He must have detected a kind of quizzical expression on my face, because Stan Remington says, "I wear a wig on stage."

Ursula nods. "He has a costume designer, too. Weirdest guy you've ever seen. And I've seen weird."

Pleasance perks up. "Really? A costume designer? I figured bands had to have a method to their fashion mayhem."

Stan widens eyes as blue as his brother's. "It's not what I got into rock-'n'-roll for, sweetheart, believe me. But these days in the industry, nothing is left to chance. Same as in everything, I guess."

"That's what I think"—I jerk a thumb at Cristoff—"but Cristoff here, our floral designer, thinks every second involves a personal choice of some sort. Have a seat."

Stan nods and sits down, first pulling a chair out for Ursula. "Now, that's something I've been reading about a lot lately. This whole who-chooses-who in regard to faith." He digs his elbows into the plum lacquer of the tabletop, his pitted, dissipated features flaring up under some youthful curiosity. "What do you think?"

Now being Episcopalian and all (and let's face it, growing up with that Hungarian resolve), well, it isn't easy to guess, if one knows anything about doctrine, where I should fall. But I don't. I got hold of Calvin's *Institutes* one day and there I went, much to Daddy's chagrin, off into what he calls, "that fatalistic camp of self-professed automatons." But what if Stan doesn't feel that way? What if he suddenly says, "Well, actually, I was leaning more toward the whole freedom-of-choice bit, so I don't think I want some absurd Calvinist planning the most important day of my life."

Ursula relaxes in her seat. "I'm a Presbyterian."

I practically scream, the relief so great.

Cristoff leans forward and pushes his binders toward the center of the table. "I'm Church of God."

Pleasance's eyes grow and she shakes her head. "Well, I'm not sure what this has to do with weddings, but I grew up A.M.E. Haven't been to church in years though."

"Peach is Catholic," I feel the need to say.

"Peach?" Stan says. "Who's Peach?"

"Our caterer. Devout man. Bristly, too. Like one of those prickly pears," I say. "But sweet on the inside. He's making us some tea."

"Tea? Lovely."

Now, I don't know if it's just me, but this rocker, who looks like some decomposition virus started eating away at him in the Great Guns glory days, saying words like, "Tea? Lovely," just plain freaks me out. I have to hold in my laughter.

Stan sits back, comfortable. "Well, while we're waiting for the tea, let's talk about doctrine for a bit then. This is still so new to me. Now Gordon here, he's been a faithful fellow for years now."

I turn to Gordon. "Really?"

He points to his prosthesis. "Even have this to show for it."

"Wow," Pleasance breathes.

"No kidding," Cristoff whispers.

Pleasance begins to fidget. Poor thing. She's not all that comfortable with religious talk around strangers. "I made something of myself all by myself," she's said to me before. But she knows better than to change a subject a client has raised.

Well, an invigorating conversation ensues, Cristoff and Gordon on the free-will-of-man side of the court, Ursula and me lobbing our shots from the God-chooses side, having a marvelous time. Pleasance excuses herself after fifteen minutes to help Peach and Gert serve the tea, and I realize afresh I forgot what faith is all about. See, I always thought of my faith as simply salvation. Well, I'm promised salvation, future tense, salvation from the flames of hell. But faith is day by day, right? Faith is about this minute, this hour, this year, this lifetime. This sin, this fault, this stumble. Faith is about victory despite that, even though the victory is not your own. I look at Stan and Gordon, Ursula and Cristoff, and they seem so excited about this stuff. And they should be. But I haven't felt like this in years.

Honestly, I think I did the whole "ask Jesus into my heart" years ago, grew in the faith with Teddy, who knelt and prayed with me one day after Bible school, and then, when he died…

Well, no wonder I feel so starved and wanting. I need to take some lessons from Cristoff, get out of bed earlier, and spend time with Jesus. I know better than to ask him to come down and have study time with me. One time, he told me this, "During my quiet time, Lillie, it's the only time I can sit before anybody and be exactly who I am. He sees me entirely, and I'm thankful He knows it all. I'm thankful that I don't have to pretend a thing."

It's lunchtime now and we're onto eschatology—end-times stuff. Rapture or not. Figurative or literal. Good grief. Now this is the stuff I stopped caring about a long time ago. What's going to happen at the end of the world as we know it? Well, it's going to happen the way God has planned it, and either I'll be right or I'll be wrong, but what I thought will not have changed a thing. Not one single thing.

And I feel fine.

So there.

This whole theological debate is why I gave up on Christian radio, although they're probably onto something else these days. Should I care more about this stuff? Probably. But mostly now I need to get back to Jesus. These people here, they just love Jesus and seem to know Him better than I do. Even Peach, who's now sitting with us, smiling and scratching his belly. I can imagine what he's thinking: "It's just good to hear people talk about God."

And I have to say amen.


Four o'clock. Versions of the Bible. Even Peach, who thinks the Douay Rheims is the only inspired version, gets in on this one.

I'm so sleepy! I need some Coke, not this tea junk.

And then, finally, Stan brings both palms down on the table and says, "You're hired!"

"What?" I shake the cobwebs out from between my ears.

"Yep. In fact, Ursula is coming on tour with me for the next six months, so Gordon will be taking care of it all."

"Just like that? You haven't even seen our ideas."

Thank You, God.

"I like you. You all have the inside scoop on what marriage is all about. And I trust Gordon implicitly with these matters. He's an artist, you know."

Gordon smiles and shakes his head, the younger brother receiving a compliment from the padre of the clan, I guess. But in all actuality, I do believe Gordon is the one to be looked up to.

We all shake hands, agree to sign papers within the next few days, and that is that. How weird is this?

I'll never forget the day the Berlin Wall fell. That day in November of 1989 I walked the halls of C. Milton Wright, so proud to be an American, so proud of Ronald Reagan, bless him. Mom is a huge fan of RR, so if that's not cool or tony or smart, well, that's just too bad. The corncob intelligentsia aren't my kind of crowd anyway. I mean, they probably don't even like a good meat loaf sandwich, you know?

I heard the news on my way to school, called Mom, and told her to turn on the TV.

When I got home that evening, all set to study my brain into the fullnesses of World History, Aunts Babi and Luca were busy in our little kitchen. Grandma Erzsèbet sat with my father in the living room playing this bilingual form of Scrabble they'd come to terms with over the years. And the smells, oh the smells, of paprika and sour cream and chicken having browned in an enameled iron pot, and the wine being poured and freedom being toasted, and a general buzz of celebration threw me right into the arms of those women, my women. Tacy jumped around, only twelve then, not at all capable of understanding the day's import, but still jumbled with a molecular gratitude.

Or maybe I'm not giving her enough credit. Maybe I'm not giving her enough credit now. I don't know what it takes to make a marriage work. Maybe she's just doing what she needs to get by.

After the meal, Aunt Luca raised her glass and Mom translated this to Grandma E: "To freedom!"

"To freedom!"

"I am proud," Aunt Babi said, "to be a Hungarian tonight. To have survived long enough to rejoice."

I remember that sometimes, when I get down on life and think about how lonely I am, how miserable and insignificant to anything that really matters. And then Babi's line comes back to me. "To surviving long enough to rejoice."

And isn't that every day? Isn't that choosing to look at life through eyes that recognize God's greatness, His goodness, and even just the simple gift of a buttercup or a conversation with a cherished friend?

## 13

## Lillie

Gordon called me at work today. I sat at my desk, going over the books in light of the new developments with Stan Remington and Ursula, and I realized that this will reach down under our armpits and pull us away from the edge. I'm not sure it will soak us in black ink, but we will survive now, long enough to rejoice, maybe?

Lord, You know I hope so.

"I was wondering if we could start making arrangements for Stan's wedding this week instead of next. I've had something come up."

"Of course." Naturally, I'm dying to know what it is, but I won't ask. I can't. I'm a professional, right? These rules about nosiness drive me crazy. I know we're supposed to mind our own business, but shoot, that's not any fun at all. And actually, I've never been all *that* nosy, but with this guy, oh man, oh man. I want to know it all.

Lillie. Lillie.

I still can't believe guys like Gordon Remington continue to inhabit the planet. "When would you like to get together?"

"Well, unfortunately the only day I have free is tomorrow and only after four. I realize it's short notice."

"No, no. It'll be fine. Let me just check my Day-Timer to make sure." I mean, I don't want to seem like a complete loser. Of course, it will be okay no matter what, this being the saving grace of Extremely Odd.

Dang! Tomorrow I was going to the climbing wall down at the Athletic Club. Pleasance and I even had a bet as to who would climb it the fastest.

"We'll be ready for you. Can you give me a direction to go in so that we might have a few options, themes, what have you, ready for you?"

"H'm. Well, actually, Stan feels obligated to his fans who have been faithful all these years, so he wants something glamorous, large, and expensive. 'Pull out all the stops, Gordon,' he told me."

I write furiously, grinning like a kabuki mask. Pull out all the stops, my mind sings, pull out all the stops.

All the stops.

All the stops.

Pull out all the stops.

Warning! Black-ink alert! Rheee! Rheee!

I suppress a giggle, a bona fide giggle.

Oh brother.

I clear my throat. "Okay, something large and glamorous."

"But...poor Ursula, well, you've seen Urs. Not particularly the Hollywood type. She wants something intimate."

Great. "Large and glamorous but intimate."

"Sorry."

"Oh, don't worry. You've seen the people who work with me. They'll figure it out."

"Believe me, after yesterday, I'm sure they'll do just fine. So tomorrow then? Say, four thirty?"

"Fine." I don't want to hang up yet. "Gordon, what's it like being an artist?"

How stupid can you get, Lillie! Is that the best you could do?

"It's like anything else. If you love it, it's wonderful."

"And you love it."

"Yes, I do."

I grip the phone. "Are you doing something arty when you go away?"

He laughs. "Ha! Something 'arty?'"

Oh man.

"Lillie, you are a pleasure. Yeah, it's something arty, a set-design project for a play out in San Francisco, actually. They tend to like high-concept."

I've got to save myself! "Well, we'll need high-concept to pull this wedding off."

"Right you are. Till tomorrow then, love."

Oh good luscious grief. This guy is a beauty.

Till tomorrow then, love.

How lovely is that?

"I've got you down."

"Lillie?"

"Yes?"

"Do you love what you do?"

H'm. "I don't know. I guess I never really thought about it."

"Shame. Till tomorrow."

And he rings off. Just like that.

I said the wrong thing. I know I said the wrong thing.

Cristoff shakes his head. "Large and glamorous but intimate?"

Pleasance rolls her eyes and shakes her head in a direct mirror image of Cristoff.

Peach says, "Food's food."

I say, "We're in for a long night."

## Tacy

My dearest daughter. She comforted me so during the dark times. She was the gift God gave me to tell me that He still loved me. So precious, so innocent. Dear Lord, be preparing a good man for her. A good man. A man who will love her for who she is, who You made her to be.

Lillie will make sure of that. I'm leaving Hannah Grace in good hands.

## Lillie

Tacy answers on the fifth ring. It always takes her so long to get to the phone, and when she answers she sounds so see-through. But she awakens after a few seconds.

"Lillie! I'm so glad you called!"

"How's the baby?"

"Wonderful! She's a nursing wonder. Latches on so well."

Well, again, I wouldn't know much about that, but I act excited. "And how's that old Rawlins doing?"

"Fine. The church, most sadly, is losing a family."

"Who?"

"Do you remember the Haversham family, when you came for the consecration service?"

"Which apostle's bench were they on?"

"John."

"Oh my."

"I know."

Dishy. "So did they fall from grace or are they leaving the area?"

When I say "fall from grace" I'm actually using their terminology. Now, granted, a lot of churches believe we can fall from grace, that we can turn our backs on Christ, having once truly, really and truly experienced His overpowering, all-consuming love firsthand. I'm sure anyone with the slightest bit of theological savvy can figure out where I stand on this one. However, The Temperance Church of the Apostles leaves the decision as to who falls from grace and when up to Pastor Cole.

"They fell from grace, Lillie, but you know I'm not at liberty to say what happened."

"Was it sexual in nature?" Big problems in the church usually fall into that category. Or we make it that way. I mean, hair-sprayed heretics spout all manner of false doctrine across the airwaves and we turn a blind eye. Not that it justifies sexual sinning, but it surely should be noted by Christians that all sorts of sins lurk in the shadows, and not just sexual indiscretions call for action. Haughtiness, prejudice, complacency, anger, gossip, laziness, self-centeredness—

"I can't say."

"Then that means it was. If it wasn't, you'd have said, 'No. But I can't tell you what it was.'"

"Okay, it wasn't. He wanted to start a Bible study and Pastor Cole said it was his job, not Bob's to interpret the Word of God for the church."

"No!"

"Yes, unfortunately. I mean Rawlins says that when Pastor Cole speaks, it's as if God is talking."

Good grief! The new pope of Baltimore County.

"Can I come up Friday after work?"

"Well, Rawlins won't be here."

"So much the better."

"I need to clear it with him."

"What? Why?"

"Just to see if we've got anything else on the schedule, Lillie. Besides, Philly's taking the afternoon off."

I hear the baby cough. "Hannah okay?"

"Oh yes. Just a little cough. Must have autumn allergies. Remember how allergic Aunt Babi gets in the fall?"

Her black eyes swell to the size of large olives every autumn. "Oh yeah. So anyway, how about Friday night?"

"Maybe I'll meet you at Mom and Dad's."

"Okay." It'll have to do.

Like she'll really show up.

"How do you feel about Mom and Dad coming to live with me?"

"..."

"Tace?"

She sniffs. But a bright voice answers. "I think it's great, Lillie. We're so busy with the church and all, and Daddy would hate being around all that."

"He's never liked that Alban Cole fellow."

"No."

Wow, she didn't defend the man.

"So you're not mad at me for suggesting it?"

"No, not at all mad."

Sad? Disappointed? For Pete's sake, Tacy, say *anything* to indicate you're feeling something.

Gordon and I sip tea down in Peach's kitchen. Man, I like this guy. He was a complete gentleman during our presentation, and he offered such great suggestions we all said more than once, "You should be working here!" Creative types energize me. Though I'm not one of them, I can feed off them, sucking their juices, sweet and fresh. I'm a three-day-old cup of coffee; they're ice-cold pineapple juice. I'm General Tsao's; they're Crispy Duck with Basil Leaves.

It's rather delightful.

"I think renting out Pier 3 is the perfect idea." Gordon tips his cup toward me. "And the barge docked there for the reception. Who thought of that?"

I raise my hands. "Not me, I assure you. I'm just the business head of this venture."

"Well, you've surrounded yourself with a great team."

"They'd probably tell you that they had the foresight to make sure they brought someone on with some common sense."

"Well, the world can sure use a little more of that."

"Really?"

"You don't think so?"

"No, I think the world can use more people like you and Cristoff and Pleasance. You bring beauty to light. People like me only manage the status quo."

"How old are you, Lillie?"

"Thirty-two. Just had a birthday."

"I'm forty-one."

"You seem younger."

He sits in a relaxed pose, wearing blue jeans, as usual, and a thick fisherman's sweater. Doc Marten boots encase his feet, but instead of the usual black, these are grass green. They look like Jackson Pollock did a number on them.

"Thanks. I feel a lot younger. Especially since my accident."

"That's odd."

"That's how God dragged me over to His side. Wanna hear about it?"

"I do. If you're willing."

"I want you to know, Lillie. It's important to me."

It is to me, too.

Drinking. Drugs. Sex. The arts community. Everything you imagine from the outside but wonder if you're right. You are. The light in the kitchen fades as he speaks. The others leave, poking their heads in to say a soft good-bye.

"And then one night, after my brother died—"

"Hale? The bass player?"

He nods. "Hale was the wildest of us. But also the most large-hearted. Do you know that I'm the youngest by far?"

"I read that after I met you at the hospital."

His brows arch. "Really?"

"Yes." I feel the heat fill my face. No one but Teddy has brought heat to my face before. And this is grown-up heat, thirty-two-year-old heat. God, You made him so beautifully. "You're a beautiful person," I say.

Where did that come from? Why did I say that out loud? Why do I feel like someone else is controlling my tongue?

"I'm sorry, Gordon! I'm sorry. I didn't mean to blurt that out like that!"

"Do you often, as you say, blurt?"

"No, never."

"Excellent. So you blurt only when I'm around?"

"It seems so."

"You seem like a very purposeful person."

"I try."

He lowers his left eyelid in a slow wink. "Well, we'll have to try and change that then, won't we?"

I feel gooey inside. A very nice gooey. A feeling that lets me know a woman actually lives inside this puff-pastry shell. Just a woman. Without the preceding words Strong or Hungarian.

"You were telling me about Hale." Good. I'm glad we left that part of the conversation unfinished.

"Yes. Well, after his death, I wanted to die too. He really took me under his wing, Hale did. My mother, well, let's just say she ran a pub and took a little too much advantage of the inventory. But Hale took care of me, brought me on the road as a lad, taught me to play bass too."

"Really? You play bass?"

"Yes, every once in a while I fill in. Although compared to Hale..."

"Didn't know that."

"Must not be on the Internet." He laughs. Hah! I respond in kind. No choice. He pulled it out of me.

"I was living in New York at the time. New York City. And I bought this motorcycle, spur of the moment, the day Hale was buried. I crashed it that night, somewhere out in New Jersey."

I suck in a breath.

"Stupid, I know. So drunk you couldn't believe I could actually climb on the bike. And I had been at those hard-rocking, psychedelic clubs, those violent, sort of futuristic joints. Private, lots of drugs."

They really exist? I thought places like that only inhabited movies like *Strange Days* or *The Matrix*.

"And that's how you lost your leg?"

"Yeah. But it wasn't until after I recovered and was back on my feet— or should I say foot?—that I met a woman named Mildred LaRue."

Great, a woman. "Sounds interesting."

"Best jazz singer I ever heard. The coolest old lady you've ever seen, but don't ever tell her I called her that. Anyway, I wandered into her club when my wave of self-pity was at its highest crest. She was singing with her band, The Star Spangled Jammers. "

"Cool name!"

"Oh yes, definitely."

"Why are you telling me all this, Gordon?"

"I'm not sure. I just think it's important you know."

"Why?"

"I like you, Lillie. It's as simple as that."

"But we only met a little while ago."

"Yeah. And I feel like I've known you for years. Isn't that great?"

"And we met at a hospital, no less."

"No, we met looking over the pulsing artery of a city night."

See what I mean?

"So what are you saying exactly, Gordon?"

"I'm saying I think this cup of tea is nice, but I'd like to take you to dinner. On a date. Right now."

Well. "Where to?" I stand right to my feet before he can change his mind.

"How about Mick O'Shea's? Reminds me of Ireland."

"And you'll tell me more about this Mildred LaRue?"

"I sure will. In fact, she'll be up for Stan's wedding. She's the soloist. And she and her band will play for the reception."

I make a mental note. One less thing to plan for. Good.

I think maybe he'll take my hand as we cross Charles Street. But he doesn't. He only looks me in the eyes as we talk, really looks at me, and he doesn't glance away even when I begin speaking about something as insignificant and boring as what it was like to grow up the daughter of a priest and a woman armed and dangerous with a four-pack of Sharpies.

Hardly sex, drugs, and rock-'n'-roll.

He asks me if I am a virgin, just comes right out and asks, and I tell him I am but ask why he needs to know.

"I don't deserve this, but you're the one," he says.

"I am?" I'm not sure what he means.

"Yes. Mildred LaRue told me not long ago something special might happen."

"How did she know?"

"She dreams."

"How does she know which dreams mean something?"

"She doesn't. She just tells me what they are, and sometimes they come back to me, like right now."

"You barely know me."

"Oh, that's only what you think, love. I'm an artist. I see more than you could ever believe."

"But how do you know I'm the one?"

"She said she saw me pluck a white lily and hold it to my breast."

I should be creeped out, really freaking here, but I'm not. I'm ready for this. So ready. I feel at peace when I'm with him.

Teddy's dead, isn't he? And if he's not, he's dead to me. He has to be.


Cristoff calls me on my cell phone around ten p.m. Yes, I have succumbed to technological peer pressure. "Well?"

"I'm on my way home. Don't worry."

"Well, of course I'm worried. I expected you home hours ago."

I ride past the Inner Harbor, thinking how few people from Baltimore really go there without someone from out of town in tow. "Yes. Well, he wanted to talk some more."

"Any ideas?"

"Well, he already has a soloist and music. A jazz band called The Star Spangled Jammers."

"Oooh, girlfriend. A jazz band on the barge. How WWII. Hey, maybe that could be the overall theme. In fact, there's that submarine docked down there, the…the…"

*"The Torsk."*

"Yepper, that's it. Maybe we can do hors d'oeuvres on the top deck before we go around to the pier."

"Definitely photographs there. I'll talk with Gordon. Maybe he'll like that theme."

"We could hire some old fighter pilots to fly planes overhead. Oh! Maybe even skywrite their names and a heart…with an arrow going through!"

Oh, Cristoff, you lovable thing you.

"There's something I need to tell you when I get home, honey. It's important."

"Sounds serious. Am I in trouble?"

"No. You know how much I love you. Too much for you to be in trouble."

"That's what I thought, baby doll."

We ring off. I chew on a fingernail as I head down Eastern Avenue through Little Italy. I have to tell him I'm different. I'm changed. That he was right. This couldn't last forever.

The overly bright smile on Cristoff's face forces my gaze somewhere else. Onto Grandma Erzsèbet's Nightmare to be exact, blooms long gone. "Sweetie, that's wonderful news! I could tell there was chemistry between the two of you."

His face breaks down, crumbling like an avalanche, and I hold him as he cries. A few minutes later he says, "I have a confession. I've prayed for years that I would change, that I could feel like that for you. Ever since I met you I've been praying that prayer." He pulls away and takes my hands.

"We love each other with a perfect kind of love, Gilbert. You'll always be my best friend."

Later as we make milk shakes in my kitchen, Cristoff says, "I'm sorry to lose you."

"You haven't lost me, honey."

He hefts himself onto the counter. "Oh, I have." He puffs one of those very gay sighs. "Even though I've never loved you *that way,* I've always needed you. I've always known you loved me more than anyone else in the world loves me."

"That won't change, I promise."

He brightens a moment. "Yeah, well, it's not like you haven't gone on dates before, right? I mean, who knows, we may still be here on Foster Avenue next year!"

I turn back to the blender and drop in a cut-up banana and a handful of raspberries. He and I both know, somehow, because we love each other, that this isn't like all those other times. This is different, vastly different.

## 14

## Lillie

I still love paprika. You'd think I'd be sick of it by now, but I'm not. Daddy says it's a genetic thing. He must be right.

I rip off a hunk of Mom's homemade bread and stroke it through the paprikash gravy. Sometimes you're just happy to be alive.

Tacy sits across from us, smiling as usual, Hannah Grace sleeping in her arms, the tiny thing. So frail and sweet. I just want to eat that baby up.

I swallow the last bite of bread. "Well, you've sure lost your baby weight, Tace."

She didn't eat a thing. Apparently Rawlins has something against pork now, and she said she ate before she came over. "Yeah. It's nursing. Takes the weight right off, thank heavens."

"Still, you look thinner than ever."

Tacy says nothing. Man, I wish I could put my finger on her these days. She's lost to us, somehow having turned into a breeze. That's as much as I can say.

Hannah coughs again. "What is with that cough, Tace?"

Mom nods as she clears the dirty plates. "I was wondering about that myself. She's so young to have that deep of a cough." Her brows knit. I can feel mine do the same.

Tacy shifts in her seat. "She's fine. Really."

Daddy asks, "Have you taken her to the doctor?"

"Oh no! We don't believe in doctors!"

"Since when?" I ask.

"Since she was born at home so successfully. Rawlins is convinced God will provide all of our health needs, that it may simply be a lack of faith that causes physical ailments."

Daddy folds his hands across his stomach. "Your church change to Christian Scientist?"

"Oh, Dad, you know we don't believe in denominationalism."

Denominationalism.

"Tace—"

"Don't say anything, Lillie. We're all just fine. See, look at her now. See how well she sleeps? That's what she really needs."

"I still don't like the sound of it." Why am I pushing so hard?

Mom butts in. "Let's go into the family room and watch *Match Game* reruns. Remember how we all loved to watch that show when you were little?"

Oh, Mother.

Tacy shoots to her feet like an exploding firework. "I love that Brett Somers!" she practically screams. "She's just so funny!"

I catch Mom's expression and am relieved it is the mirror image of my own.

Tacy leaves as soon as the game show is over. In fact, she takes one look at her watch and flies out the door with Hannah in her arms with nothing more than a "Bye!" yelled over her shoulder.

## Tacy

The day Rawlins found out I had dinner at Mom and Dad's without asking him, he told me I must never leave the house without him. So a man named Buck began walking the grounds, watching every move I made. He was stoic. A walking cardboard person whose jacket flapped in the wind like a bird's wings. He was my raven who never left the ledge above my chamber door.

I found refuge in the Psalms, unable to write a word myself anymore. So, in the library, behind the couch, the moonlight ribboned across my page. Rawlins slept so lightly, I could only pray that he wouldn't find me. The turning of the onion skin pages sounded like thunder. But, oh dear Jesus, I would pray, do not take this from me. Hide me here between the pages. Hide me in Your love. Send Your Spirit to me and make me whole again. Let our love unite us in grace and truth. Let the fire of Your mercy rain down upon me. Purify me. Burn me to nothing, so that in You I will find all.

## Lillie

We sit in a row in the front pew. Mom, me, Gordon, Cristoff, Peach, and Gert. We didn't mention Tacy's absence. In the pew behind us, Pleasance and her two boys sing my father's favorite hymn, "Of the Father's Love

Begotten." How she knows that hymn is beyond me. I doubt many A.M.E. churches sing that song with its odd meter, its Gregorian feel. But her voice rings out in the tiny chapel where I busted open my knee for the first time, where I learned to sing a husky alto in the choir, where I fell asleep during the sermon every Sunday until I was eight, head in my mother's lap.

I can hardly believe it's Daddy's last sermon here at Saint Stephen's. Or should I say Father Carl, the boy who everyone thought "should have" died all those years ago.

He approaches the pulpit, led by no one. No need. If there's a path my father can see without his eyes, it's this approach. He prays silently. I know this because I asked years ago. He asks God to make his words God's own. God assures him that even if only one heart is touched, if only one mind is set on a more glorious course, it is worth all those hours of preparation.

My father has always believed the best of humankind. He enjoys such hope for all, such potential. And he realized years ago that God desires a better path for all men. That He wants to help us, to pick up our slithering, floundering souls and guide them back to the time and place when we were hatched, surely not perfect, but innocent enough to trust again.

The sanctuary is packed, current parishioners and members from years gone by gathered to hear my dad one last time.

Cristoff leans forward, around Gordon. "It's okay to cry, sweetie."

I nod. But I don't feel like crying. I feel like rejoicing. I feel like standing up, rotating my fist, and doing the "Woof-woof!" Yes, this was a calling well done. *Well done.* My father lived for his flock and was content to minister to a few, knowing that if He was faithful to God in the small things, those few would venture out and do the hard work of the kingdom.

He was right.

I look around at many of my own compadres of the church playground. Boys and girls who sat about Mrs. Reisenwebber's Sunday-school table and heard stories of David and Goliath and the burning bush. Joey's a pediatrician. Linda's an advocate for children. Connie goes to Africa every summer with a group of optometrists to give people glasses. Becka homeschools her four kids and sits in Mrs. Reisenwebber's chair now.

Thanks to God and His servant, Daddy.

He preaches and all I hear are these words: Love God, for He loves you. Be merciful, as God has been merciful to you. Extend grace to all, as God extended grace to you when His Son died on the cross. Rise above it all, as Christ arose on the third day, leaving death behind forever. Live. Obey. Love. Love deeply and forever.

Now I am crying.

Tomorrow we will begin packing their things.


They offer Daddy a chair, but he refuses to sit down as the flock files slowly by. We all recognize an era in our lives has ended and we are sad, yet expectant, knowing that old adage is true: When one door closes another opens. That's what Dad's been saying for the past few days.

"I'll have time to write, Lillie. In fact, I might start writing a novel."

"Wow, Dad. Something literary?"

"No. Crime."

Well, there you go.

"I need to start pulling in a little money, Lil. My devotionals don't bring in nearly enough. Your mother and I won't want to rely on your good graces forever. We'll need long-term care insurance, which is quite expensive, and I'd hate for her to go back to work without wanting to. Yes,

I believe crime novels sell well. Or suspense. I just read Dean Koontz for the first time, you know. Terrific."

But there he stands now, knowing people by their scent, their feel, their sounds. Mrs. Halsey and her cellophane-covered Bible crackling away. Bill Goins's arthritis cream. The short, pillowy form of Betsy Freitag and her L'Air du Temps. He gives them his trademark, life-giving hugs, and a thought comes to me: I won't have to share him anymore.

Well, now.

This is good news.

## 15

*Lillie*

I'm about to see Gordon's home for the first time. We've dated awhile now, lots of dinners at Mick O'Sheas, slow walks wherever, and movies and plays. It's fun dating an artsy guy because something of interest is always going on. And while I, as has been thoroughly established, am not artsy, I love the scene and appreciate the minds from which such life springs, thanks to Daddy, really, and my love of literature. I'm leading the life I always thought Tacy would.

So here we ride up the long, cobblestone drive of his 1920s estate. I can't imagine what he paid for this property. This area here on the water in Anne Arundel County is some of the priciest in Maryland. If I'd known he had this property, I'd have never invited him in for milk shakes at Grandma Erzsèbet's row house last week.

So far, the landscaping is overgrown, but it is almost December and spring will yield improvement, he quickly states, apologizing.

Oh yes, dahling, I'm thoroughly offended.

"Like you even need to apologize for this. My gosh, it's lovely and I haven't even seen the house."

"I'm going to try and keep a lot of the greenery that's already here. You know, when people tear down everything and start from scratch, you lose that settled feel. You lose the anchorage."

Well, yeah. Like I would have even thought of that.

"Lots of azaleas and forsythia," I say. At least I recognize *those* bushes. "Will be a pretty spring here."

"Beautiful. And look at all the fruit trees over to your left. There's even an apple orchard just beyond that rise. And a grape arbor. Concord grapes, they say."

I love Concord grapes, the way you pinch them between finger and thumb and pop the innards into your mouth. "So, do you eat the seeds, too? Or separate them out with your tongue?"

"I eat the seeds," he says.

Oh well. We can't be exactly the same.

He tells me he's on twenty acres, at least ten wooded, and has plans to place a few cabins back there for friends needing to retreat, to restore their creative juices.

"I want this place to thrive with life, Lillie."

No doubt it will.

We round a bend and there it stands, a magnificent brick home, with wings of Palladian windows on either side of the entry. A sturdy slate roof hovers atop the home. It all rather reminds me of the homes you see in movies that take place in the Hollywood of yore, the stately home of the producer or the studio head. I picture Robert Redford in *The Way We Were,* playing tennis with the pretty dark-haired girl and Barbra Streisand at a house much like this one. I remember thinking it was only a matter of time before Barbra's character and her communism were out the door and Robert would end up in the arms of the pretty, Gentile woman.

I turn to him. "There's got to be a classical-looking pool out back."

"Naturally. And it overlooks the water. But it needs a lot of work. Been neglected for years. Luckily for me, it's something I can hire out. I can't do it myself."

This has mystified me. "Why do you insist on doing so much of the work yourself, Gordon? You can surely afford to hire workmen to carry out your vision, can't you?"

"Oh yeah, naturally. But, well, I've never owned my own home before. I've always lived in apartments."

"Always? Even when you were little?"

"We lived over the pub, remember?"

I nod.

"So it's important for me that this be mine, really mine." He brakes to a stop. "Let's go in the front door so you can get the full impact. Such that it is at present."

I wait as he circles around the car and lets me out. Oh, wow! The first time I let myself out of his car he was thoroughly insulted, which was thoroughly cool. "That's my job, Lillie," he said. "Not because you can't, but because you shouldn't have to."

The slate path leading to the double doorway is bunched up like a pleated skirt. Errant threads of yellow grass poke up between the slabs.

"Mind the path, sweetheart. I almost killed myself the day the agent showed me this place."

"Did you trip?"

"Ha! Went down face first. I'd forgotten how embarrassed a guy can feel!"

Another reason to love him even more. Gosh, I'm a sentimental fool over this man.

He opens the door. "Ready?"

"Show me the way."

"All right then. Here we go." And he swings the door in a sweeping arc. "My lady…"

I step inside. Oh, my goodness! A double staircase curlicues symmetrically up to the gallery of the second floor. "Oh, Gordon!"

"Magnificent, isn't it?"

"More than that."

"Now it still needs a lot of work, but I'm trusting you to visualize things as we go."

I'll give it my best shot. "Tell me your plans."

"I will."

Room upon room upon room. Eleven bedrooms in all. Servants' quarters. And all sorts of "specialty rooms." Music room, day room, sunroom, receiving room, den, and what promises to be a fabulous kitchen.

"The woodwork is wonderful, Gordon. I can't believe the craftsmanship here."

"Oh yeah. I don't think I could settle down in anything else. There's something so noble about people creating such beauty with their hands."

"Like you," I say.

He smiles but continues on. "I've only just started, as you can see. But what you can't see has already been finished. New wiring and plumbing, central air, all those hidden, modern conveniences. They did that work before I moved in."

"I love it."

"I thought you might."

"How about Stan? Where did he fall?"

He points to the wall surrounding the front doors. "Right there. We were painting the foyer. By the way, do you like the color? Stan thought it might be a bit much, but Ursula loved it."

It's caramel. Like the dress Pleasance made for me. "I love it too."

"The front rooms here will be neutral but vibrant, golds and warm greens, but wait until the back rooms of the house are complete. I'm going to exhaust every color of the rainbow in this place."

"Like in your artwork."

He smiles broadly. "You got it, love."

"What about your studio? Where is that?"

"Up in the attic."

I shouldn't ask this, but I do. I should respect his privacy, but I can't. "Can I see it?"

"It's a mess."

"Probably why it's in the attic, right?"

He points toward the steps. "Right. Let's go up then."

Daddy always says that women are judged by who they are and men are judged by what they do. But with Gordon, I'd say both apply.

The attic is unfinished and his easel rests near a large window on the side of the house. Dormers provide a great deal more illumination, and track lighting tacked to the rafters supply the rest. It's bright and nourishing. One portion of floor supports an extremely large canvas, much too big for the easel. It is blank. "What's that going to be, Gordon?"

"Don't know yet. Have to live with the white space for a while before I know what happens next."

"What do you mean 'what happens'?"

He walks around the canvas. "Each space cries out for its own purpose, Lillie. I let it be, as is, for a while, and let it speak its mind."

"You don't decide?"

"Oh, definitely not. I'm just here to serve the work."

Is he the coolest guy in the world or what?

A crew of workmen found a skeleton buried beneath a condemned home in Canton. They're clearing half that block for new condominiums, only a few blocks from my home in Highlandtown.

It's all over the news. I think of Teddy and wonder, "Could he have really been taken all the way down to the city and disposed of?"

Nah. It isn't him. Is it? It couldn't be.

"Right over there, Gordon, take that little lane."

He turns his ancient International to the left and I see Grandma's polished tombstone. I loved that woman though we rarely shared words. But I felt her touch and knew she loved me, much more than words could have said. Nobody coddled a stubbed toe better than Grandma. And for a child with perpetually skinned knees, "Grandma" meant soothing love and tender compassion. You'd think, after all she endured, the small hurts would mean little. I don't think about it all much because it aches still, after these five or so years. But for the first time desolation stands at bay, just over Gordon's left shoulder.

A light snow fell last night, frosting up the Christmas lights, icing the shrubbery. I am in love and have been for two entire months. Better than lights and tinsel. Tomorrow I'm flying with Gordon to England to meet the rest of the Remington boys and Gordon's drunk (but cheerful, he assures me) mother, Roberta. His dad skipped out on Roberta halfway during her pregnancy with Gordon. He grew up in their pub, The Rowdy Boar, suckling Guinness and when old enough, wiping down the bar, polishing the glasses. Before Hale rescued him.

Hale.

The grass pokes through the powder, and once again no one bothered to weed-whack around the headstone before mowing season ended. "That makes me mad," I say.

He stops the car and turns off the engine. "I know."

"Do you even know what I'm talking about?"

"The grass, right?"

"Yeah."

"No respect for the dead."

"Exactly."

It's a sad little cemetery.

"Do you want me to wait here?"

"Do you mind?"

"Of course not."

So Gordon opens my door and I walk through the light snow and look down at the tombstone. All that bravery and here she lies. How inappropriate. If I thought for a minute her spirit was dead, that she wasn't living on in the way God planned, I think I'd hop in the coffin with her.

I hate death. I mean that. When people die we always act like it's so natural. "It happens to us all."

But it wasn't supposed to. We were supposed to inhabit a beautiful garden and walk with God in the cool of the evening. We were supposed to know no death. To live forever. Death seems wrong because it is wrong.

Yet when a life is well-lived, like Grandma Erzsèbet's, a life of home-cooked meals, close hugs, cleaning out ears with a bobby pin, rolling up shiny, slick young hair in foam curlers, birthday cards with ten spots tucked inside, and games of Candyland, well, how can you end up doing anything but rejoicing?

For minutes I stand in the cold and I trace the crisp letters with my index finger, but soon my mind fills with daily moss. I lose my focus.

I turn away, but I don't return to the truck. I simply walk down the cemetery lane, one woman amid the company of the dead.

I love the wind. The cold. The song of the winter birds. The way the late-morning sun melts the snow on the trees, small clods tumbling to the ground.

Live. Obey. Love deeply and forever.

Grandma knew how to do that. And I am her seed.

A small bench rests beneath the skeleton of a large maple tree, and I sit and I pray and my heart is large, pulsing with thankfulness. I close my eyes and commune and rejoice and remember from whence I came.

When I open them, I stand to my feet and head back toward Gordon and his big old truck. He is on his knees by Grandma's tombstone, his shoulders shifting, arms shoving.

"What are you doing?" I cry out.

But he doesn't hear me. And when he stands to his feet I notice a pair of rusty old grass clippers hanging in his hand.

So this is what it's like when deep meets forever.

He walks toward me, smiling a little sheepishly. "I hope you don't mind, but I took the liberty to take care of things a bit. I keep my gardening things in the truck. Makes it easier to care for my grounds."

God, You know I love this man.

## 16

## Lillie

When Gordon said his mother tipped the bottle with verve, he wasn't kidding. I haven't seen her sober yet, and we've been in England for three days. Of course, we're always up well before dawn with the brutal time change, breakfasting down in the pub on the previous night's special, shepherd's pie or roast beef with a gravy made from Gordon's grandfather's recipe. We leave well before Roberta arises and, home by six that evening, find she's already tied on more than a few.

Roberta Remington is a quiet drunk. She sits at the bar, smoking cigarettes, cooking to a looser and looser consistency, starting out a dried strand, ending up spaghetti, arms limp and fragile. She wears little makeup and plain skirts and blouses. By eleven, the bartender carries her upstairs to her bed. Night after night.

I'm not sure why Gordon wanted me to see this, really, unless he wanted me to know exactly where he came from. See, I see him in paint-spattered clothing and driving a decrepit International. But he's a darling in his own peculiar world. And no wonder. His artwork pulls your breath right out of your lungs. I can't call it realistic, yet it's not abstract either. But color and life and the love of life play with exuberance across his canvases. I've watched him in his studio, and let me tell you, it is unbelievably sexy to see him lose himself in his work like that. To be honest, there are times I believe I would give myself to him. I'm thirty-two and a bundle of yearning. But no, I'm his white lily, by gum, and he's going to do nothing to mess that up. I'm glad, honestly, but when his hands caress my back and sides and move just a bit too close to my breasts, I want to scream, "Just do it!"

And then they move away as softly as they approached and more than not, he gets up and fixes a cup of tea.

Englishmen.

God love him.

Perhaps I'm here in England because he respects his mother still, after all these years.

So it's early, early Christmas morning. I can't believe I'm already awake at six fifteen a.m. Nothing stirs here in the apartment over the pub, except the cat. I hear her jump down onto the wooden floor from whichever perch she has chosen. She's a tiny, little black creature named Holiday.

I wonder if Mom and Dad are back from midnight mass yet? Tacy always spends Christmas Eve and Christmas Day with Rawlins and the church people, it being a holy day and all. Tomorrow, Aunts Babi and Luca will visit my house, whip out the paprika and sour cream and celebrate with a good wine and perhaps a viewing of *Miracle on 34th Street*.

I miss them.

They're probably back from church by now, so I throw back the covers, slip on my robe, and sneak out to where Gordon sleeps on the sofa. I slide his cell phone out of the charger on the lamp table.

"And what do you think you're doing?"

His eyes remain closed.

"I'm stealing a cell-phone call from you. I didn't want to wake you. In fact, keep your eyes closed. You look beautiful in repose."

"Oh dear. How poetic."

"Well, I do have my moments."

"More of them than you think."

I don't deserve this affirming man. Not one bit.

"Keep them closed." I kiss his lips, then his eyelids. "I'll be right back."

"Nobody's awake. We could make out for a while."

I laugh. "I want to be the first to tell my parents Merry Christmas."

"Go, then, stick-in-the-mud."

But he's smiling and before I even raise my derrière off the couch, he's back asleep.

I hurry down the steps and into the pub. A lone bulb above the bar mirror lights my path in the dim room. I slide into a booth near the window and begin dialing.

"Merry Christmas to all!"

"Daddy!"

"Lil!"

"Merry Christmas."

"You're up awfully early."

"It's Christmas, Daddy."

He laughs. "Oh, right. Miss Up-at-Four-A.M.-Christmas Morning!

You wouldn't believe the food they have planned for tomorrow, Lil. They've invited everybody in the neighborhood."

"No."

"Yes. Even Cristoff's coming down to this one. After church down on Erdman Avenue, of course."

"How's he doing?"

"All right. Lonely."

"Oh, Dad. How do you pray in a situation like this? I mean, in order for him not to be lonely—"

"You pray for God's sufficiency. It's all any of us can pray for. Even marriage can't fill that kind of hole."

There you have it. The grace of God may not always seem to be enough, but in the end, it is.

A gentleman ambles by the window, large terrier at the leash, for an early morning constitutional. "I miss everybody."

"We miss you."

"How's Tacy?"

"Fine, I suppose. Making excuses as to why she can never come and see us. And here we sit, our granddaughter getting older by the day. I don't understand it."

"Have you talked to Rawlins?"

"Never returns my calls."

"Figures."

"Let's not ruin Christmas with talk of that guy. I'm rejoicing in the birth of the Savior. What about you?"

"Well, I've only been out of bed for five minutes, Daddy."

His warm chuckle bears up almost as good as a hug. "Then I'm even more thankful for the call."

Gordon slips into the seat opposite me. "I've got your coffee on," he whispers.

"So are you having a good time, Lillie?"

"The best. We've seen all the sights you'd imagine."

"Tower of London?"

"Check."

"Westminster Abbey?"

"Check."

"Houses of Parliament? Buckingham Palace? Saint James Park?"

"Check, check, and check."

"Great! Saint Paul's?"

"Oh, Daddy! That was transcendent. God bless Christopher Wren."

"Amen."

Gordon whispers, "Amen," too and reaches into his jeans pocket.

"I saw it before I lost my sight," Daddy says. "I think that's helped me accept my blindness. I remember so many beautiful sights."

Gordon takes my hand and I feel so happy.

"British Museum yet?"

"No, that's tomorrow."

"Going out to the Cotswolds?"

"We're just doing London this time around. Gordon knows this city so well. He says he can't claim to be a country boy."

Daddy laughs. "Well, to be honest, if you've seen one Cotswold village, you've seen them all."

"Give everybody my best," Gordon whispers.

"Gordon sends his best."

"And ours back."

Gordon squeezes my hand and before my eyes, he slides a square-cut diamond onto my finger.

Oh, wow. Wow. Wow. Oh my gosh. Wow.

"Lillie?" Daddy's voice sounds farther away than Maryland.

I can't say anything, I just stare at Gordon, knowing my mouth yawns open like a garage door.

"Lillie?" Daddy says again.

"Well?" Gordon asks. "I'd get down on one knee, but with this leg…"

I exhale a great breath. "Wow."

"Lillie, dear? What in the world are you doing?"

"Daddy, I just got engaged."

Gordon sags in relief. "Yes, then?"

"Oh yes. Of course yes!"

"Right now?" Daddy asks. "As in, right this moment?"

"Right now."

"You've got to go, Lil! Call us later after you've kissed that man with all the soundness a bride-to-be can muster! Your mother will be thrilled."

I lay the phone on the table and practically throw myself across the tabletop, colliding chest to chest with Gordon. I hit my nose on his collar-bone, but I don't care.


The pub celebrates our engagement, all the regulars slapping Gordon on the back, saying, "It's about time, mate."

Roberta pulls me into her pickled arms, giving me a pickled kiss and a pinch on the cheek. "Lovely," is all she says. "Simply lovely."

Hey, if Gordon's dealt with all of this, God bless him. I'm so over-joyed, even the prospect of a drunk mother-in-law doesn't daunt me in the least. The fact that she lives here in England probably has something to do with that. I'll never really know her. Oh, I'll try. But in the end, she'll die "in her cups" as they say. Somehow the fallout will descend on my shoulders because Gordon can't have come to complete terms with something like this. But right now, I'm rejoicing.

Fitz, Stan, and Ursula, too, toast to our future and we sit down to a bona fide Christmas goose and plum pudding, and how cool is this?

## Tacy

The last Christmas should have been the happiest. And in some ways it was. My greatest gift was Hannah Grace. We went to church in the barn, sang carols, and listened to a sermon. No gifts were exchanged and no tree, of course, it being of pagan origin. But I sat on the bench and praised the Lord of heaven and earth, the sweet baby Jesus, in my heart. And I felt so thankful.

When we had all been dismissed, Pastor Cole told Rawlins to come with him back to his house. He had things to discuss. The flicker of disappointment across my husband's eyes comforted me, but he obeyed. He always did.

He came home at two the next morning and wouldn't tell me a thing.

## Lillie

I love my basement pad. Darn it if Cristoff and Mother didn't redecorate the entire room during my absence. Pleasance helped out despite the fact they had two weddings to deliver. Gert wielded brush, Peach wired track lighting. They really don't need me. Not at all.

I am a genie in a bottle. I love it. Truthfully, I'm feeling rather more like Pollyanna these days. Great living quarters, business doing wonderfully, Mom and Dad here—Daddy working furiously on his cozy mystery, having decided he didn't really have a violent bone in his body from which to draw a proper crime story, the world being what it is these days. I'm engaged with a fat whopper of a ring to a man who says he loves me just as I am, extra thirty pounds (okay, forty-five) and all, a man who says, "Honestly, Lillie, Reubens has always been one of my favorite painters." That's a remark at which a girl could laugh or cry. I choose to laugh. And pass the butter, baby!

The hubbub of the holidays has calmed down, and during it all, not a flicker from Tacy.

Well, it's been a long day preparing for Stan's wedding. Permits to obtain, agents to contact regarding the celebs in the wedding party. All the drudge work the others hate. Thank God for Gert. Now there was a good deed well rewarded. Maybe I'm needed after all.

I slip off my jeans and sweater, roll into some sweats, and head upstairs for my nightly cup of hot milk with Mom and Dad. They're already sitting at the kitchen table. Mom hops to her feet. "I just put your mug in the microwave."

"Thanks."

The air seems weighted with a discussion pushed suddenly in the deep freeze. "What's wrong?"

Daddy shakes his head.

Mom says, "Rawlins called here."

"Why?"

"Well, the baby's cough is getting worse, so I made an appointment for her at Dr. King's office. I called Tacy this morning and told her I'd be up and we'd go out to lunch. I figured I could talk her into the appointment over a sandwich at The Fusion Grille."

"She's always liked it there," Daddy says.

"So, what happened?"

"Well, I talked her into it. And we drove over to the office. Let me tell you, every time that child coughs it sounds like rusty bedsprings. It's horrible."

"So what did the doctor say?"

"We didn't even get in the door. Rawlins followed us there."

"No!"

Daddy rubs his eyes. "It's true. Apparently one of his thugs called him on the cell phone and out he came."

"I can't believe I didn't notice him." Mom shakes her head. "There was quite a scene in the parking lot. I've never seen eyes like that, Lillie. I didn't know what to do. He pulled Tacy to him and ushered her to the car. They drove away and there I stood. I should have just taken that baby from her arms and run in with her!"

Daddy felt for her hand, then wound his fingers in hers. "Don't blame yourself, Kathy. I'm sure it all happened so fast."

"It did!"

And then Mom broke down. I have never in all my life seen my mother cry. Curse that man! Curse him, and his pastor and his "god."

"To make matters worse," Daddy says, "Rawlins called here an hour ago and said he has forbidden Tacy to see us anymore. That she had disobeyed his authority, and before God, he cannot knowingly put her into situations where she will stumble into sin."

"Seeing her own parents?!"

Mom nods and wipes her nose. "Maybe I went too far, but, Lillie, you've heard Hannah Grace. Something's wrong with that child! She's wheezing now, too."

The clock above the oven says eight fifteen. "Mom, put the milk in the fridge. I'm going out."

"To Tacy's?"

"You'd better believe it."

"Be careful," Daddy says.

Mom nods. "He scares me."

Daddy sets down his mug. "Let me go with you."

"I'll be all right, Daddy. What can he do to me?" I kiss their cheeks. "Don't wait up."

Dad sighs. "As if that's a possibility."


Well, I'm praying my head off, I can tell you that, because there's something about Rawlins that scares the breath out of me, something that has always said, "Don't cross me." He's one step away from insane. I mean, if you have to keep yourself behind bars under lock and key twenty-four hours a day, what's hidden inside the cell? And is that padlock as strong as it seems? Would it take just the right pair of snippers to spring it open?

I would say yes. And it is one of the few things I can say for certain.

Rawlins is a self-assembled Frankenstein, portions of his twisted ideals bolted together to form only God knows what.


I drive out of the city and north through Baltimore County. The white fences glow, all I can really see in the dark of the country, but I know this stretch well. It's normally great fun zipping along here.

How am I going to do this? I breathe in and out like a boxer ready to spring into the ring. Psych yourself up, Lillie, you can do it, come on girl. You're strong. You're Hungarian. You're a mean, lean confrontation machine.

...

Okay, so that didn't help at all.

Maybe I should pray some more, ask God for good words to say, because He sure knows I am one of His children who says, "If only I had said..." five minutes after a conversation ends. Or five hours. Or five days. I hope one day to stop doing that sort of thing. That horrible mulling that takes up way too much of my time. I am a broken record, hear me whine.

So, God, give me words. You know how he's going to twist things around, and now that I'm talking to You, I have to wonder why I'm even going at all. This is ridiculous. We both know Rawlins won't budge. So why try to push at this mountain?

Because Mom and Dad need someone to stand up for them, and Tacy needs to know we care. There's no other way to do that now. This isn't just about Rawlins. It's about them. Help me to yell loud enough so she'll hear me from wherever she is locked inside that prison. Does she even know she's in prison?

I call Gordon on my cell phone, for which I now am grateful, especially with my parents at home.

"Sweetheart!" he answers. Caller ID.

"Hi, Gordon. You need to be praying."

I tell him why. He knows all about Rawlins.

"Want me to come up?"

"Nah. It'll take too long. I'll be all right." Gordon's home is too far away for a quick jaunt. "Besides, I've never seen Rawlins actually lose it."

"We can do this together tomorrow."

"Believe me, I'd rather have you here, but I've got momentum going right now and I don't want to lose that."

"Call me as soon as you're finished."

"I'll need to."

I swear I'm not driving all *that* far above the speed limit, but the miles evaporate. I am Warp-Speed Woman. Whatever the heck warp speed is. Maybe that's when God is traveling with you. I hope so. Oh, Lord, You know I hope so.

All too soon their stone-pillared entryway appears on the left. Well, here we go then.

God, go with me.

I pull the car up by the barn, climb out, and slam the door as hard as I can on a '63 car without doing something scary to the poor thing. Good, the bang echoed off the barn and house and soon, the motion detector will throw on the light at the corner of the porch as I stride up to the house.

Bingo. There it goes.

Yes, I stride. I ball my fists. I fool myself into believing that yes, I am the quintessential Strong Hungarian Woman. If only for this second.

Rawlins, you creepy man! I work up some lather. You horrible, controlling misogynist. You big bully, you.

You freak.

Tace, you deserve to have somebody at least try.

The freak meets me on the porch.

"Lillian."

"Rawlins."

"I can guess why you're here."

"Just a guess?"

"I *know* why you're here, Lillian."

We stand before the door. "How could you, Rawlins? What the heck did they ever do to you?"

"I'll accept no interference. And your euphemism isn't appreciated either."

My gosh! Stay calm.

"But your child is in danger, Rawlins."

"I'll be the judge of that."

"Why not? You're awfully good at that, aren't you?"

He crosses his arms. "If you came thinking to change my mind, you're wasting your time. My mind is made up."

"With a little help from Pastor Cole?"

"He's a man of God. Of course I went to him for counsel."

"And here I thought you were your own man."

A crude-oil hate fills me, and I am sinning. God, help me, but I hate this man standing before me.

"So you're actually cutting her off from her parents?"

"Yes. To keep her from sinning yet more."

"Going against rules *you've* made, rules that have nothing to do with Scripture?"

"I happen to think they do."

"Chapter and verse, Rawlins. Chapter and verse."

"This is neither the time nor the place."

"Yeah, right. Plus, your lord and master, Alban, isn't around to feed you the answers, is he? You know, my father is every bit as much a man of God."

"I don't doubt that."

"I want to see Tacy."

"She's retired for the night."

"Bull."

He places a hand on the doorknob. "This is going nowhere, Lillian, and furthermore, it's going to keep going nowhere."

"Because your kooky pastor says so?"

"Because *God* says so."

"You are so *blind!*"

"You'd better leave, Lillian."

"I *want* to see my sister. You're beating her, aren't you? You punished her for going with my mother, didn't you? Perhaps I should just give a little call to social services? Perhaps a social worker needs to come out, because, by golly, when they hear that child's cough, they'll whisk her away so fast you'll wonder if she ever existed in the first place."

My own passion scares me. And I hate my own words. This is his child, not some doll. And I'm throwing around words like "social services" as if they are nothing more than confetti.

"Show me my sister!" I scream.

He opens the door and calls up the steps. "Anastasia, could you come here please?"

I force my way in.

There she stands at the top of the stairs, wearing a beautiful white silk nightgown and robe. Their bedroom is above the porch on which we stand. Did she hear?

"Lillie! What are you doing here at this hour?"

She's heard nothing. Darn, darn, darn!

"Are you okay?"

"I'm fine." And she smiles like an angel, Rawlins not taking his eyes off her.

"Rawlins called Mom and Dad."

"That's enough, Lillian."

I advance toward the stairs. "He told them he forbids you—"

"I said that's enough, Lillian!" He puts his arms around my waist and lifts me off my feet. "Tacy, get back to our bedroom!"

She turns without question.

As he propels me to the door, I yell behind me. "Tacy! Can't you see what's going on?"

He sets me down on the porch. "Don't try and come here again. Better she be dead than to be dragged into sin by her own family."

He turns and walks back inside. The door clicks softly behind him.

And here I stand with nothing left to say, and nothing left to do. Tonight anyway. I scream in frustration.

Gordon's International is parked down the street and I know he's already inside with my parents. God love him. Surely by now Cristoff sits down there too, and they're all wondering what to do next.

I enter the kitchen, the March chill blowing everybody's hair before I shut the door. Suddenly, I'm shivering and I just can't stop, and I know I failed, and what will happen to Tacy now?

I feel my shoulders sagging and Daddy says, "It's okay, Lillie. You did what you could."

How did he know?

Gordon hugs me. "It was a start, sweetheart."

Cristoff grabs that concept. "That's right, sweetie, think of tonight as a building block."

Mom hugs me next. "You are a good girl, Lillie. We've just begun to fight, eh?" She pulls back and smiles into my eyes. "Now, let's have that milk."

"Okay."

"So, he didn't bite?" Daddy asks.

"It was on the verge of getting really ugly. But he allowed me to view Tacy at the top of the steps and she looked fine. Her usual monotone self."

Mom removes my mug from the refrigerator. "That's the frightful part. Dear Lord, you raise a child to respect herself, to be a capable, vibrant human being, and then some lunatic comes along…" She places the milk in the microwave and punches the keypad. "Not that I could see it then! Heavens no! I was so charmed by the money, the chances he offered Tacy for a better life, God forgive me."

"Kathy, dear, we were all fooled."

Well, not *all* of us. "I'm thinking about calling social services," I say.

Cristoff taps the rim of his cup. "Wow, Lillie, that's drastic."

Daddy says, "Maybe it's a little too soon for that."

Gordon says nothing. He just reaches for my hand beneath the table and rests it, still held in his, on his thigh.

I tell them what Rawlins said about Tacy being better off dead. "That sounds even more drastic to me."

Dad sighs. "I should go see him myself. I shouldn't have let you run off like that. It was my job, really."

"It's okay, Daddy. I think it was better I go first, you know, a big-sisterly reaction. It also helped to see how firm he is on this whole thing."

"And?" Mom's brows raise.

"Very."

"Not surprising," Cristoff says.

The microwave beeps and Mom removes my mug. "Why don't you call him tomorrow, Carl, and set up an appointment?"

"All right, babe."

How can they be so calm?

"I'll drive you," I say, bewildered but unwilling to squash their attempt at action with my doubts.

Daddy shrugs. "He won't let you in, I'm sure. But at least he'll know I'm still around, that no matter what he does or says, I'm still her father."

Fifteen minutes later, I walk Gordon toward his truck. "What a night," I say.

"Yeah. But you did the right thing. I'd have done as much for one of my brothers."

"I know."

The chill wind hits us full-on front. Gordon wraps his arms around me as we stroll down the street to where he parked the car. I nuzzle into his side, trying not to throw him and his prosthesis off kilter. "You know, nights like these have a strange quality, don't they?"

"Yeah, they do, sweetheart."

"Dark and large."

"Hollow yet important."

"I love you, Gordon."

"I love you too, Lillie."

"You came tonight."

"Yeah, I did. You'd have done the same."

17

## Tacy

The morning after Lillie came, I woke up late. Rawlins had already left for work. Something hard pressed into my ribs and I rolled to the side. My cuff bracelet was still warm when I reached for it. I slid it up my arm and pressed the sides completely together. It slid back down. I tried again. Once more, it ended up around my wrist.

So be it, I thought, and set it in the deepest drawer of my jewelry chest. The rest of the day seemed a little lighter. I was no man's slave.

Rawlins is still alive as I look down on him. He's beating on the window of the car, trying to open the door.

## Lillie

I absolutely need a little distraction right now, and Stan's wedding proves more than muscular enough. Around Christmastime we decided to definitely go WWII. The invitations just arrived, the words engraved on the wingspan of model Vickers Wellingtons, heavy bombers used in the war.

I did not think of this.

Peach did. He saw lots of planes close up during the war and declared these perfect. The rest of us knew nothing and therefore offered no argument.

Now, there you go. Peach is already moving away from me into the realm of the creative ones. Soon, no one but myself, in my sad and lonely world of facts and figures, will paddle in the waters of the mundane.

Well, I've still got Mom. She's pretty much standard transmission too.

We all sit around the conference room, laying the models into sky-blue tissue-paper nests, sealing the boxes and addressing labels by hand. We've achieved a regular assembly line and for only one thousand guests! The invitations alone cost more than most of our customers pay for their entire wedding. Fifteen percent.

Fifteen percent.

Yeah boy.

This is a five hundred thousand dollar wedding easy, really easy, and already two more high-profile customers have signed with us: Stan's financial manager's brother's girlfriend's sister, who is a film producer, as well as a New York socialite patron-of-the-arts diva who's supported Gordon's work for years. Oh, Genevieve is the coolest person I've ever met! Why Gordon never captured her for himself is beyond me. I asked him this and he twisted up his face and said, "Yeah, right, sweetheart. It would be like marrying my sister. Genevieve and I have been good friends for so many years, we'd hate to risk losing that."

H'm.

*"And,"* he added, "she never gave my heart a good tumble like you did."

Okay, that was the answer I had been looking for.

Thank heavens my romance and my business worries subsided before Tacy's life took on this toothless quality. If you removed her from that gorgeous house and stuck her in the hollows, I swear you'd see a Flannery O'Connor story in surround sound, Technicolor, and VistaVision. Honestly, her life deserves a poor, rural setting in some "holler" somewhere. We've got the weird traveling prophet and a sick child. Where are the rundown farmhouses and the walks along dusty roads to some hidden creek or stump? Where is the sister who is really the mother? Where is the obese woman who runs the tattered boarding house with closed shutters? Where is the dead fly?

As I am a plane nester, holding by far the least creative job on the assembly line, I keep asking people to repeat themselves over the crackle of my tissue paper. "What did you say, Cristoff?"

"Any word from Tacy?"

Of course, the whole gang is aware of the tragedy, and it's easy to tell it's never far from their thoughts. This situation has that haunting quality to it, like a holocaust movie or that Dylan Thomas poem, "A Refusal to Mourn the Death, by Fire, of a Child in London." Oh, it's literary all right, and that's what gets me. Grappling with this stuff is so much easier when it's in a book.

"No word."

"Figures."

"I know."

Pleasance looks up from where she addresses labels in her elegant yet artistic script. "I still can't believe he wouldn't even let your father in the house!" That really angered Pleasance.

*She has every right to be furious.* Rawlins met Daddy on the porch a few days after our confrontation, almighty Alban present as well. Naturally, my being excommunicated already and being female in general, they forbade me to draw nigh unto the holy presence. Believe me, I tried, but Rawlins nodded at Cole, who said, "This man will not deal with you again, woman. You stay there or he will not speak to your father either." And then Rawlins took Dad's arm, very tenderly, too, and respectfully, which made me cringe in a way because it shows how easily he can divorce himself from himself, and led him onto the deck.

Cole glared at me like some possessed character in a (you guessed it) Flannery O'Connor novel, a character more like a metaphorical agent of theological twistedness than an actual human being.

Judging by their posture as they sat around the glass-topped patio table, the discussion grew intense, but they kept their voices under control, because you can believe me I was straining to hear whatever I could.

After fifteen minutes Rawlins stood up and helped Daddy down off the deck and to the car. He said nothing to me.

"Just drive me home, Lillie," Daddy said, and I pulled away.

"Wanna talk?" I asked.

"Not right now."

He shook slightly, trembling like a leaf in the rain, and in that moment, he took on the aura of a character actor, that odd pathetic man who never gets a break, whose smile trembles but never wanes as the bully of a world slaps him in the face and kicks him in the hind parts.

In that moment I hated Rawlins. I thought I hated him before but not like this. It wasn't just a righteous indignation or a fear for my sister. It was hatred a Christian shouldn't feel, and not only did I fail to push it from me, I decided to stroke it and feed it and change its litter pan every single day.

The next day I called social services and told them everything I knew.

My father remains silent, only answering questions and saying grace, and I believe he talks to Mom but not as much. They removed something from him there on the deck, and I have a horrible feeling that I'll never know exactly what it was. And maybe I hope I don't.

Of course, Gordon knows all about Teddy. He hired a private investigator. The bones in Canton weren't Teddy's.

"He's the best, Lillie. Good on cold cases and is in with the police. He's our best bet."

*Our* best bet.

And now, we're just waiting for news.

The social worker's voice sounds like she's talking to a pile of slime. "Do you realize how backed up we are, and you send us out on a phony charge?"

I focus on my desk blotter. Someone drew a four-leaf clover and two bows. "Didn't you hear the baby's cough?"

"Yes. It's not good but not too troubling at this point. I'm also a nurse, Ms. Bauer, and I believe that child has acid reflux, which she aspirates when she naps. Your sister and brother-in-law have said they will gladly change the routine and feed her as soon as she wakes up from her naps and keep her upright as she digests. Beyond that, the child is well cared for, loved greatly, and her parents want to do the right thing."

"Didn't you feel something wasn't right though? I mean, Rawlins is—"

"We are done with this investigation, Ms. Bauer. I tell you, there are times when I wish people who send us out on false alarms were fined. You need to work out family difficulties on your own. We're overworked as it is."

There's nothing left to say, so I politely end the call and hang up the phone. I have to mull. I have to be shocked at what she said, because she talked so fast I could hardly compute. I mean, *I'm* the bad guy? *I* should be fined? What's going on here?

Years ago, I remember hearing the conversations of the parents of my friend who took me to the Creation talks. Boy, did they mistrust the government, or "the bureaucracy" as they called it. They didn't trust anyone really, not even God, now that I think of it, the way they were so scared of everything. But after this, I'm wondering if maybe they had a point!

My father always said to me, "The government isn't evil, Lil. It's just stupid."

Man. What in the world am I going to do next? Rawlins won't change Hannah Grace's schedule. The schedule is king, the schedule is god, the schedule is his, and he's the authority and to disobey his schedule is to disobey his authority, and to disobey his authority is to disobey *God, God, God!*

Oh, God, where are You?

She's just a baby, Jesus, a sick little baby.

18

## Lillie

Someone keyed my car down both sides, poured acid on the hood and trunk, and slashed the rag top to strings. I found the damage this morning and vowed to try and stop sleeping with my fan on high. How could I have not heard that? Of course, I should call the police, and they'll ask who could have done this. I'll them about my brother-in-law, and they'll say they will check it out.

Like that will do a thing. The detective, a female with my poor luck, will call me two weeks later and say, "I went out and talked to Rawlins McGovern," and the next words will have this meaning: "And I was bowled over by his charm and the way he really looked at me when he was talking to me and how could this nice man do something like this?" And then her brows will knit in accusation as if to say, "And I can't believe you called social services on this perfectly nice family. This car damage is probably another scheme to make the poor dear look bad."

So I don't report this. The car is ruined, the acid having eaten through the body so thoroughly I'd basically have to replace all the panels, which I can ill afford even if I could find them. It won't bring the car back. Nothing can bring that car back. A vacant cab rolls near, and I hail it, riding to work and hoping I can at least sell the darn thing for parts. I decide not to breathe a word of this to Mom and Dad.

## Tacy

I told the social worker I would do what she said, but Rawlins wouldn't let me. So I lied in effect. I felt black with sin. Maybe Rawlins is right about me, I remember thinking.

I don't know why I was so stupid. I told him just after she left that I had been changing the schedule on my own during the day. I was so proud I was already doing the right thing. Me. Just me, Tacy. I was so happy that I had maternal instincts of my own. I thought he'd be proud of me.

But he tightened his jaw and breathed in and out and he left the room. I heard him call Pastor Cole. Then he shut his study door. That man had some kind of control of my husband, more than just something a firm, demanding pastor could command. But I wouldn't have dreamed of asking Rawlins about it. Was he demanding sexual favors? Dear heavens, I didn't know how I could even think such a thing. Maybe it was money. Maybe he was extorting Rawlins for something Rawlins was hiding. He did seem to be hiding something. Even from the beginning.

That night, once again, I sat behind the couch. The moonlight spilled onto the pages of my Bible and I wished, oh yes, I wished I might turn into a silver beam and stream up to heaven and take Hannah with me. The thought of a murder/suicide used to horror me. But Hannah and I were dying by inches. It might have been a merciful alternative to the hell we inhabited.

Look now though, God has taken care of it. Lillie will say, "Tacy was too good for this earth, Daddy."

Daddy will nod and cry. And Mother will fix a pot of coffee and cover her grief with activity.

I never got to paint those murals in the cottage.

I don't know why my spirit isn't ascending yet. I feel the presence of my Savior, an undeniable peace, yet I watch the scene below me. Lillie's stopped her car and is sliding down the hill toward the Rover.

Rawlins screams for help again, and I wonder what my sister will do. Is Hannah asleep in her car seat in Lillie's station wagon? Is Gordon comforting my little one?

## Lillie

With a June wedding of my own nearing, to a rich guy no less, money coming in from the business, and very little personal expenses to begin with, I figure I can spring for a nice car. I mean, nothing too flashy, nothing that says, "Hey, fiancé, you've got a bucketload, so I'm just going to go whole hog and get this cute Mercedes-Benz convertible." Then again, this is going to have to last me awhile, so I don't want to go for anything that I'll get sick of a year from now, either, like a minivan or a sedan. I need a little speed. I really do.

Gordon shuffles along beside me as we walk the lot at the Volvo dealership in Hunt Valley. "You know, I'm not a violent man, sweetheart. But I feel like something needs to be done to send Rawlins a message. I can't believe what he did to your car."

"What kind of message? Any message I can think of is illegal, and besides, I always get caught."

"God must really love you, then."

Never thought of it like that before.

"What about a restraining order?" he asks.

"We can't prove he did anything. And I wouldn't be surprised if he files a restraining order on me first."

"Just a thought… He's not done with this, Lillie. You know that, don't you?"

M'm. "Yeah, I do."

But I don't want to think about King Rawlins VIII just now, and I tell Gordon that.

I run my hand along the sun-warmed bumper of a silver Volvo wagon. "What do you think about a wagon? I mean, maybe we should be practical."

As in kids.

Wow-wee.

"There's a little seat in the back there," I say.

"Yeah." He winds his arms around my waist from behind. He kisses my neck. "Wanna start right away?"

"I'm thirty-two. You're forty-two. What do you think?"

"Okay. Kids right away. I'm with you there. And in the meantime, the car will be more than practical for your business, running stuff on-site."

"Let's test-drive it."

The car salesman photocopies our licenses, and we head off in the

April sunshine, sunroof open, radio blaring—believe it or not, a Pink song. "I'm a hazard to myself," she sings in her rugged, controlled voice. "Don't let me get me."

I love Pink. She asks the questions I ask and feels much the same about herself as I do. If she didn't sound off with such foul language, I'd hand her CD out on the streets to pubescent girls searching for their own identity. If she didn't have such a potty mouth, I can guarantee that mothers everywhere would be waiting in line for her next CD.

I sing with gusto. "Don't wanna be my friend no more—"

"Hey, you don't have a bad voice," Gordon says, tattooed arm resting on the open window sill. The tattoo is of a once bare-breasted mermaid, attesting to what we'll do to ourselves when we're young. She wears a red bikini top now. What a hoot.

"Thanks. Been singing in church choirs all of my life. Alto."

"You have that lyrical quality to your speaking voice. I'm not surprised. Hey, if Stan ever needs a backup singer—"

"No way! With this figure?"

He laughs and takes my right hand off the gear stick. "You are perfect. Why would you think I'd want to share my bed for the rest of my life with a stick figure?"

I shrug.

He squeezes my hand. "You know, Lillie, men on the whole don't like skinny. I don't know where women get this idea."

"Well then, I guess I'm the one for you."

There, that should stop this vein of conversation cold. Although I internally obsess about my figure, I hate talking about it.

"And you're not a hazard to yourself either," Gordon says. "I know you're thinking that the song is just how you feel."

I just smile a little.

"Really, Lillie. Believe me, ask any of the remaining Remington brothers, and they'll tell you what being a hazard really is."

"I guess hazards take many forms. I mean when you think of hazards, you think of sharp rocks or cliffs or windy roads beside ravines. But what about soft hazards, like waterbeds and featherbeds and thick down pillows that can smother a baby's breath?"

Where did all that come from?!

"Tacy and Hannah."

"Yeah."

For some reason, I negotiate the eastern road away from Hunt Valley, planning out a rather large, circuitous route back to the dealership. Hey, the tank's full.

Gordon turns to look at me. "We're going by Tacy's house, aren't we?"

"Maybe Rawlins isn't home. Maybe we could pull in for just a bit?"

"I'm game."

"I just need to see her."

"I know."

Five minutes later I turn off Jarrettsville Pike and navigate this car, which I've decided to buy since it has a turbo engine that rocks more than even Pink, between the stone posts on either side of their driveway.

"I feel sick, Gordon."

"I don't blame you. We need to send some kind of message though. That we're not afraid of him."

"Maybe showing up here will do just that."

I doubt it. But it sounds good, right?

The tires crunch on the gravel of the drive as I pull onto the parking area near the Queen Mother of All Decks. Rawlins's car isn't in sight, thank

You, God. I exit the car as quickly as possible and run up to the back door, not waiting for Gordon. Time is definitely of the essence and all.

I knock. Philly, the housekeeper, a tiny woman of Greek descent, real name Philadelphia, frowns at me through the window. But she opens the door anyway. "You can't come in here, Lillie. You know that."

"Is she all right?"

"She's upstairs, napping." Philly's from the city. No nonsense.

"I mean the baby."

"She's napping too."

Well, let's see if Rawlins did as he promised. "Did Tacy nurse her to sleep?"

"Get on out of here before I get fired for talking to you."

I've always liked Philly. Gruff but bighearted.

Hannah's cough echoes even from upstairs.

"Philly, how can you stand this?"

"You better get on, Lillian."

"Philadelphia!" a foreign voice calls from the top of the steps. "Who is that?"

"Just a salesman!"

I whisper. "Who is that?"

"The new nursemaid."

"A nursemaid? What does Tacy need a nursemaid for? She doesn't *do* anything?"

"Just go!"

"Philly—"

"Mr. McGovern brought her in a few days ago. A church lady. There's a guard coming on duty any minute too. Now get going!" She shakes her head as she shuts the door, and I stare at the cross dividing the panes of glass and see the crucified Christ and wonder, "Did Jesus die for *this?*"

And I know the answer is yes. And right now, like when I think of the sins of the Hitlers and the Husseins, it just kinda makes me mad. Shouldn't some behavior just be beyond redemption?

Grandma Erzsèbet never remarried. After Teddy disappeared, despite the language barrier, Grandma brought me through. She'd lost her greatest love to a work camp; she knew the reason for separation didn't much matter: disappearance…gone is gone.

So Grandma held me for hours on end as I cried out tears of loss and frustration for three years, and a tenderizing fork poked my heart again and again with each news report, each false hope. She whispered Hungarian things in my ear, words my brain couldn't translate. But my heart did. "I know. I understand."

That was the thing about Grandma. She'd been through so much, my grandfather being taken away, my Uncle Istvàn in the work camps. She knew. More than anybody else, she knew. And that soothed me. Kissing my hair, she hummed songs I would never understand but would never forget either.

Several years later, my mother interpreting, I asked Grandma why she never remarried. She said she'd married a loving man, taken from her by a cruel master. She figured her chances of finding another man like my grandfather were slim and she refused to end up with a cruel master.

"I have more respect for myself than that."

Tacy, Tacy. How did you agree to give yourself, your *self* away to a mere man? Teddy's gone, but I'm not. Rawlins is still here, but Tacy has disappeared.

As much as I feel sorry for my sister, there are times I want to shake her silly, knock some sense into her, scrape that vapid expression off her beautiful face and scream for her to go back to the spot where she laid herself down and walked away. And now a nursemaid? Or a warden?

Philly's standing on my doorstep, cussing me out good, and I guess I don't blame her.

The name-calling stops. "Don't you think I saw what was going on, Lillie? Don't you think I was doing my best to run interference when I could? But you had to come poking around. Now that man has hired another housekeeper, not to mention the fact that the other women from that spooky church, and that guard, are there, keeping a watchful eye when Rawlins is gone. So, thanks to you, now nobody remains for Tacy."

"Come on in off the doorstep, Philly. We'll talk about it inside."

She enters the house. "I could sure use a cup of coffee."

"I just put on a pot a little while ago."

She takes off her jacket, folding it neatly and laying it across the back of the living room chair. "And a job. I sure could use a job."

"I know." I pick up the jacket and hang it in the closet near the door. "I'll help you."

"You'd better."

I usher her back to the kitchen. My folks are breakfasting at Aunt Luca's this morning, thank goodness. Daddy's been coming around just a tad, and I don't want him hearing this stuff right now. See, I've got plans. I'm not sure how all the details will work out, but I'm going to try. Or I think I am. I mean, I *am* a Strong Hungarian Woman. Right?

I pick out the prettiest mug I've got, a delft blue-and-white pedestal mug. "I've got a job for you."

"How much you pay?"

I fill the mug and set it in front of her. She takes a sip of it, black. I'm not surprised. "Eight bucks an hour?"

Her brows raise. "Oh!" Then her eyes narrow. "How about nine?"

"Eight-fifty."

"You gotta deal."

We shake.

I ask, "It's none of my business but—"

"Minimum wage."

"No!"

"Yes. He's a cheap one, that rat."

"What about your living quarters? Did you move out of your rooms there?"

"I'm at my mother's house, temporarily."

"Do you like being a housekeeper, Philly?"

"If I like the lady I work for."

"What if that lady was a guy?"

She shrugs. "Don't know."

I make a mental note to call Gordon and inform him of his great need for a full-time lady like Philly. Oh gee, that's going to be fun. A new marriage to a British, one-legged artist, with Philadelphia Kosmakos right there to render things even more surreal.

I tell her it's Gordon she'd be working for, and then soon after, me as well.

She examines the kitchen. It's basically clean, but of course, the small bit of counter to the left of the sink is relegated for a pile of junk mail and hair bobs. And there's the obligatory napkin holder that's void of napkins but stuffed full of more flyers and inserts and invoices. An iffy basket of bananas resides near the fridge. Just your regular kitchen mess. "I think I could do that. You don't seem too particular. And after that Rawlins…"

That Rawlins.

"I can't seem to think of his name either without *that* in front of it. It's like he's not really human."

She picks up her coffee. "He's a thing."

"You lived there for years, Philly. Surely he's got an Achilles heel? Other than the control thing."

"I couldn't find a thing. And believe me, I looked. Even jigged open the desk drawers. Nothing."

"No kidding."

"Yeah. You'd think there'd be *something*, wouldn't you?"

"What about his mother? You ever have talks with her?"

"She's not allowed there anymore either. She was bugging them about the baby not going to the doctor for checkups."

Wow. Come to think of it, she hasn't had tea with Mom in a while either. "Did she ever give you any insight into him?"

"Just once. She told me once, when I was ready to quit one of the dozens of times I threatened it, that Mr. McGovern, her husband, isn't really Rawlins's dad."

"Really? Tacy's never told me that."

"Tacy doesn't know. She said Rawlins's real father died when Rawlins was little but was a good father. I'm not sure when she remarried, but obviously he adopted the boy."

"Well, Mr. McGovern seemed nice enough at the wedding," I say.

"Oh yeah, nice old guy. But always working. Still, better than no one, you know?"

"…"

"The man really has no excuse."

We all want that, don't we? We want terrible people to be that way for a reason, some cruel childhood, abuse, neglect. But isn't always the way life goes. Some people view others as a commodity, pure and simple, and never look into another human's eyes and see a real person with a life and a future and the right to at least be respected. Unless, of course, they act like Rawlins, and then they deserve nothing.

"How did he get religion?"

She shakes her head. "Beats me. That Alban Cole might have had something to do with that. They both think he's a man of God, but how can he be? He's a fruitcake."

"Exactly."

"I try to imagine him as having once been a sweet little baby, but I just can't."

I'm so proud of myself, I call Gordon on the phone. "Guess what I did?"

"With you, Lillie, I have no idea."

Well, huh. I can't imagine anybody sees me as the spontaneous type.

"I bought a cell phone today. For Tacy."

"Oh yeah? Why?"

"So she can call us without Lord Rawlins finding out."

"Great idea."

"I know. I can't believe I thought of it. I've got my home number, office number, and cell number already programmed into it. I mailed it today. I know Tacy gets the mail. She always did at home, anyway. She always loved to get the mail."

I'm so excited. I believe God gave me this idea so it's going to work! It has to. Please God, let her still get the mail.

19

## Tacy

I tried to kidnap my own child. God help me, I tried. I wish, now that I'm gone, somebody could find this out, that I wouldn't be judged by how I appeared. I tried to save the family from worry; I tried to seem happy. But now that I'm going away they're all going to wonder about me, wonder why I didn't do anything before this.

The church woman left for the night, and I stole into the nursery at two a.m. Rawlins seemed to sleep most heavily around then. I dressed Hannah Grace, praying the entire time, Dear God, keep this child alive until I get her to someone who can help. Her wheezing was getting so much worse.

He locked the deadbolts by then, with his key, but I figured it out. I decided to go through the living room window and onto the front porch. One good thing about Pastor Cole was that he said security systems were a lack of trust in God.

I got the cell phone from Lillie, but only because the new guard didn't know he shouldn't leave the mail on the kitchen counter. Though I couldn't get a moment alone to call her, I knew she'd come pick me up at a moment's notice. I couldn't risk calling inside the house, so I figured I'd grab Hannah Grace, walk a mile or two, and call then.

But she cried out. I was going through the window, and I banged her little head on the frame. Oh, God. I couldn't believe I did that. I was trying to be so careful. And she cried out.

So I ran. I longed to comfort her and stop her crying, knowing how it would bring on an asthma attack. But I had to run. I was halfway through the pasture when he caught me, wrenching Hannah from my arms.

He hit me. Across the jaw. It stunned me and I lay there freezing in the field until morning, when he came walking toward me, backlit by a rising sun, like some dark angel. I wanted to run, but I couldn't. I couldn't leave. I couldn't leave my baby in the hands of that monster.

The next day another guard came on duty for the nighttime. He sat on the porch, on the deck, walked the grounds, and watched. When one of the church women arrived for duty, he checked a list and let her inside the house.

I feel so light now though. I can see so much. There's Rawlins, looking at me, his eyes growing round. And I see fear in his eyes for the first time ever. But I am looking down on him. That's a first.

I wonder, are my eyes open in death, or did I close them on the roll? Do I stare lifeless at him now?

# *Lillie*

Good-bye, April. This spring is flying by, and it's a good thing my friends are all in the wedding-planning business because planning my own nuptials is akin to me modeling in boat shoes without falling off the runway. I found a pair of orange sandals yesterday. What a buy!

I'm sitting at David and Dad's eating a grilled cheese, bacon, and tomato, on rye of course, going over the accounts for the Remington wedding.

I never knew.

Really. I mean, you watch those Hollywood entertainment shows, and they report the wedding of "Hollywood's Hottest Couple," tallied in at a million dollars or more.

I used to laugh. I used to think, "What kind of idiots would spend a million bucks on a wedding?"

Well, now I know. Not only does the day itself figure into the package, but several parties are planned beforehand, airfare galore, hotel bills galore, incidentals galore, and well, just conjure up the word "galore" and you might begin to grasp the true scope of a wedding of this magnitude.

Oh, the layers of this monstrous, beastly machine in the area of the guest list alone. Family and friends, of course, but don't forget the agents, the record company execs, the managers, the crew, the Who's Who of Galore. Lots of British rockers, musicians, and singers I'd have given my right arm to meet a year ago are today merely large annoyances.

Now I know why some entertainers choose those tiny weddings in obscure chapels in the middle of nowhere with a barefoot bride in a simple Vera Wang sheath. Because you are afforded but two choices in weddings like this: invite everybody or invite nobody.

Stan—the Kleenex, the Jell-O, the Band-Aid of rock-'n'-roll—chose the former, and now, with the wedding next week, we're all running around like raving roly-polies after the rock's been lifted up. I wish somebody would touch me so I could curl up into a ball and lie still.

Every day, more and more invoices crowd the box. Cristoff received a one-hundred-thousand-dollar budget for the flowers alone and is almost in a state of euphoria. He's using a lot of live shrubbery for the reception, gardenia bushes, and hibiscus for stage setting, and some tropical plants I don't recall the names of because, let's face it, I only have so much brain space to spare right now. And the table arrangements for the reception on the barge are low and sprawling so the guests can converse across the table. I never knew so many varieties of roses existed; however, Cristoff says we're limited to varieties popular in the '40s. He's a bit disappointed he can't do those soaring arrangements, but again, we're tied to authenticity and I'm reasonably sure, after a great deal of research at the library, they weren't yet dreamed of years ago. Gordon and I will plant the majority of the shrubs at the house so it isn't a complete waste of money, or plant life for that matter. You should see the landscaping plans for the house. Magnificent. The Garden of Eden rises again!

Pleasance floats in the heavenlies as well. The silk for the bridesmaids' gowns—from France, hand-embroidered, and eight-hundred dollars a yard—has been cut and sewn into gowns Edith Head would envy. Ursula's ensemble steals a whole lot more than the breath. She chose a dusty ivory color for a more vintage look. Not only that, it sets off her coloring. One of the prominent Hollywood makeup artists will apply her makeup, so even dowdy Ursula and the word "stunning" will flawlessly intersect.

What heroics will be employed on Stan, however, remains to be seen. He will take a miracle, although he promised Ursula he wouldn't wear the wig. The white dinner jacket will help too. Gordon's wearing the same. I may not recognize any of the Remington boys cleaned up and spit-polished.

Peach has been scouring old cookbooks, and while he can't possibly attend to all the food himself, he's assembled a crew of ten local catering companies and is "large and in charge," as Pleasance says.

Gert shares her sanity in generous helpings, which is probably the biggest, most important job of all. I want to be like Gert when I grow up.

I punch figures into my portable calculator, amazed a bank account capable of sustaining this kind of expenditure exists in the world. "Wow," I breathe aloud.

"Good thing he got a good financial manager right away."

I turn my head. "Hey, baby."

Gordon kisses my cheek. "Here's someone I'd like you to meet." He pulls the chair out opposite me. An older African American woman stands beside him. "Lillie, this is Mildred LaRue, jazz singer extraordinaire and lead voice of The Star Spangled Jammers. And one of my dearest, closest of friends."

Mildred shakes my hand as I stand to my feet. "This boy is way too much of somethin', isn't he? Still tryin' to figure out what though."

She gathers me into these long brown arms, skinny and strong as a heavy wire coat hanger. I hug her right back if only to keep the breath from being knocked out of me.

"Now then"—she pulls away—"sit back down and let me look at you. Gordon, you just feel free to sit over there with your ladylove. I want to see the two of you together, and will this David or this Dad be able to provide me a decent cup of coffee?"

Gordon kisses her cheek. "I'll get you one, love."

I say the inevitable. "Gordon's told me so much about you."

"And I feel like I already know you. That boy called me the first night he met you! Three o'clock in the morning! I said, 'Son, you've flipped your lid!'"

"Sounds like Gordon." The first night? Wow.

I examine him as he stands at the counter, chatting with the attendant as she rings up the coffee, smiling, so at ease and naturally charming. She's blushing and I'm not jealous because I'm sure of him.

"He sure is easy to love," I say.

Mildred reaches into her green clutch purse and pulls out a bleached-white, ironed handkerchief. "My late husband was like that. He was a dynamic preacher. We had a church down in the town of Mount Oak for years. Ever heard of that town?"

I shake my head.

"Anyways, I directed the music. Still sang jazz on the side. Much to the dismay of *some,* if you know what I'm talkin' about." She wipes moisture from her brow. So she's the type that sweats. I like her already.

"Oh yes."

"That's right. You a preacher's kid, aren't you?"

"Well, a priest's kid. But close enough."

"Episcopalian."

"Yep. We have our difficult members too."

"Know me a little Episcopalian girl down where I live. Wears leather jackets and rides around in a red Beetle that's been painted to look like a ladybug."

"No kidding?"

She shakes her head. "No, I'm not. One of those creative types."

"My sister was like that."

"Yep. Writes music. Draws. Plays umpteen instruments. I keep telling her to find her a man, but I think she may be bent backward, if you know what I'm saying. So she's determined to just be married to Jesus."

Too bad Tacy didn't decide that. Cristoff did, and he's far better off than she is. "Can't fault her for that."

"No. I say the same. I even introduced Gordon to her a couple of years ago. Nothing there. And Gordon's too passionate to enter into anything but a whirlwind relationship."

Whirlwind? Well, yes. I guess it has been. Never thought of it like that, but here we are, set to be married in a month, and we only met last October.

Very cool.

I say, "Well, when it's right, there's no sense in bumbling around. The first time I saw him, I knew there was something special. Especially after he just reached down, pulled up his pant leg, and showed me his prosthesis!"

Mildred laughs. "He did that to me, too."

"What did I do?" Gordon sets down the coffee in front of Mildred.

"Your fake leg," she says. "You aren't exactly shy about it."

He scrapes out the chair next to me and sits. "Why not? After having gone through all that pain, I deserve to wave the blasted thing over my head!"

I place my hand on his thigh, loving the warmth of him. God, I want to make love with him so badly. Just another month. Just another month. I squeeze and he looks over at me.

Yeah boy!

Gordon begins to pick away at a napkin. "I just believe in letting people know who you are right up front."

We chitchat for a while. I really like Mildred. She is very dark and very thin, a living cigarillo, and her white hair, swirled up into a french twist, sits upon her like sculpted ash. She wears nothing but green, Gordon once told me. Except on stage with the Jammers, where it's nothing but red, white, and blue.

She's extremely orange, it's plain to see.

"My Jesse David was in your face, like you, Gordon. You knew who he was a mile away."

Later that day, after we dropped Mildred off at her hotel, I asked Gordon, "Am I like that? Can you tell who I am a mile away?"

"I could."

"Good." The shopfronts of Aliceanna Street slide by. We open the windows and sunroof of the Volvo. Gordon had dropped me off earlier and taken the car in to have a ten-disc CD player installed, which is just another example of his ways. How filled up I've become.

He's playing Gert's *Best of Bread* tape though. Go figure.

"By the way, I did something last night, Lillie."

Gordon's a night owl. "How late were you up?"

"Only until two."

"Okay."

"So anyway, love. I think we need to work on your self-esteem."

A great bark of a laugh escapes me all on its own. The guttural equivalent of "good luck."

"I do, sweetheart. What's so funny about that?"

"Oh, Gordon. Please."

"Anyway, look in the front pocket of my knapsack there by your feet. There's a list in there. It's on drawing paper."

I push aside a doughy eraser and two pencils.

"See it, Lil? I had it laminated."

A small spiral sketchpad, a Starbucks gift card, three different size bottle caps.

"It's small. Wallet-size," he says.

Still searching. "Gordon, I never know what to expect from you."

"Good. Get it yet?"

"Yep. Here it is. It was stuck inside that little notebook." I slide out what looks like a flimsy credit card.

"Okay. That's for you to keep with you in your wallet."

I start to read down a list of stellar qualities written impossibly small in his beautiful hand. Hard-working, Intuitive, Intelligent, Caring, blah, blah, blah, Pretty, Sparkling Eyes, blah, blah, blah, and I think that the saying is true, love really must be blind. And finally, the last one reads, A Really Nice Derrière.

Another laugh shoots out. "Gordon! A nice derrière? I'm overweight, for gosh sakes! My butt is *huge!*"

"Oh no. It's perfect. Men like nice round butts. They really do."

No kidding.

"No kidding, Lillie," he says. "Who wants a pile of bones sitting on his lap? Ouch."

We ride toward the house and I stare at the card. It didn't really matter what he had written; the fact that he'd written it at all held me captive.

That and one word.

*Brave.*

"Brave? You think I'm brave?"

"The way you went out to Tacy's to confront your brother-in-law? The way you went back? Of course."

"That wasn't brave. Hannah Grace could be dead now for all I know." And it all goes liquid inside of me, like cold butter dropped in a hot skillet.

He pulls into a space near my house. He takes my hand. And he gathers me to him as I sob, mouth open and wet against his shirt. Even though we try to busy ourselves, to keep situations at arm's length, they still progress inside our souls. They don't stop eating at the lining. He breathes steadily, and after a minute I realize I've adjusted my sobs to his rhythm, or perhaps he adjusted his breathing to mine. And that quick observation stills my crying, and I turn my cheek to his chest and rest in the beating of his heart.

"Whatever you have to do, you do. I'll be right there with you, Lillie."

I sit up and shuffle in my purse for a tissue. "Stan's wedding is in two days. The next day, that Sunday, I'll go out there."

"I'll go with you."

"I'd like that. Thank you." I don't want to talk about this anymore. So I blow my nose then put on some Chapstick. "I thought sure she'd use that cell phone by now."

He smiles, then says, "The Admiral Fell Inn should be filling up now. Are you sure we booked enough rooms?"

Man, he's good.

"Positive. And don't forget, the majority of the guests are making their own arrangements. You sure you don't want me to ride with you down to the airport to get your mom?"

"Oh yes. Definitely. She'll be three sheets to the wind anyway. I mean, some things you don't mind waving around for all the world to see, but some things you do."

There are times when I look at him, a weakness unfolds. More to the point, a fragility, like the moist glittering wings of a butterfly uncurling from its cocoon, and I love him even more.

20

*Lillie*

The rehearsal dinner, given by Ursula herself, is the only normal thing about this affair. We are sitting in a private dining room at Sabatino's in Little Italy, eating pasta and drinking wine, patiently biding our time until the desserts—cannoli, Italian wedding cake, gelati, tiramisu, and only Ursula knows what else—arrive. The Italian owners hover, aloof, dark men who give off that peculiar Mediterranean vibe when talking with the women they deem merely the female means to an end, not the end itself.

My cell phone rings as the dinner plates are cleared.

I read the caller ID. "It's Tacy's phone," I whisper to Gordon. "I'll be right back."

In the hallway, on the third ring, I punch the button. "Tacy?"

"Stay away from my wife." Rawlins's voice sounds calm, but it scares me. My heart races.

"I can't do that."

"You will. I'll make sure of it."

"Are you threatening me, Rawlins?"

"I'm protecting my family. Nothing more."

I hear a crash in my ear, and the line goes dead. He destroyed the phone. I know it.

On shaky legs I walk back into the dining room.

"How is she?" Gordon asks.

"It was Rawlins."

"Blast."

Exactly.

"Let's go out there tonight. Just to scope out the scene. I've got to get them out of there, but I've got to know what I'm up against. I feel this is bigger than we know, Gordon."

"I do as well."

So it grows.

"Maybe we should just try and get them out of there."

Gordon nods. "You're the boss."

Pleasance accompanies us. Truth is, she can whip me at rock climbing any day of the week. And she runs faster, too.

It's three a.m.

I turn around in the passenger seat of the Volvo. She sits quietly in the back. "I know this is asking a lot the night before our biggest gig ever."

She shakes her head and waves a hand. "This is more important. No matter what happens, Gert's got everything under control. And she's handy with a needle if we need any last-minute adjustments. Let's just hope things don't turn violent."

Pleasance wears all black, climbing shoes snug on her feet if she needs to get up to the second floor.

"Thank you, Pleasance."

"Sometimes we just have to do this sort of thing, Lillie. If there is any way possible, I'll get that baby down."

I picture her, Hannah Grace strapped to her back as she carefully locates proper footholds. I imagine myself wanting to cry out time after time, "Be careful!" and forcing myself mute. So I'll dance like a boxer on the ground, left foot to right, right foot to left, ready to break any fall that might occur. Gordon holds my hand. "You just get your sister out of there, love. Pleasance and I will take care of the rest."

It's grown in the last few hours, this mission. If we get in, we might as well do what needs to be done. "I've never in all my wildest dreams imagined this."

"Who does?" Gordon says. He's ready as our driver. He's pulling up along the side of the road, near the end of the driveway, where we'll keep the engine running for our return.

I grab the door handle. "Ready then?"

Pleasance nods. "Let's go, Lillie Pad."

Over the border. Over the border. You can do this.

We work our way through the brush and onto the property, staying close to the bushes once we emerge. We watch for a while, checking the movement of the guard. His circuit becomes predictable. Around the house and out to the barn. Around the back of that building to the stables. That takes him about three minutes.

"We don't have much time," I whisper. And we make our plans.

As arranged, Pleasance runs toward the front porch to look inside the windows and check the locks on the front door. I run toward the almighty deck to do the same at the back entry.

I fear the boards will creak, but I should have known better. Not on Rawlins's deck. How dare they?

Breathe. Breathe.

The motion sensors have illumined the scene, but I meld as far into the shadows as possible. There they are, three deadbolts above the doorknob. Wow. There's no way.

I peer into the window. The light in the oven hood shines warmly, all looks clean and normal. A real-life kitchen. It all looks so normal.

Ouch!

A pair of iron arms circles me.

"Gotcha!"

I look down. They are large arms, covered in dark hair. They are not Rawlins's arms.

Pleasance hollers and kicks as she is dragged up the porch steps by Rawlins. Dear God, he's holding a gun. Why didn't I bring mine?

"You didn't know about the cameras, did you, Lillian?" he hisses. "You don't get it, do you?" Will this be the day of his unstitching? He pushes Pleasance toward me. "Let her go, Anthony."

The arms free me.

Rawlins leans against the deck railing. "You've given me no choice, Lillian. I've tried to be a good sport about this."

"No choice? What do you mean, 'no choice'?"

"Get out of here now, before I shoot you."

"I want my sister!"

He moves forward, pointing the gun at me. "I said, *get out*."

Gordon materializes.

"Who's that?" Rawlins asks.

"My fiancé."

Rawlins points to Gordon's cane and laughs. "Wonderful. An invalid."

Gordon steps forward. "You might consider a more rational approach to this, Rawlins."

"I'm perfectly rational. Furthermore, this discussion is done." He turns his back on us and places his hand on the screen door. He turns back to look at us.

"Come on, Lillie," Pleasance says, breathing heavily. "There's always tomorrow." She stares Rawlins down, but he doesn't budge.

"This isn't the end of the matter," I tell him. "Not nearly."

"Oh yes, it is. You'll see. Take them to their car, Anthony. You brought this on yourself, Lillian. It was one thing to battle this on your own, but now you've brought others into the situation. You'll be sorry."

He enters the house before I can retort.

We walk back to the Volvo, Anthony three steps behind, gun one step closer. He remains in the shadows as we climb inside the car.

Gordon speeds away. "I'm in this now, sweetheart. All the way."

"Me too," say Pleasance. "That man is scary. We've got to get them out of there."

"Oh, we will," I promise them and myself. "No mistake about it."


Six a.m. I jam down the button on my old, wind-up alarm. Sorry, but nothing wakes me up like that shrill bell, only two hours of "sleep" notwithstanding.

Throwing back the covers, I jump out of my cozy bed and begin throwing on my jeans and T-shirt. This is our uniform today, until the wedding, of course. The T-shirts, bright orange for clear visibility, declare us EXTREME in purple letters on front and back. I ordered them and thoroughly enjoyed the groans as I unpacked them. My wedding clothes, the caramel dress and bone pumps, are already hanging in Gordon's suite at The Admiral Fell.

Oh man. Tacy. I picture Rawlins and his big gun. A Glock no less.

I try to shove it out of my mind as I pour a cup of strong coffee into my travel mug. Thank You, God, for timers on coffee makers. Thank You, God, Mom and Dad are still asleep and none the wiser.

Out the door and in the car, I make my way down to the floral tent setup on the pier. Cristoff didn't come home last night as he and his team prepared the bouquets, which are quite amazing. It saddens me to think they'll be dead by tomorrow. But a pallor has overshadowed all of this. I just need to make it through the day. I slow my steps and remember to pray, and I wonder what God will do, how I'll ever be able to make the needed rescue. I long for the woods behind the manse, for the circling buzz of bees, for the rustle of a squirrel in the trees, but only traffic and the shutting of car doors sing along with my prayers. I feel no comfort, but a meaty resolve begins to build inside me, conceived by a muscular panic, hearty and unable to be restrained forever. I wish God would take care of Rawlins without my aid, but the collection of strength has begun, and more will arrive. To whom much is given, much is required, and my heart cries out, "Why me?" But I know the answer, spoken by my own voice. *Because there's no one else who can.* I have failed in my own strength and now, while a different strength collects, I must wait on God.

Ten minutes later, I step inside the green-and-white striped tent. Cristoff runs over. "We finished thirty minutes ago. We're set to go."

"Good. Let's get going on the reception setup. The rental companies should be arriving at eight."

"Got it. Can you believe this? Did you ever, sweetie?"

"Not in a million years."

"Let's go. It's going to take at least an hour to put the plants around."

So we walk up the brick pier toward the barge. A mammoth white tent, the harbor purple with morning behind it, sails like a galleon. Streamers of flowers and ribbons scalloping the temporary handrails we circled around the barge's perimeter—safety first for this sue-happy crowd—will lend the barge a sumptuous yet protected quality. Cristoff's words, not mine. In other words, large but intimate. See? Anything's possible.

"This is going to be great, honey."

Cristoff already occupies the zone. "Let's start with the magnolia trees. We strung the lights last night."

The reception is set to begin at seven p.m., dotted with lots of twinkle lights and candles galore. Galore.

"How about the church?"

"We're going over after this to start setting up the candelabra and the pew decorations. It should take several hours."

You can imagine, right? Tulle, silk ribbons, ivy, roses, and all the rest I can't remember and am not paid to.

"How about the table decorations?"

"On schedule. We've got the major portion of them together. The delicate blooms will go in during the ceremony."

"The *Torsk?* How about that?"

"The flags are on, Lillie, and beyond that, there's just not room for anything but the bar. I still can't believe they're even letting us use it."

"Hey, money talks."

He leans down and grabs the pale pink foil-wrapped pot of a magnolia tree. "Ready?"

"Oh yeah."

Gordon arrives fifteen minutes later.

"What are you doing here, babe?" I ask.

"You don't think I'd let you do this all by yourself, do you? I do feel like an unofficial member of Extremely Odd these days."

Cristoff and his crew begin placing plants at light speed, consulting his carefully drawn diagrams. "It's not like I don't have help!"

"Then at least share a cup of coffee with me." He holds up a basket. "They made this up for me at The Admiral Fell." He pulls out a muffin the size of a footstool and holds it under my nose.

"You're too much."

"Yeah. Isn't it fun? I'll even tear the paper off for you."

After last night, I could use a little pampering.

Okay, so I could list all the movie stars, rock stars, artists, and overall famous people, but I won't. Suffice it to say, "Everybody is here."

Everybody, dahling.

The wedding itself went off without mishap other than the fact that Ursula poked a heel through her long veil five minutes before her walk down the aisle of the church. Pleasance, a sea of calm during these times, sewed another length of tulle on in less than two minutes.

From where I sat with the family, a new experience for me (and a very hard one as I knew nothing about anything going on behind the scenes), I couldn't help but cry. Stan sang her a song he'd written, and stodgy Ursula, looking gorgeous, actually wiped away a tear. Gordon squeezed my hand and whispered, "I honestly thought I'd never see this day."

Miracles never cease, do they? I can only pray that's true.

## 21

## Lillie

So, picture those *E! Entertainment* shows about celebrity weddings and you've got the picture. I realized while sitting at the reception with Gordon, watching the dancing, watching Miss Mildred and The Star Spangled Jammers, watching my team do a bang-up job, that our little business is capable of great things. So cool. And I felt proud and capable of almost anything.

Cristoff runs up to me and hands me his cell phone. "Call for you."

"What?" I look in my bag and fish out my own phone. Out of juice. Figures. I can't believe I forgot to charge it. Wait, yes I can. "Who is it?"

"Your dad."

I take the phone. "Daddy?"

"Oh, Lil. You've got to get home right away."

"Why?"

"Someone has set fire to the house."

Dear Lord.

"Are you and Mom all right?"

"We're fine. They contained it to our house. It's almost out now."

"I'll be right there." My stomach thickens and I press the Off button. Dear, sweet Lord. "I've got to go."

Gordon says, "What's wrong?"

"The house. Somebody torched it. Guess who?"

"I'm going with you."

"But it's your brother's wedding."

"Yes, and it's over. This is going to get scary here in a little while. Trust me."

Cristoff grabs my hand. "You going to be okay?"

"Cristoff, it's your home too."

"I have nothing, Lillie. You know that."

"But—"

"Just go, girlfriend! And don't worry about a thing, sweetie. It's all under control."

Boy, do I wish that was the truth.

The neighbors turned out in force, comforting my parents, running toward me as I get out of the car.

"It was definitely arson." Mom hugs me. "Started around back. The gas can is still there. Everyone's on their way." Meaning my aunts and uncles and, well, everybody. Coming when we need them. Everyone but Tacy.

I look on the smoking remains of this life, Grandma Erzsèbet's life.

"I'm sorry, Lil," Daddy says.

And we stand together, watching it.

"Come around back, sweet pea." Mom weaves her arm through mine. "I've got something to show you."

It's all gone now. All soggy and cold. A skeleton of a house.

We walk around the block and up the alleyway. And there it stands by the back gate, still thriving, Grandma's rhododendron bush. "See here? All wasn't lost."

And the sight of that ugly old bush becomes my undoing and I weep in my mother's arms. We weep together. Too many tears nowadays.

Minutes later I pull back. "I'm so glad you and Daddy are okay. What happened?"

"We smelled the smoke. We were sitting at the kitchen table and I saw flames leaping up outside. I grabbed the phone and called 911 as I led your father outside."

"All his books. His new novel."

"All gone."

"What are we going to do, Mom?"

She smiles. "Oh, Lillie. I've lived through far worse."

Gordon's apologizing all over the place for the state of the bedrooms. The only finished one, which he's been using until I move in, he gives to Daddy and Mom. "I'll hire workmen," he tells me after I kiss my parents good night. "It'll get some of these rooms in shape more quickly."

"There's no need, Gordon, really. Man, I hate to put you out like this."

"You're not. I'm here for the good and bad. And really, this was going to happen in a month, wasn't it?"

"Well, they were just planning on living at the row house."

"For how long? Imagine it, Lillie, the walks they'll take, the food Philly will cook for them. They deserve a nice, easy life now."

"The Lord knows you're right."

He kisses my cheek. "Right. Now, let's get you settled."

Philly comes up the back steps, arms full of sheets and towels. "Lucky I brought some extra sets with me."

"I'll do some shopping tomorrow," Gordon says.

"Cristoff and Pleasance will help," I say. I feel like a stuffed doll.

"What rooms?" Philly asks.

"Put Lillie at the end of the hall. It's the only other one with a bed. I'll sleep on my couch up in the studio."

Of course I protest.

Philly jerks her head toward Gordon. "He sleeps up there four nights out of five anyway, Lillie."

Gordon nods in agreement. "It's true."

I am convinced. I follow.

"You can't keep a secret from that woman, can you?" he asks.

"Nope."

We enter the bedroom. It is dismal and pink and there are already signs of renovation work being done to the plaster.

Philly begins to make up the bed. "I know you're tired. But you won't sleep. I've poured some milk into mugs and they just need a zap in the microwave. Give me some time to get this room in some sort of shape."

We obey and soon sit at a huge wooden table in the kitchen, mugs of heated milk warming our hands.

"Your dad's taking things really well," Gordon says.

"I know. He's a priest, remember? They do well at times like this."

"You're lucky to have the parents you do."

"I know. They're feeling pretty impotent right now though, I'm sure."

"Do they suspect Rawlins too?"

"I think so. Daddy was pressing the investigator pretty hard."

"Good."

"You got a phone?"

He leans the chair back and grabs one off the counter. "Here."

I dial Tacy's number. I could care less that it's now one thirty in the morning. Rawlins answers, of course.

"How could you?" I say.

"I don't know what you're talking about, Lillian."

"Bull. You're an evil man. Evil, Rawlins. You and that pastor of yours."

"Good night."

The line goes dead.

I dial back, and it rings and rings.

He picks it up and hangs up right away.

I call back. Again and again until finally the rings keep going. And I'm sure he's unplugged the phone.

"Do you think Tacy's safe, Gordon? Have I put her life in jeopardy?"

He only shakes his head and takes my hand.

I am sick.

22

## Lillie

Well, as they say, when it rains it pours. Sorry, I'm beyond a tricky turn of phrase right now. The detective Gordon hired to find Teddy has called. I like this guy, Nathan Dovey. He's a black man dressed like a Southern gentleman. Specializes in missing persons. We sit before him now in Gordon's kitchen. He found a record of Teddy's death in Ohio. Murdered. Not long after graduation.

"I'm sorry if the news causes you pain."

"It's not your fault."

"True. But I'm usually such a bearer of ill tidings."

"Does Mrs. Gillie know?"

He nods.

Mrs. Gillie moved away years ago. I wish I might have been with her when she heard the news.

"How did he get all the way to Ohio?"

"They're not sure. I sent his picture around and somebody from the sheriff's office up there in the town of Delaware recognized it."

"After all these years?" Gordon asks.

"Yep. Apparently he's a man who never forgets a face."

Teddy's dead.

Teddy's dead.

Teddy's dead.

Teddy's dead.

I want to ask him about the details of Teddy's murder. But I can't. I can't tote that much weight around now. And once I pick up the truth in that bag, I'll never be able to put it down again.

No. It won't change matters at all. And maybe Teddy wouldn't want me to know. Maybe he'd wish to keep the details from tainting my memory of him.

Gordon says, "Thanks, Dovey. It's good to finally know. Right, Lillie?" His apprehension screams at me. Oh, Gordon.

"Yes. Thank you." I turn to Gordon and lay my hand on his shoulder.

The detective slides his small, light-blue, spiral-bound notepad into his breast pocket. "If you ever need me again, you know where to call." He takes his leave after some handshaking.

"Well?" I say to Gordon.

"I should be asking you that."

"Yeah. I'll let you know in a couple of days."

He embraces me. "Are you at least relieved to know?"

"I guess so. But that makes me feel very selfish."

Mom and Dad cry with me that night. Tacy should know this, but it's impossible. We talk about our Teddy long after our mugs of milk are empty.

"Do you have Mrs. Gillie's number, Mom?"

"My book was lost in the fire."

"I'll find out how to reach her."

Gordon knocks on my door later to see if I'm okay. We sit down at the foot of the bed. "I am. I've been thinking, Gordon. And I'm glad I fell in love with you before I knew anything. I'm glad you weren't a tonic. I'm glad you weren't 'the next best thing.'"

"Thanks, sweetheart."

"You're not, you know. You're *the* thing. The only thing. But you know, I'm thankful you were around when I found out the truth."

"Let's take a walk," he says.

"I'll get out of my pajamas."

"Don't bother, love."

He ushers me down to the water. My fingers find his and we watch in silence as the circle moon wings into the darkened sky, tinting the river gold and peaceful.

## Tacy

I could hardly believe I pulled it off. Rawlins showed me the letter from Lillie, asking me to come to her wedding, to be her honor attendant. She apologized for the rush and made copious promises to appease Rawlins. I could tell by her words that she had to muster some fortitude to send it. Not to mention that it was so late. Lillie was always so punctual.

It killed me to hear her supplicate herself before Rawlins, because I knew it killed her to do it. Lillie was always so proud.

And after that scene when she came to the house in the middle of the night, doing Lord knows what, I knew she'd do whatever it took to protect me and Hannah. And I was right.

I see Lillie now, crawling to the Rover as Rawlins continues to scream. Somehow, I can actually smell something burning.

Rawlins refused to let me take part in the wedding. I starved myself for a week to change his mind. It's really true—you can't make a person eat. He actually was forced to use the Heimlich maneuver when he tried to shove food down my throat. That man was so predictable.

## Lillie

So, obviously, my wedding plans are totally and unapologetically boring compared to most of the weddings around this place. This miffed the gaggle at first, but after Stan's wedding, they eventually confessed relief to simply glide on through.

And I don't blame them. If the setup on the Remington affair was akin to hiking Pikes Peak, the tear down and cleanup was nothing short of scaling Mount Everest. Cristoff reported 250 bags of trash. Can you believe that? And three-quarters of the guests were probably staunch environmentalists. I'd like to know how much energy is used to produce, distribute, and project just one movie? And does the world really *need* movies? We went along for millennia without them. Talk about "the pan calling the skillet burned," as my Aunt Babi used to say before Mom finally corrected her.

Jaime Pickerson calls me just before a Tuesday morning breakfast meeting. "Still friends with me, Lil?" Her raspy voice tickles my ear.

"Hey, you paid your bill. I've got no quarrel."

"I always clean up after myself."

"How are you and Brian? It's been over six months."

"Separated."

Oh man! Our first marital failure. Wait, we didn't actually *do* the wedding, did we? That's a relief. "I am so sorry to hear that."

"Well, whatever, you know. I always suspected I wasn't really the marrying type. I'll be fine."

"You always are." It's time to let the conversation drop right there. I don't know Jaime well enough to dive with her into her well of pain. Then again, maybe there isn't one. "Hey, I loved what you said to that population explosion guy the other day!"

Her laughter grates across her vocal cords. "It's the truth! If everybody who was worried about it made the personal sacrifice—*blam!*—we'd be fine!"

"Talk about putting your money where your mouth is."

"Exactly. You going to be out at the shooting range?"

"I should go up, but I'm getting married soon."

"No stuff!"

Why should that be so surprising? "Nope. Small affair by the water."

"Cool. Well, the news is almost done and my board is lit up like a Christmas tree."

Jaime's not really creative in her imagery.

"Thanks for the call."

"Good luck on your marriage."

"Thanks."

Good luck? Luck? Oh, sheesh, no wonder they're separated!

Gert shadows the doorway. "Lillie, dear, your eggs are getting cold."

"Be right there, Gert."

"Okay, first order of agenda is the Newton wedding." I push my plate of bacon and eggs forward. Gert cooked today as Peach has an appointment with the ophthalmologist regarding his upcoming cataract surgery. "Who wants to go first?"

Pleasance raises a hand, then begins to fill us in on the gowns, Renaissance, and the men's doublets. Thirty minutes later we're onto the Martins and then the Graveses, the Kalines, and the Neubauers.

I'm telling you, business booms, booms, booms!

Finally, "Now the Gordon Remington wedding."

"Yeah boy," Pleasance says. "This is a piece of cake. Your gown is almost finished, Lillie Pad. I'll mark the hem today if you don't mind."

"And your gown, Pleasance?"

"Honey, I had that done a week after you asked and the color was decided."

That would lead one to believe a decision existed. I told her to pick whatever color she wanted. She chose pale green. It's slim and svelte and perfect for her.

For some reason, Rawlins, upon conversing with Daddy on the phone, said that Tacy could be in the wedding, marriage being "ordained by God and pleasing to Him." We didn't want to go crawling to him, but we did it for Tacy, hoping he'd view the gesture as a peace offering.

Now, I agree with him about marriage and am thankful he can at least see the importance of this day to the family, but I hate it when he does the right thing for the right reason. In three days, I'll see my sister at the rehearsal dinner. I can't wait. Her gown is pale pink. They sent her measurements through the mail.

"The tuxes?" I ask her.

"All ordered and ready for pickup." Needless to say, there will be many more groomsmen than bridesmaids. Stan and Fitz, an artist friend named Brig, and, because Cristoff would make a frightening maid of honor, he'll line up with Gordon and the guys. It was Gordon's idea. I swear that man can read my thoughts even before they've arrived in my brain.

"Girlfriend," Cristoff says, "they are fabulous."

The tuxes are actually kilts accompanied by those beautiful short jackets decorated with silver buttons. I don't know what they're called. It's not my department. But Gordon told me his mother's family hails from Scotland, so there you go. Works for me.

Gert, filling in for Peach, picks her teeth with a folded, empty packet of Sweet'n Low. "The wedding breakfast will be just perfect. Scones and cream and jam and casseroles like you have never seen before, and Maryland food, too: sautéed crab and Smithfield ham, crab cakes and your favorite, Lillie, fried chicken."

I love fried chicken. I really do. My favorite dinner consists of fried chicken, mashed potatoes, and biscuits. I read once this is Liz Taylor's favorite meal too. I can safely say, other than breathing and your basic bodily functions, this is the only thing the two of us have in common. Well, and maybe the propensity to gain weight. The poor woman must die when she views old photos of herself. At least, I've always been chubby.

Cristoff reports on the flowers, lots of lilies and roses and my mother's favorite, the gardenia.

What a gang!

"So it looks like everything is set then?"

Pleasance waves a hand. "Honey, we are more than good to go. And we've hired enough staff so we can enjoy ourselves, be part of the wedding party. That sure will be weird."

Cristoff nods. "Tell me about it, girlfriend."

Cristoff and Pleasance sure have been getting along great lately. This pleases me. Cristoff has no need for a woman, and Pleasance doesn't want a man. Both need a new best friend.

## 23

## Lillie

Mom's asleep, Gordon's busy in his studio, and only Daddy and I sit in the kitchen drinking our warmed milk.

I take a sip. "We get to see her tomorrow."

"I know."

"Scared, Daddy?"

"Yeah, of what I'll say to my son-in-law, the arsonist."

"Me too. I guess I'm glad I'll just be too preoccupied with myself. That's okay, right?"

"Of course. Your wedding day only comes once. We hope." He winks his wink. "Hopefully the circumstances will be enough to staple my mouth shut."

I hope so too. I picture a bride in white, cursing profusely at someone, and it sure isn't pretty.

"So, how do you like the computer setup Gordon had installed,

Daddy? Did you ever think you'd be able to talk your stuff right into a computer?"

"No. It's making this book a whole lot easier, that's for sure, honey."

Daddy returned to us after the fire. I don't know why and I'm afraid to ask, because I might set him back. It probably has something to do with realizing the fragility of our existence, of not letting someone else steal the life from you. Maybe. Who knows? If he wants to talk about it he will.

"So, how's your pastor-detective doing these days?"

"Oh, he's gotten himself into a pickle with the Magillicutty sisters."

"I should say!"

I enjoy hearing about this cozy mystery. Dad's fashioned his own town on the Eastern Shore inhabited by eccentric people, many of them Hungarian in descent. Write what you know, right? Truthfully, the writing isn't as good as either he or I thought it would be, but I just tell him, "It's a first draft, Daddy, and you're speaking it! Surely that's an entirely different brain function than writing."

"I sure hope so. Unfortunately, it's all I've got."

"I mean, Henry James wouldn't have been able to do it."

He laughs. "But Somerset Maugham would have."

"Here, here."

The kitchen is almost remodeled, the contractors working overtime. The bedroom suite Gordon and I will share—once three bedrooms but now a large bedroom, a massive bath, dressing room, and a sitting room—is done. Gordon painted it himself, each room a different sky. The bedroom an ink-blue night sky with stars, the bathroom a sunrise, and the sitting room places us in blue skies!

Man, I hope it doesn't rain tomorrow.

The pool is finished as well, as is the veranda where the wedding breakfast will take place after the ceremony near the water. Daddy will conduct the service. I think that, more than anything, pleases me the most. A minister's child must make many sacrifices throughout her childhood, but this is a most precious reward. Almost worth the endless parade of hand-me-downs.

While Stan invited everybody, we have invited only the closest of friends and family. I know each of my aunts will arrive bearing some Hungarian dish for the reception, so I warned Peach ahead of time. He scratched his belly and said, "I've always wanted to learn to cook Hungarian."

So that's that.

The rehearsal dinner, just the wedding party and family, will be a crab feast on picnic tables near the water. I already ensured prime rib as an available option for Rawlins and Tacy, since they adopted the Old Testament dietary laws last fall. The steak will be well done, naturally. I hope this lifestyle at least makes them feel better about themselves. I mean, in the end, isn't that what legalism is all about?

Daddy drains his mug. "I think I'm ready for bed now. I'm still not used to the layout, Lil. Will you guide me upstairs?"

"Of course, Daddy."

I place our mugs in the sink and help him from the table. He begins to mumble a song, one we've sung together since I was a little girl.

"You can't always get what you want."

We stop at their bedroom door. "It's true, Lil," he says, still holding onto my arm. "You get what you need."

"Some of us do anyway, Daddy."

"Oh, I think we all do. One way or another."

If this comforts him, so be it.

I kiss his cheek and guide him toward the bed. Mom has already laid out his pajamas. She's sleeping.

One always takes a chance with an outdoor function. But as I sit here on the veranda with my morning cup of coffee, I am thankful many prayers have been answered. The normal Maryland humidity lies low. The breeze ruffles the treetops beneath a deep sky, and our rehearsal dinner is this evening.

Cristoff calls me on my cell phone. "I'm sitting out on my deck, drinking a cup of coffee in this gorgeous breeze. Where are you?"

"On the veranda doing the same."

"Girlfriend, you couldn't have special-ordered a more beautiful day, and the forecast promises the same all weekend long."

I choose to believe the weatherman this time.

Cristoff bought a row house on Foster Avenue, a block down from Grandma Erzsèbet's. He has no plans for the place, other than some cans of stark white paint and refinished floors. He's already got a roommate, an eighty-two-year-old childless woman from the church on Erdman Avenue. He calls her Granny. You've got to love it.

He brings her flowers. She makes him soup and is already crocheting an afghan for his bed.

"You excited, sweetie?" he says.

"Honestly, honey, did you ever think this day would come?"

"I had my doubts."

A kiss alights upon the back of my neck. Gordon. I turn and smile at him, mouthing the word, "Cristoff."

"Tell him I said hi," he whispers.

"Gordon says hi."

"Hi, Gordon."

"Hi, Gordon," I say.

Gordon chuckles and walks into the kitchen. Probably to fix a cup of tea.

"So, you nervous?" Cristoff asks.

"I can't believe she'll be here in"—I check my watch—"three hours."

"Me either. I've been praying all morning."

"Thanks."

"Don't worry about a thing, sweetie. This is your time to shine. There are plenty of days ahead to worry about your sister."

I can only hope that's true.

I hold her to me tightly. "Oh, Tacy, Tacy."

She laughs. "I'm here! I'm here! Rawlins was so nice to let me come after all that's been going on."

I let it slide. She doesn't know the half of it. She doesn't know who's really being nice here. And right now she doesn't need to. Let her enjoy some freedom.

She pulls away. "You look wonderful, Lillie. It's amazing what love does for a woman."

"You're as pretty as ever."

And I realize I can't truthfully use the word beautiful anymore. She's almost emaciated and her eyes shine like polished onyx.

"Let's go try on your gown."

Pleasance set up her machine at the kitchen table. She's sewing a rolled hem around my veil. It's a walking-length veil attached to a small rhinestone comb. The whole getup is simple elegance at its finest, bless her.

"Pleasance! Tacy's ready for her fitting!"

Pleasance takes one look at my sister, spits a mouthful of pins into her hand and says, "Girlfriend, you are definitely *not* a size six!"

Tacy cries, "Oh no! Have I gained weight?"

Is she *serious?*

"Hardly. Get over here, strip down to your underwear and we'll take those measurements again. I have a feeling I'll be sitting at this machine for a while."

Tacy looks like she's going to cry.

"It's okay, baby doll," Pleasance says. "I'm a whiz on this machine. Right, Lillie?"

"A downright whiz," I say. "Don't you worry about a thing, Tace. It's all going to be great."

Rawlins walks in. "Lillian."

"Rawlins." You creep.

"Congratulations on the forthcoming nuptials."

Pleasance almost chokes.

"Thank you. We were just going to retake Tacy's measurements. We think the gown will be too large for her."

He sets down the car seat. Hannah must be sleeping. She's swaddled in several receiving blankets, only her nose visible. I long to hold her, but I don't dare ask.

"Absolutely not," he says. "I already sent the measurements."

"But Pleasance here is an expert seamstress. She took one look at her and said the gown will be much too big."

"Your father told you the parameters of our agreement, did he not?"

"Yes, but the gown will be much too—"

"She wears it as is or she doesn't wear it at all."

"But Rawlins, this is my wed—"

"Let's go, Anastasia."

"Okay, okay. The gown stays as is."

"Come with me outside, Anastasia. You're finished in here."

Tacy smiles at him. "All right, Rawlins."

He leads the way, back turned to us. As Tacy passes by, she squeezes my shoulder twice, tighter than a death grip. But she continues on, saying nothing else.

"I'll eyeball it, Lillie Pad. It won't be perfect, but it'll be better than nothing."

The whir of the machine follows me up to my room.

Later that night, at the crab feast, I sneak a peak at Hannah while Rawlins uses the restroom. I guess he couldn't hold it any longer, because it's the first time I know of he's relieved himself since he arrived.

She still sleeps, and I swear they drugged the child or something. Around her mouth a bluish ring has formed, and her breath comes in raspy gasps.

I quickly replace the covers as they were and seek out Gordon. "Something must be done."

"Let's think on it, sweetheart. We'll come up with a plan."

As Tacy hugs me good-bye, she whispers, "No guard on tonight, back door unlocked," in a quick burst.

If any doubt remained, it flies away. God has spoken through the lips of my sister.

"Family conference," I whisper to Daddy as the last guest leaves. Of course, it includes Cristoff and Pleasance. We sit around the kitchen table,

Philly fixing coffee and wiping down any horizontal surface. We'll need her insight.

"Okay, let's count the costs. We could lose the wedding tomorrow." I look at Gordon.

"Tomorrow's only a day, love. We'll have plenty more."

"Sure?"

He takes my hand.

"Okay." The hall clock chimes ten deep bongs. "First of all, I'll need a car seat."

"I got it," Cristoff says. "I passed an all-night Wal-Mart on my way here."

"We need to make sure Rawlins will be sleeping. Or at least try."

Mother says, "Two a.m. Any earlier and he may be up late working. Any later and he may be getting up early."

"I agree."

"Take your gun, Lil," Daddy says.

" . . . "

" . . . "

"It was destroyed in the fire."

"I have one," Gordon says, voice quiet.

Wow. Now I'm really scared. Everything swells.

I clear my throat. "So, we should probably get them right to the hospital. Tacy looks starved, and if Hannah doesn't have some kind of bronchial infection, I'd be shocked."

"Your father and I will meet you there," Mom says.

"Saint Joe's will be closest."

Mom nods.

"I'm up for another run, Lillie Pad," Pleasance says.

"You go ahead on home to the boys, Pleasance." I turn to Gordon. "You'll go with me, won't you?"

"You couldn't tear me away, sweetheart."

Just as I thought.

Cristoff rises from his chair. "I'll go get the car seat. And some baby blankets."

"Get some formula and bottles, too," Mom says.

Cristoff turns.

"Hold on a minute, Gilbert, son," Daddy says. "I wasn't a priest for that many years to think we can do this alone. Let's pray together and may God go with us all, especially Lillie and Gordon."

I want to break down. I want to heave my sobs upon the table. But I can't.

I won't.

24

## Lillie

One a.m. already and I'm shaking.

The car seat Cristoff rushed out to buy is strapped into the backseat of the Volvo. Three blankets and a cooler holding a bottle lie ready. Gordon's gun sits in its case on the floor. Cleaned and loaded.

"I went by the old lot and cut this for you." Cristoff hands me a stem of Grandma Erzsèbet's Nightmare, the end wrapped in a moist paper towel and tinfoil.

"It's still there?"

"Yeah, it sure is. But they're clearing the lot next week. Grandma E would want to come along."

As we climb into the car, dew already moist on the ground, I touch the branch on the console beside me. I recall Mom all those years ago traveling across the border. I think of Grandma Erzsèbet and even Tacy. Two hard squeezes. No guard tonight. And I pray.

I click the gearshift into drive. "Ready, Gordon?"

"Yes, Lillie."

"Did you ever think you'd find yourself in a situation like this?"

"Not for a minute."

Somehow, deep in my mind, I always knew I'd be called upon for something bold and scary. If tonight isn't that time, I'm in trouble.

I cut the engine as soon I think the car will drift up to the house. The farmhouse has never looked so impenetrable before. A strong wind has arisen and the humidity floats on the darkness. Gordon readies the pistol. "I'll stand guard on the deck."

"Okay." I turn off the inner lights. "Ready?"

"Let's go."

We open our doors and climb out, each foot tenderly meeting the drive. After opening the back door and pressing down the lock, I ready the belts of the car seat. We leave our doors ajar and locked as well. Just a quick slip over the tiny head, a snap of the buckle, and we'll be on our way.

Although I delicately place each foot on the gravel, each footstep thunders into the darkness. My heartbeat thrums a loud bass beat. I feel like walking noise. My lungs begin to constrict and I pray the wheezing won't give me away.

I place a hand on Gordon's arm and reach into my pocket. He stops as I puff on my inhaler. Dear God, don't let me get lightheaded, please. We wait several seconds, then continue forward again.

The back door is unlocked as promised. I don't know how she managed it. The hood light shines above the range. All is spotless, shining, and looking new. Antiseptic and chilling. I picture the church ladies going about their ministrations, the new housekeeper cooking meals, all their voices hushed in reverence to Rawlins McGovern, or more to the point, Pastor Alban Cole. The grim face of the preacher comes to mind.

We can do this.

I turn back and look at Gordon standing by the door, gun in his hand. He shouldn't have to deal with this. No one should.

I start to negotiate the back stairs leading up next to Hannah's bedroom, placing a ginger foot on the first step.

Praying, praying. Dear God, let me do this. Help me do this.

I tread up the steps in my sneakers, black clothes hopefully rendering me invisible. I can't believe I'm here doing this. Give me strength.

The door stands open. A baby monitor glows on the changing table and in the corner, the ghost-white figure of my sister sits in the rocking chair.

She rises, completely dressed. "We're ready," she whispers.

I simply nod. Feeling my lungs constrict at the apprehension, choosing now to breathe instead of whisper. My wheeze scrapes the silence.

"She's ready." Tacy barely breathes the words and reaches down into the crib. She hands me the limp, almost lifeless form of her child. Hannah Grace's breathing is so shallow and exhausted she doesn't waken.

Oh, God, she's so beautiful. Help us help her. Help me help them.

As I take the little body, a rattle falls out of the folds of the blanket.

No!

"Anastasia!"

No! No!

"Go!" she hisses. "Go!"

"Anastasia!"

"It's just me, Rawlins!"

Panicked, I bolt down the darkened staircase, caring little about noise now, hearing commotion behind me.

Go, Lillie. Go. Go. Go. Get out of here.

Through the kitchen door and halfway down the deck steps, I hear Rawlins yell, "Stop!"

But I don't. I can't. I'm propelled by something bigger than myself. Something that rests inside us all.

I run past Gordon. "Now, Gordon! Hurry!"

Gordon follows, his limping gait slowing him down.

I lay Hannah on the car seat and buckle her in. Her eyes open wide. "It's okay, baby. It's Aunt Lillie, dear. Only Aunt Lillie."

She gasps a raspy breath, and her face screws up.

Don't cry. Please don't cry. I know it will set off a coughing fit.

Gordon catches up and I reach in to stroke her face. "It's okay, baby."

Rawlins is off the deck now, thundering toward the car. "Stop or I'll shoot, Lillian!"

I slam the door and start to climb in.

Rawlins catches up with me. "No!"

"Oh yes."

"No." And his fist slams into my jaw. I reel back as he goes for the handle of Hannah's door.

I kick out and my foot finds the soft spot of his groin. He cries out, doubles over, and I slide in, shut the door as Gordon follows suit.

Throw the car into reverse.

Back out, gravel flying, and I'm tearing down the driveway.

Oh, Tacy! What will become of you?

"What's happening behind us, Gordon?"

"He's shoving Tacy into the Rover."

And his pursuit begins, tires spinning, gears raging.

Thank God for a car that hugs the road.

"Hang on, Gordon."

I peel out onto Jarrettsville Pike, wishing this was a manual transmission, but the turbo kicks in, and we shoot forward like a rocket. Hannah begins to cry.

"I'll climb in the back," Gordon says.

"How?"

"Watch this. It'll be all right, Lillie. We have her." He pulls up his pant leg and unhooks the prosthesis.

We race on the night wind, Hannah's cries picking up speed as Gordon climbs in the back.

"Buckle in! I'm about to make a quick turn."

Darn this automatic transmission! I want to downshift! Downshift!

I brake heavily and turn down a small road. Can I lose him?

Headlights round the corner after me.

"How's the baby?"

"I gave her that bottle."

"She shouldn't drink lying down."

"Lillie!"

He's right.

Engine roaring, I thrust forward down the dark country road. I think all sorts of thoughts. We needed Tacy here to make this work. We needed the word of the mother, we needed to know she was on board. Oh, I can see it now. Mrs. Mannequin standing there, nodding to the police, agreeing with Mr. Monster that I kidnapped their child. It doesn't matter now. I need to get her to Saint Joe's, but I need to lose him first. He'll never let me in the door of that hospital if he can help it.

Rawlins would rather die first.

There's a thought.

Soon I turn on the road surrounding Loch Raven Reservoir, famous for its twists and turns. Surely I'll lose his clunky Range Rover here. The dark is so peaceful, and no cars witness our chase scene.

"How close is he, Gordon?"

"He's keeping up."

"I'm going as fast as I can and still be safe."

"Go faster."

That's all the encouragement I need.

I brake and accelerate, brake and accelerate, and here it comes, the worst hairpin of them all. The ravine beside us falls dark and deep, a steep, wooded drop to the water below.

"What's happening, Gordon?"

"I can't see."

A car approaches. Probably some kids out too late. Lord, let's hope they're not drunk. And their high beams are on. I press on the brakes as they blind me temporarily.

"I can see her! She's fighting him! She's hitting him around his face!"

I look in my rearview mirror.

"She's grabbing the steering wheel."

Time quagmires and their car lurches and swerves as Rawlins tries to right the vehicle.

"She's hanging on. Darn. I can't see anything now!"

The Rover lurches again, bucks and sways and swerves and hangs in suspension, then tumbles into the ravine.

Oh, dear God. Dear God.

I brake, skidding to a halt. Slamming the car into park. "Stay with Hannah, Gordon!"

In the dimness below, the white Rover lies belly up. I skid down the slope. The driver's side is pinned against a tree.

"Tacy!"

But no answer comes from my sister. Only Rawlins's cry, "Help us!" bleeds into the darkness. He screams and screams and screams. Branches and brush scrape my face and hands and I dive toward the ground.

Oh, Tacy. God, help me get to her. Get me to that little girl with the blond braids who begged me year after year to let her play Mom in "the bicycle game." There we'd be, flying down the path between the house and rectory, the house Hungary, the rectory Austria. Standing up, I'd pedal like mad while she held on tightly to the seat with her small hands, eyes as big as baseballs. But she wouldn't yell in fright. Not Tacy.

But she took that ride tonight. She told me when to come and I followed her lead and felt her strength.

## Tacy

You're here now, Lillie. Oh, you're here!

She's looking at me. I want to tell her it's okay. But I'm leaving and I cannot stop myself now. I'm almost finished.

## Lillie

I belly up to the window and in the moonlight I see her, neck at an impossible angle, eyes open, seeing nothing.

No!

I smell smoke.

"Lillie!" Rawlins screams. "You've got to get me out of here! My legs are pinned."

"Tacy's dead."

"Help me, please. This car is going to explode."

I can't. I can't.

I feel my head shaking at him.

"No, Lillie! Don't do this!"

"Tacy's dead!" I am frozen.

"Dear God, help me! Please, Lillie."

"My sister is *dead!*"

"Please!"

"The car is going to explode. Your door is up against a tree."

I double around to Tacy's side, and God help me, I open her door and climb in to retrieve the monster. I pull and pull. "I can't! I'll call 911."

"No!" he screams. "Don't leave me!"

Smoke begins to thicken the air. My own voice screams inside my head. "Get out! Get out! Get out!"

I peer into the dead face of my sister one last time.

Oh, God. I didn't want it to end like this. You know I didn't!

"Don't leave me! Please!"

I slide back and scrabble up the bank, feet pedaling on the decaying leaves. I run across the asphalt. "Gordon, call 911!" And as I open my door, the explosion rocks me. There's the rhododendron branch. O Tacy, Tacy.

I reach in, grab it, and hurl it down onto the flaming mass.

Hannah starts choking on the formula.

"We've got to get her to the hospital, Lillie." Gordon's voice brings me home.

No time to watch it burn. No time. No time.

Back in my seat, I jam down the accelerator and leave my sister behind.


## Tacy

*It's finished. It's finally over. I can leave now, Jesus. He's gone.*


## Lillie

I punch 01 into the cell phone. Mom, already waiting at Saint Joe's, answers Gordon's phone. "You got them?"

"Just Hannah. She's in bad shape."

"I'll tell the team to be ready for her. Tacy?"

"Mom, you're breaking up. I'll be there soon." I hang up. I can't tell her. Not now. I punch the accelerator to the floor and mutter mumbled, senseless prayers. It's all I can do.

Gordon's holding Hannah now, rubbing her tiny back, doing all he can to make the coughing stop.

I'm dying inside. We've saved her. But at what expense?

"Lillie?"

"She was already dead, Gordon. Broken neck."

"So she didn't know what hit her."

"I hope so."

We are silent for a while. Finally he speaks from there in the backseat, his voice so far away. "You know she would have gladly sacrificed herself for this child. I think your sister was stronger than she appeared."

"She died fighting."

She exceeded our expectations. Maybe we all did tonight.

25

"They're dead," I tell the officer the next morning. I relate the entire story, leaving out no detail, ending with, "I suppose I'm going to be charged with kidnapping, reckless endangerment, and manslaughter, aren't I?"

"Her mother handed her to you, Miss Bauer." He shakes his head. "Your niece was in bad shape. But thanks to the doctors…and you…"

I don't know what will become of Hannah. But for now, she's alive. Thank You, God, she's alive.

Gordon slips an arm around my waist.

"Don't worry ma'am. I don't see how there will be any charges made against you. I've already talked with your brother-in-law's mother, and she says you did the right thing. Tried to do it herself on numerous occasions."

Relief trickles into me. I picture the funeral in several days. Closed casket and no one from The Temperance Church of the Apostles in attendance, if I have anything to do with it.

I gaze out the window of the hospital room. Hannah sleeps, breathing with the help of a ventilator, but breathing. They vacuumed out her lungs and some IV is pumping medication into that tiny, fragile arm.

The officer excuses himself.

The clock says two p.m. Over twelve hours have passed since I left the house. Seems like twenty-four. Seems like two.

"Well, we missed our own wedding, Gordon."

"Well worth it. Look how pink she is."

"Yeah." I take her hand, petting the delicate fingers. "Yeah." And a torrent of tears sweeps me away as I weep for my sister over her little child. My poor Tacy. I think of her as she is right now, finally free to be God's glorious creation. Maybe she shares a cup of heavenly wine with Grandma. Maybe they know the end from the beginning and, as part of that great cloud of witnesses, watch and approve. I can only hope I will not disappoint them. I will try my best not to.

Mom and Dad seek one another in their agony. At five o'clock the family will descend on Gordon's and we will weep, we will grieve, we will remember. And we will ingest paprika and sour cream as the Bajnoks have always done. We will go on from here. Somehow. Because deep inside of us, we know that God has willed us to carry on. And He will provide the strength.


The Temperance Church of the Apostles disbanded. When we went through Rawlins and Tacy's effects we were enlightened far more than any of us wanted to be. Alban Cole was nothing more than a con man, raised in a religious home, who knew the Bible, knew the lingo, knew how to grind people to dust beneath his heel.

He extorted millions of dollars from his congregation, much of it from Rawlins. He disappeared, but Nathan Dovey is on the job, courtesy of Stan and Gordon Remington. When he's found, I can only pray to God I'm not there. Over a hundred letters from Almighty Alban threatening hellfire, damnation, and sacrifice were found in hollow books in the library at the farmhouse. Rawlins was in so much debt, it's a good thing he's dead.

Daddy was relieved Cole wasn't really a minister, but I said, "Daddy, what does that matter? There are plenty of pastors who do the same thing to their congregations. It's just not for money." The lust for power is just as perverting.

I found a couple of beautiful canvases in Tacy's studio. They hang in our dining room, so when the family gathers together, as I know we will, Tacy will in some way be present.

But today, we pay tribute to Grandma Erszèbet.

"For someone with one leg, you sure did a good job digging that hole, Gordon."

His wedding band glints on the hand that holds the shovel. "Oh, I'm handy all right."

After two weeks of marriage, a hasty solemn ceremony by the water, just me and him, the family, and the Extremely Odd gang, I know just what a handy fellow he is. I always suspected artists' hands would know just what to do. It was so worth the wait.

"I can't believe you found the Nightmare at the landfill."

And only after about seven phone calls to try and see who had hauled the mammoth bush away. It's barely alive, but I'm confident Gordon can coax it back to life. He has a way with living things.

"It deserves to be here. Hey, the spirit of Grandma E lives on in you, sweetheart."

For the first time in my life, I know that's true.

The August sun shines hot on our heads. "I need to get Hannah a hat." I heft her up on my hip. Ten months old and doing just fine now. Skinny, but completely on the mend.

"Just one more second while I put the root ball in. I want you to shovel in the first spade of dirt. It's symbolic, you know."

He lifts the massive bush and sets it in the hole. "Ready?"

"I am. I really am."

I lean down and set her on my lap and I shovel in the dirt, and more and more. I want to do it all. And I pat it down with my skeleton hand. Hannah reaches out and pats it too, a tiny little skeleton growing inside of her. I'll do my best to make sure she comes to terms with that sooner than I did.

# About the Author

Lisa Samson lives in Maryland with her husband, Will, and their three children. As of this writing, three book-selling college boys live in the spare bedroom, and their conversation brightens up the ten p.m. hush. Her husband has recently completed his master's degree, and Lisa is still recovering, but she's not complaining, remembering how much political capital she's banked over the past year. She is busy procrastinating over her next book.

OTHER BOOKS
BY LISA SAMSON

*The Living End*
*Songbird*
*Women's Intuition*
*The Church Ladies*
*Indigo Waters*
*Fields of Gold*
*Crimson Skies*

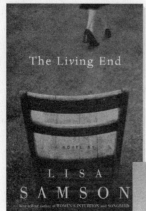